BOOKS BY RITA MAE BROWN

The Hand That Cradles the Rock
Songs to a Handsome Woman
The Plain Brown Rapper
Rubyfruit Jungle
In Her Day
Six of One
Southern Discomfort
Sudden Death
High Hearts
Starting from Scratch:
A Different Kind of Writers' Manual
Bingo
Venus Envy
Dolley

AND WITH SNEAKY PIE BROWN

Wish You Were Here
Rest in Pieces
Murder at Monticello

Rest in Pieces

RITA MAE BROWN
& SNEAKY PIE BROWN
ILLUSTRATIONS BY WENDY WRAY

BANTAM BOOKS NEW YORK · TORONTO · LONDON · SYDNEY · AUCKLAND

REST IN PIECES

A Bantam Book / September 1992
Bantam paperback edition / July 1993

Library of Congress Catalog Card Number: 92-7257

ISBN 0-553-56239-8

Published simultaneously in the United States and Canada

Bantam Books are published by Bantam Books, a division of Bantam Doubleday Dell Publishing Group, Inc. Its trademark, consisting of the words "Bantam Books" and the portrayal of a rooster, is Registered in U.S. Patent and Trademark Office and in other countries. Marca Registrada. Bantam Books, 1540 Broadway, New York, New York 10036.

PRINTED IN THE UNITED STATES OF AMERICA

OPM   0 9 8 7 6

To the Beegles
and their dalmatians

Cast of Characters

Mary Minor Haristeen (Harry), the young postmistress of Crozet, whose curiosity almost kills the cat and herself

Mrs. Murphy, Harry's gray tiger cat, who bears an uncanny resemblance to authoress Sneaky Pie and who is wonderfully intelligent!

Tee Tucker, Harry's Welsh corgi, Mrs. Murphy's friend and confidant; a buoyant soul

Pharamond Haristeen (Fair), veterinarian, formerly married to Harry

Boom Boom Craycroft, a high-society knockout

Blair Bainbridge, a handsome model and fugitive from the fast lane in Manhattan. He moves to Crozet for peace and quiet and gets anything but

Mrs. George Hogendobber (Miranda), a widow who thumps her own Bible!

Market Shiflett, owner of Shiflett's Market, next to the post office

Pewter, Market's fat gray cat, who, when need be, can be pulled away from the food bowl

Susan Tucker, Harry's best friend, who doesn't take life too seriously until her neighbors get murdered

Ned Tucker, a lawyer and Susan's husband

Jim Sanburne, mayor of Crozet

Big Marilyn Sanburne (Mim), queen of Crozet and an awful snob

Little Marilyn Sanburne, daughter of Mim, and not as dumb as she appears

Fitz-Gilbert Hamilton, Little Marilyn's husband, is rich by marriage and in his own right. His ambition sapped, he's content to live very well and be a "gentleman lawyer"

Cabell Hall, a trusted figure in Crozet, is preparing to retire from the bank where he is president

Ben Seifert, Cabell Hall's protégé, has come a long way from a callow teller to a bank officer. He was a year ahead of Harry in high school

Rick Shaw, Albemarle sheriff

Cynthia Cooper, police officer

Rob Collier, mail driver

Paddy, Mrs. Murphy's ex-husband, a saucy tom

Simon, an opossum with a low opinion of humanity. He slowly succumbs to Harry's kindness. He lives in the barn-loft along with a crabby owl and a hibernating blacksnake

Dear Reader:

Here's to catnip and champagne!

Thanks to you my mailbox overflows with letters, photos, mousie toys, and crunchy nibbles. Little did I think when I started the Mrs. Murphy series that there would be so many cats out there who are readers . . . a few humans, too.

Poor Mother, she's trying not to be a grouch. She slaves over "important themes" disguised as comedy and I dash along with a mystery series and am a hit. This only goes to prove that most cats and some dogs realize that a lighthearted approach is always the best. Maybe in a few decades Mom will figure this out for herself.

The best news is that I was able to afford my own typewriter. I found a used IBM Selectric III so I don't have to sneak into Mother's office in the middle of the night. I even have my own office. Do you think I should hire Pewter as a secretary?

Again, thank you, cats out there, and the dogs, too. Take care of your humans. And as for you humans, well, a fresh salmon steak would be a wonderful treat for the cat in your life.

All Best,

SNEAKY PIE

1

Golden light poured over the little town of Crozet, Virginia. Mary Minor Haristeen looked up from the envelopes she was sorting and then walked over to the large glass window to admire the view. It seemed to her as if the entire town had been drenched in butter. The rooftops shone; the simple clapboard buildings were lent a pleasing grace. Harry was so compelled by the quality of the light that she threw on her denim jacket and walked out the back door. Mrs. Murphy, Harry's tiger cat, and Tee Tucker, her corgi, roused themselves from a drowsy afternoon slumber to accompany her. The long October rays of the sun gilded the large trotting-horse weathervane on Miranda Hogendobber's house on St. George Avenue, seen from the alleyway behind the post office.

Brilliant fall days brought back memories of hotly contested football games, school crushes, and cool nights. Much as Harry loathed cold weather, she liked having to buy a new sweater or two. At Crozet High she had worn a fuzzy red sweater one long-ago October day, in 1973 to be exact, and caught the eye of Fair Haristeen. Oak trees transformed into orange torches, the maples turned blood-red, and the beech trees became yellow, then as now. Autumn colors remained in her memory, and this would be that kind of fall. Her divorce from Fair had been final six months ago, or was it a year? She really couldn't remember, or perhaps she didn't want to remember. Her friends ransacked their address books for the names of eligible bachelors. There were two: Dr. Larry Johnson, the retired, widowed town doctor, who was two years older than God, and the other, of course, was Pharamond Haristeen. Even if she wanted Fair back, which she most certainly did not, he was embroiled in a romance with Boom Boom Craycroft, the beautiful thirty-two-year-old widow of Kelly Craycroft.

Harry mused that everyone in town had nicknames. Olivia was Boom Boom, and Pharamond was Fair. She was Harry, and Peter Shiflett, who owned the market next door, was called Market. Cabell Hall, president of the Allied National Bank in Richmond, was Cab or Cabby; his wife of twenty-seven years, Florence, was dubbed Taxi. The Marilyn Sanburnes, senior and junior, were Big Marilyn, or Mim, and Little Marilyn respectively. How close it made everyone feel, these little monikers, these tokens of intimacy, nicknames. Crozet folks laughed at their neighbors' habits, predicting who would say what to whom and when. These were the joys of a small town, yet they masked the same problems and pain, the same cruelties, injustice, and self-destructive behavior found on a larger scale in Charlottesville, fourteen miles to the east, or Richmond, seventy miles beyond Charlottesville. The veneer of civilization, so essential to daily life, could easily be dissolved by crisis. Sometimes it didn't even take a crisis: Dad came home drunk and beat the living shit out of his wife and children, or a husband arrived home early from work to his heavily mortgaged abode and found his wife in bed with another man. Oh, it couldn't happen in Crozet but it did. Harry knew it did. After all, a post office is the nerve center of any community and she knew, usually before others, what went on when the doors were closed and the lights switched off. A flurry of legal letters might cram a box, or a strange medley of dental bills, and as Harry sorted the mail she would piece together the stories hidden from view.

If Harry understood her animals better, then she'd know even more, because her corgi, Tee Tucker, could scurry under porch steps, and Mrs. Murphy could leap into a hayloft, a feat the agile tiger cat performed both elegantly and with ease. The cat and dog carried a wealth of information, if only they could impart it to their relatively intelligent human companion. It was never easy, though. Mrs. Murphy sometimes had to roll over in front of her mother, or Tee Tucker might have to grab her pants leg.

Today the animals had no gossip about humans or their own kind. They sat next to Harry and observed Miranda Hogendobber—clad in a red plaid skirt, yellow sweater, and gardening gloves—hoe her small patch, which was producing a riot of squash and pumpkins. Harry waved to Mrs. Hogendobber, who returned the acknowledgment.

"Harry," Susan Tucker, Harry's best friend, called from inside the post office.

"I'm out back."

Susan opened the back door. "Postcard material. Picture perfect. Fall in central Virginia."

As she spoke the back door of the market opened and Pewter, the Shifletts' fat gray cat, streaked out, a chicken leg in her mouth.

Market shouted after the cat, "Damn you, Pewter, you'll get no supper tonight." He started after her as she headed toward the post office, glanced up, and beheld Harry and Susan. "Excuse me, ladies, had I known you were present I would not have used foul language."

Harry laughed. "Oh, Market, we use worse."

"Are you going to share?" Mrs. Murphy inquired of Pewter as she shot past them.

"How can she answer? Her mouth is full," Tucker said. *"Besides, when have you known Pewter to give even a morsel of food to anybody else?"*

"That's a fact." Mrs. Murphy followed her gray friend, just in case.

Pewter stopped just out of reach of a subdued Market, now chatting up the ladies. She tore off a tantalizing hunk of chicken.

"How'd you get that away from Market?" Mrs. Murphy's golden eyes widened.

Ever ready to brag, Pewter chewed, yet kept a paw on the drumstick. *"He put one of those barbecued chickens up on the counter. Little Marilyn asked him to cut it up and when his back was turned I made off with a drumstick."* She chewed another savory piece.

"Aren't you a clever girl?" Tucker sniffed that delicious smell.

"As a matter of fact I am. Little Marilyn hollered and declared she wouldn't take a chicken that a cat had bitten

into, and truthfully, I wouldn't eat anything Little Marilyn had touched. Turning into as big a snot as her mother."

With lightning speed Mrs. Murphy grabbed the chicken leg as Tucker knocked the fat kitty off balance. Mrs. Murphy raced down the alleyway into Miranda Hogendobber's garden, followed by a triumphant Tucker and a spitting Pewter.

"Give me that back, you striped asshole!"

"You never share, Pewter," Tucker said as Mrs. Murphy ran between the rows of cornstalks, moving toward the moonlike pumpkins.

"Harry," Mrs. Hogendobber bellowed, "these creatures will be the death of me yet."

She brandished her hoe in the direction of Tucker, who ran away. Now Pewter chased Mrs. Murphy up and down the rows of squash but Mrs. Murphy, nimble and fit, leapt over a wide, spreading squash plant with its creamy yellow bounty in the middle. She headed for the pumpkins.

Market laughed. "Think we could unleash Miranda on the Sanburnes?" He was referring to Little Marilyn and her equally distasteful maternal unit, Mim.

That made Susan and Harry laugh, which infuriated Mrs. Hogendobber because she thought they were laughing at her.

"It's not funny. They'll ruin my garden. My prize pumpkins. You know I'm going to win at the Harvest Fair with my pumpkins." Miranda's face turned puce.

"I've never seen that color on a human being before." Tucker stared up in wonderment.

"Tucker, watch out for the hoe," Mrs. Murphy yelled. She dropped the drumstick.

Pewter grabbed it. The fat swung under her belly as

she shot back toward home, came within a whisker's length of Market and skidded sideways, evading him.

He laughed. "If they want it that bad I might as well bring over the rest of the chicken."

By the time he was back with the chicken, Mrs. Hogendobber, huffing and puffing, had plopped herself at the back door of the post office.

"Tucker could have broken my hip. What if she'd knocked me over?" Mrs. Hogendobber warmed to the scenario of damage and danger.

Market bit his tongue. He wanted to say that she was well padded enough not to worry. Instead he clucked sympathy while cutting meat off the chicken for the three animals, who hastily forgave one another any wrongdoing. Chicken was too important to let ego stand in the way.

"I'm sorry, Mrs. Hogendobber. Are you all right?" Harry asked politely.

"Of course I'm all right. I just wish you could control your charges."

"What you need is a corgi," Susan Tucker volunteered.

"No, I don't. I took care of my husband all my life and I don't need a dog to care for. At least George brought home a paycheck, bless his soul."

"They're very entertaining," Harry added.

"What about the fleas?" Mrs. Hogendobber was more interested than she cared to admit.

"You can have those without a dog," Harry answered.

"I do not have fleas."

"Miranda, when the weather's warm, everyone's got fleas," Market corrected her.

"Speak for yourself. And if I ran a food establishment

I would make sure there wasn't a flea within fifty yards of the place. Fifty yards." Mrs. Hogendobber pursed her lips, outlined in a pearlized red that matched the red in her plaid skirt. "And I'd give more discounts."

"Now, Miranda." Market, having heard this *ad nauseam,* was prepared to launch into a passionate defense of his pricing practices.

An unfamiliar voice cut off this useless debate. "Anyone home?"

"Who's that?" Mrs. Hogendobber's eyebrows arched upward.

Harry and Susan shrugged. Miranda marched into the post office. As her husband, George, had been postmaster for over forty years before his death, she felt she could do whatever she wanted. Harry was on her heels, Susan and Market bringing up the rear. The animals, finished with the chicken, scooted in.

Standing on the other side of the counter was the handsomest man Mrs. Hogendobber had seen since Clark Gable. Susan and Harry might have chosen a more recent ideal of virility, but whatever the vintage of comparison, this guy was drop-dead gorgeous. Soft hazel eyes illuminated a chiseled face, rugged yet sensitive, and his hair was curly brown, perfectly cut. His hands were strong. Indeed, his entire impression was one of strength. On top of well-fitted jeans was a watermelon-colored sweater, the sleeves pushed up on tanned, muscular forearms.

For a moment no one said a word. Miranda quickly punctured the silence.

"Miranda Hogendobber." She held out her hand.

"Blair Bainbridge. Please call me Blair."

Miranda now had the upper hand and could intro-

duce the others. "This is our postmistress, Mary Minor
Haristeen. Susan Tucker, wife of Ned Tucker, a very fine
lawyer should you ever need one, and Market Shiflett,
who owns the store next door, which is very convenient
and carries those sinful Dove bars."

"Hey, hey, what about us?" The chorus came from
below.

Harry picked up Mrs. Murphy. "This is Mrs. Murphy, that's Tee Tucker, and the gray kitty is Pewter,
Market's invaluable assistant, though she's often over
here picking up the mail."

Blair smiled and shook Mrs. Murphy's paw, which
delighted Harry. Mrs. Murphy didn't mind. The masculine vision then leaned over and patted Pewter's head.
Tucker held up her paw to shake, which Blair did.

"I'm pleased to meet you."

"Me, too," Tucker replied.

"May I help you?" Harry asked as the others leaned
forward in anticipation.

"Yes. I'd like a post box if one is available."

"I have a few. Do you like odd numbers or even?"
Harry smiled. She could be charming when she smiled.
She was one of those fine-looking women who took few
pains with herself. What you saw was what you got.

"Even."

"How does forty-four sound? Or thirteen—I almost
forgot I had thirteen."

"Don't take thirteen." Miranda shook her head. "Bad
luck."

"Forty-four then."

"Thirty-four ninety-five, please." Harry filled out the
box slip and stamped it with pokeberry-colored ink, a
kind of runny maroon.

He handed over the check and she handed over the key.

"Is there a Mrs. Bainbridge?" Mrs. Hogendobber brazenly asked. "The name sounds so familiar."

Market rolled his eyes heavenward.

"No, I haven't had the good fortune to find the right woman to—"

"Harry's single, you know. Divorced, actually." Mrs. Hogendobber nodded in Harry's direction.

At that moment Harry and Susan would have gladly slit her throat.

"Mrs. Hogendobber, I'm sure Mr. Bainbridge doesn't need my biography on his first visit to the post office."

"On my second, perhaps you'll supply it." He put the key in his pocket, smiled, and left, climbing into a jet-black Ford F350 dually pickup. Mr. Bainbridge was prepared to do some serious hauling in that baby.

"Miranda, how could you?" Susan exclaimed.

"How could I what?"

"You know what." Market took up the chorus.

Miranda paused. "Mention Harry's marital status? Listen, I'm older than any of you. First impressions are important. He might not have such a good first impression of me but I bet he'll have one of Harry, who handled the situation with her customary tact and humor. And when he goes home tonight he'll know there's one pretty unmarried woman in Crozet." With that astonishing justification she swept out the back door.

"Well, I'll be damned." Market's jaw hung slack.

"That's what I say." Pewter cackled.

"Girls, I'm going back to work. This was all too much for me." Market laughed and opened the front door. He paused. "Oh, come on, you little crook."

Pewter meowed sweetly and followed her father out the door.

"Can you believe Rotunda could run that fast?" Tucker said to Mrs. Murphy.

"That was a surprise." Mrs. Murphy rolled over on the floor, revealing her pretty buff underbelly.

"This fall is going to be full of surprises. I feel it in my bones." Tucker smiled and wagged her stumpy tail.

Mrs. Murphy gave her a look. The cat was not in the mood for prophecy. Anyway, cats knew more of such things than dogs. She didn't feel like confirming that she thought Tucker was right. Something *was* in the air. But what?

Harry placed the check in the drawer under the counter. It was face up and she peered down at it again. "Yellow Mountain Farm."

"There is no Yellow Mountain Farm." Susan bent over to examine the check.

"Foxden."

"What? That place has been empty for over a year now. Who would buy it?"

"A Yankee." Harry closed the door. "Or someone from California."

"No." Susan's voice dropped.

"There is nothing else for sale around Yellow Mountain except Foxden."

"But, Harry, we know everything, and we haven't heard one word, one measly peep, about Foxden selling."

Harry was already dialing the phone as Susan was talking. "Jane Fogleman, please." There was a brief pause. "Jane, why didn't you tell me Foxden had sold?"

Jane, from the other end of the line, replied, "Because

we were instructed to keep our mouths shut until the closing, which was at nine this morning at McGuire, Woods, Battle and Boothe."

"I can't believe you'd keep it from us. Susan and I just met him."

"Those were Mr. Bainbridge's wishes." Jane held her breath for a moment. "Did you ever see anything like him? I mean to tell you, girl."

Harry fudged and sounded unimpressed. "He's good-looking."

"Good-looking? He's to die for!" Jane exploded.

"Let's hope no one has to do that," Harry remarked drily. "Well, you told me what I wanted to know. Susan says hello and we'll be slow to forgive you."

"Right." Jane laughed and hung up.

"Foxden." Harry put the receiver in the cradle.

"God, we had some wonderful times at that old farm. The little six-stall barn and the gingerbread on the house and oh, don't forget, the cemetery. Remember the one really old tombstone with the little angel playing a harp?"

"Yeah. The MacGregors were such good people."

"Lived forever, too. No kids. Guess that's why they let us run all over the place." Susan felt old Elizabeth MacGregor's presence in the room. An odd sensation and not rational but pleasant, since Elizabeth and Mackie, her husband, were the salt of the earth.

"I hope Blair Bainbridge has as much happiness at Foxden as the MacGregors did."

"He ought to keep the name."

"Well, that's his business," Harry replied.

"Bet Miranda gets him to do it." Susan took a deep

breath. "You've got yourself a new neighbor, Sistergirl. Aren't you dying of curiosity?"

Harry shook her head. "No."

"Liar."

"I'm not."

"Oh, Harry, get over the divorce."

"I am over the divorce and I'm not majoring in longing and desire, despite all your hectoring for the last six months."

"You can't keep living like a nun." Susan's voice rose.

"I'll live the way I want to live."

"There they go again," Tucker observed.

Mrs. Murphy nodded. *"Tucker, want to go over to Foxden tonight if we can get out of the house? Let's check out this Bainbridge guy. I mean, if everyone's going to be pushing Mom at him we'd better get the facts."*

"Great idea."

2

By eleven that night Harry was sound asleep. Mrs. Murphy, dexterity itself, pulled open the back door. Harry rarely locked it and tonight she hadn't shut it tight. It required only patience for the cat, with her clever claws, to finally swing the door open. The screen door was a snap. Tucker pushed it open with her nose, popping the hook.

For October the night was unusually warm, the last flickering of Indian summer. Harry's old Superman-blue Ford pickup rested by the barn. Ran like a top. The animals trotted by the truck.

"Wait a minute." Tucker sniffed.

Mrs. Murphy sat down and washed her face while Tucker, nose to the ground, headed for the barn. *"Simon again?"*

Simon, the opossum, enjoyed rummaging around the grounds. Harry often tossed out marshmallows and table scraps for him. Simon made every effort to get these goodies before the raccoons arrived. He didn't like the raccoons and they didn't like him.

Tucker didn't reply to Mrs. Murphy's question but ducked into the barn instead. The smell of timothy hay, sweet feed, and bran swirled around her delicate nostrils. The horses stayed out in the evenings and were brought inside during the heat of the day. That system would only continue for about another week because soon enough the deep frosts of fall would turn the meadows silver, and the horses would need to be in during the night, secure in their stalls and warmed by their Triple Crown blankets.

A sharp little nose stuck out from the feed room. *"Tucker."*

"Simon, you're not supposed to be in the feed room." Tucker's low growl was censorious.

"The raccoons came early, so I ran in here." The raccoons' litter proved Simon's truthfulness. *"Hello, Mrs. Murphy."* Simon greeted the sleek feline as she entered the barn.

"Hello. Say, have you been over to Foxden?" Mrs. Murphy swept her whiskers forward.

"Last night. No food over there yet." Simon focused on his main concern.

"We're going over for a look."

"Not much to see 'ceptin for the big truck that new fellow has. That and the gooseneck trailer. Looks like he means to buy some horses because there aren't any over there now." Simon laughed because he knew that within a matter of weeks the horse dealers would be trying to stick a vacuum cleaner hose in Blair Bainbridge's pockets. *"Know what I miss? Old Mrs. MacGregor used to pour hot maple syrup in the snow to make candy and she'd*

always leave some for me. Can't you get Harry to do that when it snows?"

"Simon, you're lucky to get table scraps. Harry's not much of a cook. Well, we're going over to Foxden to see what's cooking." Tucker smiled at her little joke.

Mrs. Murphy stared at Tucker. She loved Tucker but sometimes she thought dogs were really dumb.

They left Simon munching away on a bread crust. As they crossed the twenty acres on the west side of Harry's farm they called out to Harry's horses, Tomahawk and Gin Fizz, who neighed in reply.

Harry had inherited her parents' farm when her father died years ago. Like her parents, she kept everything tiptop. Most of the fence lines were in good repair, although come spring she would need to replace the fence along the creek between her property and Foxden. Her barn had received a fresh coat of red paint with white trim this year. The hay crop flourished. The bales, rolled up like giant shredded wheat, were lined up against the eastern fence line. All totaled, Harry kept 120 acres. She never tired of the farm chores and probably was at her happiest on the ancient Ford tractor, some thirty-five years old, pulling along a harrow or a plow.

Getting up at five-thirty in the morning appealed to her except in darkest winter, when she did it anyway. The outdoor chores took so much of Harry's free time that she wasn't always able to keep up with the house. The outside needed some fresh paint. She and Susan had painted the inside last winter. Mrs. Hogendobber even came out to help for a day. Harry's sofa and chairs, oversized, needed to be reupholstered. They were pieces her mother and father had bought at an auction in 1949 shortly after they were married. They figured the furniture had been built in the 1930's. Harry didn't much care how old the furniture was but it was the most comfortable stuff she'd ever sat in. Mrs. Murphy and Tucker could lounge unrestricted on the sofa, so it had their approval.

A small, strong creek divided Harry's land from Foxden. Tucker scrambled down the bank and plunged in. The water was low. Mrs. Murphy, not overfond of water, circled around, revved her motors, and took a running leap, clearing the creek and Tucker as well.

From there they raced to the house, passing the small cemetery on its knoll. A light shone out from a second-story window into the darkness. Huge sweet gum trees, walnuts, and oaks sheltered the frame dwelling, built in 1837 with a 1904 addition. Mrs. Murphy climbed up the big walnut tree and casually walked out onto a branch to peer into the lighted room. Tucker bitched and moaned at the base of the tree.

"Shut up, Tucker. You'll get us both chased out of here."

"Tell me what you see."

"Once I crawl back down, I will. How do we know this human doesn't have good ears? Some do, you know."

Inside the lighted room Blair Bainbridge was engaged in the dirty job of steaming off wallpaper. Nasty strips of peony paper, the blossoms a startling pink, hung down. Every now and then Blair would put down the steamer and pull on the paper. He wore a T-shirt, and little bits of wallpaper stuck to his arms. A portable CD player, on the other side of the room, provided some solace with Bach's Brandenburg Concerto Number One. No furniture or boxes cluttered the room.

Mrs. Murphy backed down the tree and told Tucker

that there wasn't much going on. They circled the house. The bushes had been trimmed back, the gardens mulched, the dead limbs pruned off trees. Mrs. Murphy opened the back screen door. The back porch had two director's chairs and an orange crate for a coffee table. The old cast-iron boot scraper shaped like a dachshund still stood just to the left of the door. Neither cat nor dog could get up to see in the back door window.

"Let's go to the barn," Tucker suggested.

The barn, a six-stall shed row with a little office in the middle, presented nothing unusual. The stall floors, looking like moon craters, needed to be filled in and evened out. Blair Bainbridge would sweat bullets with that task. Tamping down the stalls was worse than hauling wheelbarrows loaded with clay and rock dust. Cobwebs hung everywhere and a few spiders were finishing up their winter preparations. Mice cleaned out what grain remained in the feed room. Mrs. Murphy regretted that she didn't have more time to play catch.

They left the barn and inspected the dually truck and the gooseneck, both brand new. Who could afford a new truck and trailer at the same time? Mr. Bainbridge wasn't living on food stamps.

"We didn't find out very much," Tucker sighed. *"Other than the fact that he has some money."*

"We know more than that." Mrs. Murphy felt a bite on her shoulder. She dug ferociously. *"He's independent and he's hard-working. He wants the place to look good and he wants horses. And there's no woman around, nor does there seem to be one in the picture."*

"You don't know that." Tucker shook her head.

"There's no woman. We'd smell her."

"Yeah, but you don't know that one might not visit. Maybe he's fixing up the place to impress her."

"No. I can't prove it but I feel it. He wants to be alone. He listens to thoughtful music. I think he's getting away from somebody or something."

Tucker thought Mrs. Murphy was jumping to conclusions, but she kept her mouth shut or she'd have to endure a lecture about how cats are mysterious and how cats know things that dogs don't, *ad nauseam.*

As the two walked home they passed the cemetery, the wrought-iron fence topped with spearheads marking off the area. One side had fallen down.

"Let's go in." Tucker ran over.

The graveyard had been in use by Joneses and Mac-Gregors for nearly two hundred years. The oldest tombstone read: CAPTAIN FRANCIS EGBERT JONES, BORN 1730, DIED 1802. A small log cabin once stood near the creek, but as the Jones family's fortunes increased they built the frame house. The foundation of the log cabin still stood by the creek. The various headstones, small ones for children, two of whom were carried off by scarlet fever right after the War Between the States, sported carvings and sayings. After that terrible war a Jones daughter, Estella Lynch Jones, married a MacGregor, which was how MacGregors came to be buried here, including the last occupants of Foxden.

The graveyard had been untended since Mrs. Mac-Gregor's death. Ned Tucker, Susan's husband and the executor of the estate, rented out the acres to Mr. Stuart Tapscott for his own use. He had to maintain what he used, which he did. The cemetery, however, contained the remains of the Jones family and the MacGregor family, and the survivors, not Mr. Tapscott, were to care for the grounds. The lone descendant, the Reverend Herbert Jones, besieged by ecclesiastical duties and a bad back, was unable to keep up the plot.

It appeared things were going to change with Blair Bainbridge's arrival. The tombstones that had been overturned were righted, the grass was clipped, and a small camellia bush was planted next to Elizabeth MacGregor's headstone. The iron fence would take more than one person to right and repair.

"Guess Mr. Bainbridge went to work in here too," Mrs. Murphy remarked.

"Here's my favorite." Tucker stood by the marker of Colonel Ezekiel Abram Jones, born in 1812 and died in 1861, killed at First Manassas. The inscription read: BETTER TO DIE ON YOUR FEET THAN LIVE ON YOUR KNEES. A fitting sentiment for a fallen Confederate who paid for his conviction, yet ironic in its unintentional parallel to the injustice of slavery.

"I like this one." Mrs. Murphy leapt on top of a square tombstone with an angel playing a harp carved on it. This belonged to Ezekiel's wife, Martha Selena, who lived thirty years beyond her husband's demise. The inscription read: SHE PLAYS WITH ANGELS.

The animals headed back home, neither one discussing the small graveyard at Harry's farm. Not that it wasn't lovely and well kept, containing her ancestors, but it also contained little tombstones for the beloved family pets. Mrs. Murphy and Tucker found that a sobering possibility on which they refused to dwell.

They slipped into the house as quietly as they had left it, with both animals doing their best to push shut the door. They were only partially successful, the result being that the kitchen was cold when Harry arose at five-thirty, and the cat and dog listened to a patch of blue language, which made them giggle. Discovering that the hook had been bent on the screen door called forth a new torrent of verbal abuse. Harry forgot all about it as the sun rose and the eastern sky glowed peach, gold, and pink.

Those extraordinarily beautiful October days and nights would come back to haunt Harry and her animal friends. Everything seemed so perfect. No one is ever prepared for evil in the face of beauty.

3

"He has not only the absence of fear but of all scruple."
Mrs. Hogendobber's alto voice vibrated with the importance of her story. "Well, I was shocked completely when I discovered that Ben Seifert, branch manager of our local bank, indulges in sharp business practices. He tried to get me to take out a loan on my house, which is paid for, Mr. Bainbridge. He said he was sure I needed renovations. 'Renovate what?' I said, and he said wouldn't I be thrilled with a modern kitchen and a microwave? I don't want a microwave. They give people cancer. Then Cabby Hall, the president, walked into the bank and I made a beeline for him. Told him everything and he took Ben to task. I only tell you this so you'll be on your guard. This may be a small town but our bankers try to sell money just like those big city boys do, Mr. Bainbridge. Be on your toes!" Miranda had to stop and catch her breath.

"Please do call me Blair."

"Then to top it off, the choir director of my church

walked into the bank to inform me that he thought Boom Boom Craycroft had asked Fair Haristeen to marry her, or perhaps it was vice versa."

"His vice was her versa." Blair smiled, his bright white teeth making him even more attractive.

"Yes, quite. As it turned out, no proposal had taken place." Mrs. Hogendobber folded her hands. She didn't cotton to having her stories interrupted but she was blossoming under the attention of Blair Bainbridge—doubly sweet, since Susan Tucker and Harry could see his black truck parked alongside Mrs. Hogendobber's house. Of course she was going to walk him through her garden, shower him with hints on how to achieve gargantuan pumpkins, and then bestow upon him the gifts of her green thumb. She might even find out something about him in the process. Some time ago Mrs. Hogendobber had borrowed some copies of *New York* magazine from Ned Tucker, for the crossword puzzles. After meeting Blair the other day, she had realized why his name was familiar: She had read about him in one of those magazines. There was an article about high-fashion romance. When he introduced himself, the name had seemed vaguely familiar. She was hoping to find out more today about his link to the article, his ill-fated relationship with a beautiful model named Robin Mangione.

The doorbell rang, destroying her plan. The Reverend Herbert Jones marched through the door when Mrs. Hogendobber opened it.

Now this curdled the milk in her excellent coffee. Mrs. Hogendobber felt competitive toward all rival prophets of Christianity. The Right Reverend Jones was minister of the Lutheran Church. His congregation, larger than hers at the Church of the Holy Light, served only to increase her efforts at conversion. The church used to be called The Holy Light Church, but two months ago Miranda had prevailed upon the preacher and the congregation to rename it the Church of the Holy Light. Her reasons, while serviceable, proved less convincing than her exhausting enthusiasm, hence the change.

A cup of coffee and fresh scones were served to Reverend Jones, and the three settled down for more conversation.

"Mr. Bainbridge, I want to welcome you to our small community and to thank you for fixing up my family's cemetery. Due to disc problems, I have been unable to discharge my obligations to my forebears as they deserve."

"It was my pleasure, Reverend."

"Now, Herbie"—Miranda lapsed into familiarity—"you can't lure Mr. Bainbridge into your fold until I've had a full opportunity to tell him about our Church of the Holy Light."

Blair stared at his scone. A whiff of brimstone emanated from Mrs. Hogendobber's sentence.

"This young man will find his own way. All paths lead to God, Miranda."

"Don't try to sidetrack me with tolerance," she snapped.

"I'd never do that." Reverend Jones slipped in that dig.

"I can appreciate your concern for my soul." Blair's baritone caressed Mrs. Hogendobber's ears. "But I'm sorry to disappoint you both. The fact is I'm a Catholic, and while I can't say I agree with or practice my faith as strictly as the Pope would wish, I occasionally go to Mass."

The Reverend laid down his scone, dripping with orange marmalade made by Mrs. Hogendobber's skilled hands. "A Lutheran is just a Catholic without the incense."

This made both Blair and his hostess laugh. The Reverend was never one to allow dogma to stand in the way of affection and often, in the dead of night, he himself found little solace in the rigors of doctrine. Reverend Jones was a true shepherd to his flock. Let the intellectuals worry about transubstantiation and the Virgin Birth —he had babies to baptize, couples to counsel, the sick to succor, and burials to perform. He hated that latter part of his calling but he prayed to himself that the souls of his flock would go to God, even the most miserable wretches.

"If you don't mind my asking, Reverend, how did you find out about the cemetery being mowed?" Blair wondered.

"Oh, Harry told me this morning as she walked in to work. Said her little doggie dashed over there as she was doing her chores and she caught her in the cemetery."

"She walks to work?" Blair was incredulous. "It has to be two miles at least, one way."

"Oh, yes. She likes the exercise. By the time she gets to the post office she's already put in a good two to three hours of farm chores. A born farmer, Harry. In the bones. She'll make a good neighbor."

"Which brings me to the subject of your renaming your place Yellow Mountain Farm." Mrs. Hogendobber composed herself for what she thought would be a siege of argument.

"It's at the base of Yellow Mountain and so I naturally—"

She interrupted him. "It's been Foxden since the beginning of the eighteenth century and I'm surprised Jane Fogleman did not inform you, as she is normally a fountain of information."

The Reverend shrewdly took a pass on this one, even though the land in question was part of his heritage. He hadn't the money to buy it nor the inclination to farm it, so he thought he had little right to tell the man what to call his purchase.

"That long?" Blair thought a moment. "Maybe Jane did mention it."

"Did you read your deed?" Mrs. Hogendobber demanded.

"No, I let the lawyers do that. I've tried to wrestle some order out of the place though."

"Pokeweeds," the Reverend calmly said as he downed another scone.

"Is that what you call them?"

"In polite company." Herbie laughed.

"Herbert, you are deliberately sidetracking this discussion, which, for the sake of the Historical Society of Greater Crozet, I must conduct."

"Mrs. Hogendobber, if it means that much to you and the Historical Society, I will of course keep the name of Foxden."

"Oh." Mrs. Hogendobber hadn't expected to win so easily. It rather disappointed her.

The Reverend Jones chuckled to himself that the Crozet Historical Society sometimes became the Crozet Hysterical Society but he was glad the old farm would keep its name.

Both gentlemen rose to go and she forgot to give Blair one of her pumpkins, a lesser specimen because she was saving the monster pumpkin for the Harvest Fair.

Blair walked with Reverend Jones to his church and then bade him goodbye, turning back to the post office. He passed a vagrant wearing old jeans and a baseball jacket and walking along the railroad track. The man appeared ageless; he could have been thirty or fifty. The sight startled him. Blair hadn't expected to see someone like that in Crozet.

As Blair pushed open the post office door Tucker rushed out to greet him. Mrs. Murphy withheld judgment. Dogs needed affection and attention so much that in Mrs. Murphy's estimation they could be fooled far more easily than a cat could be. If she'd given herself a minute to think, though, she would have had to admit she was being unfair to her best friend. Tucker's feelings about people hit the bull's-eye more often than not. Mrs. Murphy did allow herself a stretch on the counter and Blair came over to scratch her ears.

"Good afternoon, critters."

They replied, as did Harry from the back room. "Sounds like my new neighbor. Check your box. You've got a pink package slip."

As Blair slipped the key into the ornate post box he called out to Harry, "Is the package pink too?"

The sound of the package hitting the counter coincided with Blair's shutting his box. A slap and a click. He snapped his fingers to add to the rhythm.

Harry drawled, "Musical?"

"Happy."

"Good." She shoved the package toward him.

"Mind if I open this?"

"No, you'll satisfy my natural curiosity." She leaned over as Little Marilyn Sanburne flounced through the door accompanied by her husband, who sported new horn-rimmed glasses. Fitz-Gilbert Hamilton devoured *Esquire* and *GQ*. The results were as one saw.

"A bum on the streets of Crozet!" Little Marilyn complained.

"What?"

Little Marilyn pointed. Harry came out from behind the counter to observe the scraggly, bearded fellow, his face in profile. She returned to her counter.

Fitz-Gilbert said, "Some people have bad luck."

"Some people are lazy," declared Little Marilyn, who had never worked a day in her life.

She bumped into Blair when she whirled around to behold the wanderer one more time.

"Sorry. Let me get out of your way." Blair pushed his carton over to the side of the counter.

Harry began introductions.

Fitz-Gilbert stuck out his hand and heartily said, "Fitz-Gilbert Hamilton. Princeton, 1980."

Blair blinked and then shook his hand. "Blair Bainbridge. Yale, 1979."

That caught Fitz-Gilbert off guard for a moment. "Before that?"

"St. Paul's," came the even reply.

"Andover," Fitz-Gilbert said.

"I bet you boys have friends in common," Little Marilyn added—without interest, since the conversation was not about her.

"We'll have to sit down over a brew and find out,"

Fitz-Gilbert offered. He was genuinely friendly, while his wife was merely correct.

"Thank you. I'd enjoy that. I'm over at Foxden."

"We know." Little Marilyn added her two cents.

"Small town. Everybody knows everything." Fitz-Gilbert laughed.

The Hamiltons left laden with mail and mail-order catalogues.

"Crozet's finest." Blair looked to Harry.

"They think so." Harry saw no reason to disguise her assessment of Little Marilyn and her husband.

Mrs. Murphy hopped into Blair's package.

"Why don't you like them?" Blair inquired.

"It helps if you meet Momma. Big Marilyn—or Mim."

"Big Marilyn?"

"I kid you not. You've just had the pleasure of meeting Little Marilyn. Her father is the mayor of Crozet and they have more money than God. She married Fitz-Gilbert a year or so ago in a social extravaganza on a par with the wedding of Prince Charles and Lady Di. Didn't Mrs. Hogendobber fill you in?"

"She allowed as how everyone here has a history which she would be delighted to relate, but the Reverend Jones interrupted her plans, I think." Blair started to laugh. The townspeople were nothing if not amusing and he liked Harry. He had liked her right off the bat, a phrase that kept circling in his brain although he didn't know why.

Harry noticed Mrs. Murphy rustling in Blair's package. "Hey, hey, out of there, Miss Puss."

In reply Mrs. Murphy scrunched farther down in the box. Only the tips of her ears showed.

Harry leaned over the box. "Scram."

Mrs. Murphy meowed, a meow of consummate irritation.

Blair laughed. "What'd she say?"

"Don't rain on my parade," Harry replied, and to torment the cat she placed the box on the floor.

"No, she didn't," Tucker yelped. *"She said, 'Eat shit and die.' "*

"Shut up, Fuckface," Mrs. Murphy rumbled from the depths of the carton, the tissue paper crinkling in a manner most exciting to her ears.

Tucker, not one to be insulted, ran to the box and began pulling on the flap.

"Cut it out," came the voice from within.

Now Tucker stopped and stuck her head in the box, cold nose right in Mrs. Murphy's face. The cat jumped straight up out of the box, turned in midair, and grabbed on to the dog. Tucker stood still and Mrs. Murphy rolled under the dog's belly. Then Tucker raced around the post office, the cat dangling underneath like a Sioux on the warpath.

Blair Bainbridge bent over double, he was laughing so hard.

Harry laughed too. "Small pleasures."

"Not small—large indeed. I don't know when I've seen anything so funny."

Mrs. Murphy dropped off. Tucker raced back to the box. *"I win."*

"Do you have anything fragile in there?" Harry asked.

"No. Some gardening tools." He opened the box to show her. "I ordered this stuff for bulb planting. If I get right on it I think I can have a lovely spring."

"I've got a tractor. It's near to forty years old but it works just fine. Let me know when you need it."

"Uh, well, I wouldn't know what to do with it. I don't know how to drive one," Blair confessed.

"Where are you from, Mr. Bainbridge?"

"New York City."

Harry considered this. "Were you born there?"

"Yes, I was. I grew up on East Sixty-fourth."

A Yankee. Harry decided not to give it another minute's thought. "Well, I'll teach you how to drive the tractor."

"I'll pay you for it."

"Oh, Mr. Bainbridge." Harry's voice registered surprise. "This is Crozet. This is Virginia." She paused and lowered her voice. "This is the South. Someday, something will turn up that you can do for me. Don't say anything about money. Anyway, that's what's wrong with Little Marilyn and Fitz-Gilbert. Too much money."

Blair laughed. "You think people can have too much money?"

"I do. Truly, I do."

Blair Bainbridge spent the rest of the day and half the night thinking about that.

4

The doors of the Allied National Bank swung open and the vagrant breezed past Marion Molnar, past the tellers. Marion got up and followed this apparition as he strolled into Benjamin Seifert's office and shut the door.

Ben, a rising star in the Allied National system, a protégé of bank president Cabell Hall, opened his mouth to say something just as Marion charged in behind the visitor.

"I want to see Cabell Hall," he demanded.

"He's at the main branch," Marion said.

Protectively Ben rose and placed himself between the unwashed man and Marion. "I'll take care of this."

Marion hesitated, then returned to her desk as Ben closed the door. She couldn't hear what was being said but the voices had a civil tone.

Within a few minutes Ben emerged with the man in the baseball jacket.

"I'm giving the gentleman a lift." He winked at Marion and left.

5

The dew coated the grass as Harry, Mrs. Murphy, and Tucker walked along the railroad track. The night had been unusually warm again and the day promised to follow suit. The slanting rays of the morning drenched Crozet in bright hope—at least that's how Harry thought of the morning.

As she passed the railroad station she saw Mrs. Hogendobber, little hand weights clutched in her fists, approaching from the opposite direction.

"Morning, Harry."

"Morning, Mrs. H." Harry waved as the determined figure huffed by, wearing an old sweater and a skirt below the knee. Mrs. Hogendobber felt strongly that women should not wear pants but she did concede to sneakers. Even her sister in Greenville, South Carolina, said it was all right to wear pants but Miranda declared that their dear mother had spent a fortune on cotillion. The least she could do for that parental sacrifice was to maintain her dignity as a lady.

Harry arrived at the door of the post office just as Rob Collier lurched up in the big mail truck. He grunted and hauled off the mail bags, complaining bitterly that gossip was thin at the main post office in Charlottesville, hopped back in the truck, and sped off.

As Harry was sorting the mail Boom Boom Craycroft sauntered in, her arrival lacking only triumphant fanfare. Unlike Mrs. Hogendobber she did wear pants, tight jeans in particular, and she was keen to wear T-shirts, or any top that would call attention to her bosom. She had developed early, in the sixth grade. The boys used to say, "Baboom, Baboom," when she went sashaying past. Over the years this was abbreviated to Boom Boom. If her nickname bothered her no one could tell. She appeared delighted that her assets were now legend.

She did not appear delighted to see Harry.

"Good morning, Boom Boom."

"Good morning, Harry. Anything for me?"

"I put it in the box. What brings you to town so early?"

"I'm getting up earlier now to catch as much light as I can. I suffer from seasonal affect disorder, you know, and winter depresses me."

Harry, long accustomed to Boom Boom's endless array of physical ills, enough to fill many medical books, couldn't resist. "But Boom Boom, I thought you'd conquered that by removing dairy products from your diet."

"No, that was for my mucus difficulty."

"Oh." Harry thought to herself that if Boom Boom had even half of the vividly described maladies she com-

plained of, she'd be dead. That would be okay with
Harry.

"We"—and by this Boom Boom meant herself and
Harry's ex-husband, Fair—"were at Mim's last night.
Little Marilyn and Fitz-Gilbert were there and we
played Pictionary. You should see Mim go at it. She has
to win, you know."

"Did she?"

"We let her. Otherwise she wouldn't invite us to her
table at the Harvest Fair Ball this year. You know how
she gets. But say, Little Marilyn and Fitz-Gilbert mentioned that they'd met this new man—'divine looking'
was how Little Marilyn put it—and he's your neighbor.
A Yale man too. What would a Yale man do here? The
South sends her sons to Princeton, so he must be a
Yankee. I used to date a Yale man, Skull and Bones,
which is ironic since I broke my ankle dancing with
him."

Harry thought calling that an irony was stretching it.
What Boom Boom really wanted Harry to appreciate
was that not only did she know a Yale man, she knew a
Skull and Bones man—not Wolf's Head or any of the
other "lesser" secret societies, but Skull and Bones.
Harry thought admission to Yale was enough of an
honor; if one was tapped for a secret society, too, well,
wonderful, but best to keep quiet about it. Then again,
Boom Boom couldn't keep quiet about anything.

Tucker yawned behind the counter. *"Murph, jump in
the mail cart."*

"Okay." Mrs. Murphy wiggled her haunches and took
a flying leap from the counter where she was eavesdrop-
ping on the veiled combat between the humans. She hit
the mail cart dead center and it rolled across the back

room, a metallic rattle to its wheels. Tucker barked as she ran alongside.

"Hey, you two." Harry giggled.

"Well, I'll be late for my low-impact aerobics class. Have a good day." Boom Boom lied about the good day part and left.

Boom Boom attracted men. This only convinced Harry that the two sexes did not look at women in the same way. Maybe men and women came from different planets—at least that's what Harry thought on her bad days. Boom Boom had attractive features and the celebrated big tits but Harry also saw that she was a hypochondriac of the first water, managing to acquire some dread malady whenever she was in danger of performing any useful labor.

Susan Tucker used to growl that Boom Boom never fucked anyone poor. Well, she'd broken that pattern with Fair Haristeen, and Harry knew that sooner or later Boom Boom would weary of not getting earrings from Cartier's, vacations out of the country, and a new car whenever the mood struck her. Of course she had plenty of her own money to burn but that wasn't as much fun as burning a hole in someone else's pocket. She'd wait until she had a rich fellow lined up in her sights and then she'd dump Fair with lightning speed. Harry wanted to be a good enough person not to gloat when that moment occurred. However, she knew she wasn't.

This reverie of delayed revenge was interrupted when Mim Sanburne strode into the post office. Sporting one of those boiled Austrian jackets and a jaunty hunter-green hat with a pheasant feather on her head, she might have come from the Tyrol. A pleasant thought if it meant she might blow back to the Tyrol.

"Harry." Mim's greeting was imperious.

"Mrs. Sanburne."

Mim had a box with a low number, another confirmation of her status, since it had been in the family since the time postal service was first offered to Crozet. Her arms full of mail and glossy magazines, she dumped them on the counter. "Hear you've got a handsome beau."

"I do?" came the surprised reply.

Mrs. Murphy jumped around in the mail bin as Tucker snapped from underneath at the moving blob in the canvas.

"My son-in-law, Fitz-Gilbert, said he recognized him, this Blair Bainbridge fellow. He's a model. Seen him in *Esquire, GQ,* that sort of thing. Mind you, those models are a little funny, you know what I mean?"

"No, Mrs. Sanburne, I really don't."

"Well, I'm trying to protect you, Harry. Those pretty boys marry women but they prefer men, if I have to be blunt."

"First off, I'm not dating him."

This genuinely disappointed Mim. "Oh."

"Secondly, I have no idea as to his sexual preference but he seems nice enough and for now I will take him at face value. Thirdly, I'm taking a vacation from men."

Mim airily circled her hand over her head, a dramatic gesture for her. "That's what every woman says until she meets the next man, and there *is* a next man. They're like streetcars—there's always one coming around the corner."

"That's an interesting thought." Harry smiled.

Mim's voice hit the "important information" register. "You know, dear, Boom Boom will tire of Fair. When he comes to his senses, take him back."

As everyone had her nose in everyone else's business, this unsolicited, intimate advice from the mayor's wife didn't offend Harry. "I couldn't possibly do that."

A knowing smile spread across the carefully made-up face. "Better the devil you know than the devil you don't." With that sage advice Mim started for the door, stopped, turned, grabbed her mail and magazines off the counter, and left for good.

Harry folded her arms across her chest, a respectable chest, too, and looked at her animals. "Girls, people say the damnedest things."

Mrs. Murphy called out from the mail bin, *"Mim's a twit. Who cares? Gimmie a push."*

"You look pretty comfortable in there." Harry grabbed the corner of the mail bin and merrily rolled Mrs. Murphy across the post office as Tucker yapped with excitement.

Susan dashed through the back door, beheld the fun, and put Tucker in another mail bin. "Race you!"

By the time they'd exhausted themselves they heard a scratching at the back door, opened it, and in strolled Pewter. So, with a grunt, Harry picked up the gray cat, placed her in Mrs. Murphy's cart, and rolled the two cats at the same time. She crashed into Susan and Tucker.

Pewter, miffed, reached up and grabbed the edge of the mail bin with her paws. She was going to leap out when Mrs. Murphy yelled, *"Stay in, wimp."*

Pewter complied by jumping onto the tiger cat, and

the two rolled all over each other, meowing with delight as the mail bin races resumed.

"Wheee!" Susan added sound effects.

"Hey, let's go out the back door and race up the alley," Harry challenged.

"Yeah, yeah!" came the animals' thrilled replies.

Harry opened the back door, she and Susan carefully lifted the mail bins over the steps, and soon they were ripping and tearing up and down the little alleyway. Market Shiflett saw them when he was taking out the garbage and encouraged them to run faster. Mrs. Hogendobber, shading her eyes, looked up from her pumpkins. Smiling, she shook her head and resumed her labors.

Finally, the humans pooped out. They slowly rolled the bins back to the post office.

"How come people forget stuff like this when they get older?" Susan asked.

"Who knows?" Harry laughed as she watched Mrs. Murphy and Pewter sitting together in the bin.

"Wonder why we still play?" Susan thought out loud.

"Because we discovered that the secret of youth is arrested development." Harry punched Susan in the shoulder. "Ha."

The entire day unfolded with laughter, sunshine, and high spirits. That afternoon, as Harry revved up the ancient tractor Blair Bainbridge drove up the driveway in his dually. Would she come over to his place and look at the old iron cemetery fence?

So Harry chugged down the road, Mrs. Murphy in her lap, and Tucker riding with Blair. Harry pulled up the fallen-down fence while Blair put concrete blocks around it to hold it until he could secure post corners. Working alongside Blair was fun. Harry felt closest to people when working with them or playing games. Blair wasn't afraid to get dirty, which she found surprising for a city boy. Guess she surprised him too. She advised him on how to rehabilitate his stable, how to pack the stalls, and how to hang subzero fluorescent lights.

"Why not use incandescent lights?" Blair asked. "It's prettier."

"And a whole lot more expensive. Why spend money when you don't have to?" She pushed her blue Giants cap back on her head.

"Well, I like things to look just so."

"Hang the subzeros high up in the spine of your roof and then put regular lighting along the shed row, with metal guards over it. Otherwise you'll be picking glass out of your horses' heads. That's if you have to have, just have to have, incandescent lights."

Blair wiped his hands on his jeans. "Guess I look pretty stupid."

"No, you need to learn about the country. I wouldn't know what to do in New York City." She paused. "Fitz-Gilbert Hamilton says you're a model. Are you?"

"From time to time."

"Out of work?"

Harry's innocence about his field amused him and somehow made her endearing to him. "Not exactly. I can fly to a shoot. I just don't want to live in New York anymore and, well, I don't want to do that kind of work forever. The money is great but it's not . . . fitting."

Harry shrugged. "If a guy's as handsome as you are he might as well make money off of it."

Blair roared. He wasn't used to women being so direct with him. They were too busy flirting and wanting to be his date at the latest social event. "Harry, are you always so, uh, forthright?"

"I guess." Harry smiled. "But, hey, if you don't like that kind of work I hope you find something you do like."

"I'd like to breed horses."

"Mr. Bainbridge, three words of advice. *Don't do it.*" His face just fell. She hastened to add, "It's a money suck. You'd do better buying yearlings or older horses and making them. Truly. Sometime we can sit down and talk this over. I've got to get back home before the light goes. I've got to run the manure spreader and pull out a fence post."

"You helped me—I'll help you." Blair didn't know that "making a horse" meant breaking and training the animal. He had asked so many questions he decided he'd give Harry a break. He'd ask someone else what the phrase meant.

They rode back to Harry's. This time Mrs. Murphy rode with Blair and Tucker rode with Harry.

As Mrs. Murphy sat quietly in the passenger seat she focused on Blair. An engaging odor from his body curled around her nostrils, a mixture of natural scent, a hint of cologne, and sweat. He smiled as he drove along. She could feel his happiness. What was even better, he spoke to her as though she were an intelligent creature. He told her she was a very pretty kitty. She purred. He said he knew she was a champion mouser, he could just tell, and that once he settled in he would ask her about finding a cat or two for him. Nothing sadder on this earth than a human being without a cat. She added trills to her purrs.

By the time they turned into Harry's driveway Mrs. Murphy felt certain that she had totally charmed Blair, although it was the other way around.

The fence post proved stubborn but they finally got it out. The manure spreading would wait until tomorrow because the sun had set and there was no moon to work by. Harry invited Blair into her kitchen and made a pot of Jamaican Blue coffee.

"Harry," he teased her, "I thought you were frugal. This stuff costs a fortune."

"I save my money for my pleasures," Harry replied.

As they drank the coffee and ate the few biscuits Harry had, she told him about the MacGregors and the Joneses, the history of Foxden as she knew it, and the history of Crozet, named for Claudius Crozet, also as she knew it.

"Tell me something else." He leaned forward, his warm hazel eyes lighting up. "Why does everyone's farm have fox in its name? Fox Covert, Foxden, Fox Hollow, Red Fox, Gray Fox, Wily Fox, Fox Haven, Fox Ridge, Fox Run"—he inhaled—"Foxcroft, Fox Hills, Foxfield, Fox—"

"How about Dead Fox Farm?" Harry filled in.

"No way. You're making that up."

"Yeah." Harry burst out laughing and Blair laughed along with her.

He left for home at nine-thirty, whistling as he drove. Harry washed up the dishes and tried to remember when she'd enjoyed a new person quite so much.

The cat and dog curled up together and wished humans could grasp the obvious. Harry and Blair were meant for each other. They wondered how long it would take them to figure it out and who, if anybody, would get in the way. People made such a mess of things.

6

The balmy weather held for another three days, much to the delight of everyone in Crozet. Mim lost no time in leaning on Little Marilyn to invite Blair Bainbridge to her house, during which time Mim just happened to stop by. She deeply regretted that Blair was too young for her and said so quite loudly, but this was a tack Mim usually took with handsome men. Her husband, Jim, laughed at her routine.

Fitz-Gilbert Hamilton's den struck Blair as a hymn to Princeton. How much orange and black could anyone stand? Fitz-Gilbert made a point of showing Blair his crew picture. He even showed him his squash picture from Andover Academy. Blair asked him what had happened to his hair, which Fitz-Gilbert took as a reference to his receding hairline. Blair hastily assured him that was not what he'd meant; he'd noticed that the young Fitz-Gilbert was blond. Little Marilyn giggled and said that in school her husband dyed his hair. Fitz-Gilbert blustered and said that all the guys did it—it didn't mean anything.

The upshot of this conversation was that the following morning Fitz-Gilbert appeared in the post office with blond hair. Harry stared at the thatch of gold above his homely face and decided the best course would be to mention it.

"Determined to live life as a blond, Fitz? Big Marilyn must be wearing off on you."

Mim flew to New York City once every six weeks to have her hair done and God knows what else.

"Last night my wife decided, after looking through my yearbooks, that I look better as a blond. What do you think? Do blonds have more fun?"

Harry studied the effect. "You look very preppy. I think you'd have fun whatever your hair color."

"I could never have done this in Richmond. That law firm." He put his hands around his neck in a choking manner. "Now that I've opened my own firm I can do what I want. Feels great. I know I do better work now too."

"I don't know what I'd do if I had to dress up for work."

"Worse than that, you couldn't take the cat and dog to work with you," Fitz-Gilbert observed. "You know, I don't think people were meant to work in big corporations. Look at Cabell Hall, leaving Chase Manhattan for Allied National years ago. After a while the blandness of a huge corporation will diminish even the brightest ones. That's what I like so much about Crozet. It's small; the businesses are small; people are friendly. At first I didn't know how I'd take the move from Richmond. I thought it might be dull." He smiled. "Hard for life to be dull around the Sanburnes."

Harry smiled back but wisely kept her mouth shut. He left, squeezing his large frame into his Mercedes 560SL, and roared off. Fitz and Little Marilyn owned the pearlized black SL, a white Range Rover, a silver Mercedes 420SEL, and a shiny Chevy half-ton truck with four-wheel drive.

As the day unfurled the temperature dropped a good fifteen to twenty degrees. Roiling black clouds massed at the tips of the Blue Ridge Mountains. The rain started before Harry left work. Mrs. Hogendobber kindly ran Harry back home although she complained about having Mrs. Murphy and Tucker in her car, an ancient Ford Falcon. She also complained about the car. This familiar theme—Mrs. Hogendobber had been complaining about her car since George bought it new in 1963— lulled Harry into a sleepy trance.

". . . soon time for four more tires and I ask myself, Miranda, is it worth it? I think, trade this thing in, and then I go over to the Brady-Bushey Ford car lot and peruse those prices and, well, Harry, I tell you, my heart fairly races. Who can afford a new car? So it's patch, patch, patch. Well, would you look at that!" she exclaimed. "Harry, are you awake? Have I been talking to myself? Look there, will you."

"Huh." Harry's eyes traveled in the direction of Mrs. Hogendobber's pointing finger.

A large sign swung on a new post. The background was hunter-green, the sign itself was edged in gold, and the lettering was gold. A fox peered out from its den. Above this realistic painting it read FOXDEN.

"*That* must have cost a pretty penny." Mrs. Hogendobber sounded disapproving.

"Wasn't there this morning."

"This Bainbridge fellow must have money to burn if he can put up a sign like that. Next thing you know he'll put up stone fences, and the cheapest, I mean the cheapest, you can get for that work is thirty dollars a cubic foot."

"Don't spend his money for him yet. A pretty sign doesn't mean he's going to go crazy and put all his goods in the front window, so to speak."

As they pulled into the long driveway leading to Harry's clapboard house, she asked Miranda Hogendobber in for a cup of tea. Mrs. Hogendobber refused. She had a church club meeting to attend and furthermore she knew Harry had chores. Given the continuing drop in the temperature and the pitch clouds sliding down the mountain as though on an inky toboggan ride, Harry was grateful. Mrs. H. peeled down the driveway and Harry hurried into the barn, Mrs. Murphy and Tucker way in front of her.

Her heavy barn jacket hung on a tack hook. Harry threw it on, tugged off her sneakers and slipped on duck boots, and slapped her Giants cap on her head. Grabbing the halters and lead shanks, she walked out into the west pasture just in time to get hit in the face with slashing rain. Mrs. Murphy stayed in the barn but Tucker went along.

Tomahawk and Gin Fizz, glad to see their mother, trotted over. Soon the little family was back in the barn. Picking up the tempo, the rain pelted the tin roof. A stiff wind knifed down from the northeast.

As Harry mixed bran with hot water and measured

out sweet feed, Mrs. Murphy prowled the hayloft. Since everyone had made so much noise getting into the barn, the mice were forewarned. The big old barn owl perched in the rafters. Mrs. Murphy disliked the owl and this was mutual, since they competed for the mice. However, harsh words were rarely spoken. They had adopted a live-and-let-live policy.

A little pink nose, whiskers bristling, stuck out from behind a bale of timothy. *"Mrs. Murphy."*

"Simon, what are you doing here?" Mrs. Murphy's tail went to the vertical.

"Storm came up fast. You know, I've been thinking, this would be a good place to spend the winter. I don't think your human would mind, do you?"

"As long as you stay out of the grain I doubt she'll care. Watch out for the blacksnake."

"She's already hibernating . . . or she's playing possum." Simon's whiskers twitched devilishly.

"Where?"

Simon indicated that the formidable four-foot-long blacksnake was curled up under the hay on the south side of the loft, the warmest place.

"God, I hope Harry doesn't pick up the bale and see her. Give her heart failure." Mrs. Murphy walked over. She could see the tip of a tail—that was it.

She came back and sat beside Simon.

"The owl really hates the blacksnake," Simon observed.

"Oh, she's cranky about everything."

"Who?"

"You," Mrs. Murphy called up.

"I am not cranky but you're always climbing up here and shooting off your big mouth. Scares the mice."

"It's too early for you to hunt."

"Doesn't change the fact that you have a big mouth."
The owl ruffed her feathers, then simply turned her
head away. She could swivel her gorgeous head around
nearly 360 degrees, and that fascinated the other animals. Four-legged creatures had a narrow point of view
as far as the owl was concerned.

Mrs. Murphy and Simon giggled and then the cat
climbed back down the ladder.

By the time Harry was finished, Mrs. Murphy and
Tucker eagerly scampered to the house.

Next door, Blair, cold and soaked to the skin, also ran
into his house. He'd been caught by the rain a good
half-mile away from shelter.

By the time he dried off, the sky was obsidian with
flashes of pinkish-yellow lightning, an unusual fall thunderstorm. As he went into the kitchen to heat some
soup, a deafening crack and blinding pink light knocked
him back a foot. When he recovered he saw smoke coming out of the transformer box on the pole next to his
house. The bolt had squarely hit the transformer. Elec-
tric crackles continued for a few moments and then died
away.

Blair kept rubbing his eyes. They burned. The house
was now black and he hadn't any candles. There was so
much to do to settle in that he hadn't gotten around to
buying candles or a lantern yet, much less furniture.

He thought about going over to Harry's but decided
against it, because he was afraid he'd look like a wuss.

As he stared out his kitchen window another terri-
fying bolt of lightning hurtled toward the ground and
struck a tree halfway between his house and the graveyard. For a brief moment he thought he saw a lone
figure standing in the cemetery. Then the darkness

again enshrouded everything and the wind howled like Satan.

Blair shivered, then laughed at himself. His stinging eyes were playing tricks on him. What was a thunderstorm but part of Nature's brass and percussion?

7

Tree limbs lay on the meadows like arms and legs torn from their sockets. As Harry prowled her fence lines she could smell the sap mixed in with the soggy earth odor. She hadn't time to inspect the fifty acres in hardwoods. She figured whole trees might have been uprooted, for as she had lain awake last night, mesmerized by the violence of the storm, she could hear, off in the distance like a moaning, the searing cracks and crashes of trees falling to their deaths. The good news was that no trees around the house had been uprooted and the barn and outbuildings remained intact.

"I hate getting wet," Mrs. Murphy complained, pulling her paws high up in the air and shaking them every few steps.

"Go back to the house then, fussbudget." This exaggerated fastidiousness of Mrs. Murphy's amused and irritated Tucker. There was nothing like a joyous splash in the creek, a romp in the mud, or if she was really lucky, a roll in something quite dead, to lift Tucker's corgi

spirits. And as she was low to the ground, she felt justified in getting dirty. It would be different if she were a Great Dane. Many things would be different if she were a Great Dane. For one thing, she could just ignore Mrs. Murphy with magisterial dignity. As it was, trying to ignore Mrs. Murphy meant the cat would tiptoe around and whack her on the ears. Wouldn't it be fun to see Mrs. Murphy try that if she were a Great Dane?

"What if something important happens? I can't *leave."* Mrs. Murphy shook mud off her paw and onto Harry's pants leg. *"Anyway, three sets of eyes are better than one."*

"Jesus H. Christ on a raft."

The dog and cat stopped and looked in the direction of Harry's gaze. The creek between her farm and Foxden had jumped its banks, sweeping everything before it. Mud, grass, tree limbs, and an old tire that must have washed down from Yellow Mountain had crashed into the trees lining the banks. Some debris had become entangled; the rest was shooting downstream at a frightening rate of speed. Mrs. Murphy's eyes widened. The roar of the water scared her.

As Harry started toward the creek she sank up to her ankle in trappy ground. Thinking the better of it, she backed off.

The leaden sky overhead offered no hope of relief. Cursing, her foot cold and wet, Harry squished back to the barn. She thought of her mother, who used to say that we all live in a perpetual state of renewal. "You must realize there is renewal in destruction, too, Harry," she would say.

As a child Harry couldn't figure out what her mother was talking about. Grace Hepworth Minor was the town librarian, so Harry used to chalk it up to Mom's reading too many touchy-feely books. As the years wore on, her mother's wisdom often came back to her. A sight such as this, so dispiriting at first, gave one the opportunity to rebuild, to prune, to fortify.

How she regretted her mother's passing, for she would have liked to discuss emotional renewal in destruction. Her divorce was teaching her that.

Tucker, noticing the silence of her mother, the pensive air, said, *"Human beings think too much."*

"Or not at all" was the saucy feline reply.

8

The rain picked up again midmorning. Steady rather than torrential, it did little to lighten anyone's spirits. Mrs. Hogendobber's beautiful red silk umbrella was the bright spot of the day. That and her conversation. She felt it incumbent upon her to call up everyone in Crozet who had a phone still working and inquire as to their well-being. She learned of Blair's transformer's being blown apart. The windows of the Allied National Bank were smashed. The shingles of Herbie Jones's church littered the downtown street. Susan Tucker's car endured a tree branch on its roof, and horror of horrors, Mim's pontoon boat, her pride and joy, had been cast on its side. Worst of all, her personal lake was a muddy mess.

"Did I leave anything out?"

Harry cleaned out the letters and numbers in her postage meter with the sharp end of a safety pin. They'd gotten clogged with maroon ink. "Your prize pumpkin?"

"Oh, I brought her in last night." Mrs. Hogendobber grabbed the broom and started sweeping the dried mud out the front door.

"You don't have to do that."

"I know I don't have to but I used to do this for George. Makes me feel useful." The clods of earth soared out into the parking lot. "Weatherman says three more days of rain."

"If the animals go two by two, you know we're in trouble."

"Harry, don't make light of the Old Testament. The Lord doesn't shine on blasphemers."

"I'm not blaspheming."

"I thought maybe I'd scare you into going to church." A sly smile crossed Mrs. Hogendobber's lips, colored a bronzed orange today.

Fair Haristeen came in, wiped off his boots, and answered Mrs. Hogendobber. "Harry goes to church for weddings, christenings, and funerals. Says Nature is her church." He smiled at his former wife.

"Yes, it is." Harry was glad he was okay. No storm damage.

"Bridge washed out at Little Marilyn's and at Boom Boom's, too. Hard to believe the old creek can do that much damage."

"Guess they'll have to stay on their side of the water," Mrs. Hogendobber said.

"Guess so." Fair smiled. "Unless Moses returns."

"I know what I forgot to tell you," Mrs. Hogendobber exclaimed, ignoring the biblical reference. "The cat ate all the communion wafers!"

"Cazenovia at St. Paul's Episcopal Church?" Fair asked.

"Yes, do you know her?" Mrs. H. spoke as though the animal were a parishioner.

"Cleaned her teeth last year."

"Has she gotten in the wine?" Harry laughed.

Mrs. Hogendobber struggled not to join in the mirth —after all, the bread and wine were the body and blood of our Lord Jesus—but there was something funny about a cat taking communion.

"Harry, want to have lunch with me?" Fair asked.

"When?" She absent-mindedly picked up a ballpoint pen, which had been lying on the counter, and stuck it behind her ear.

"Now. It's noon."

"I barely noticed, it's so dark outside."

"Go on, Harry, I'll hold down the fort," Mrs. Hogendobber offered. Divorce troubled her and the Haristeen divorce especially, since both parties were decent people. She didn't understand growing apart because she and George had stayed close throughout their long marriage. Of course it helped that if she said, "Jump," George replied, "How high?"

"Want to bring the kids?" Fair nodded toward the animals.

"Do, Harry. Don't you leave me with that hoyden of a cat. She gets in the mail bins and when I walk by she jumps out at me and grabs my skirt. Then the dog barks. Harry, you've got to discipline those two."

"Oh, balls." Tucker sneezed.

"Why do people say 'balls'? Why don't they say 'ovaries'?" Mrs. Murphy asked out loud.

No one had an answer, so she allowed herself to be picked up and whisked to the deli.

The conversation between Fair and Harry proved des-

ultory at best. Questions about his veterinary practice
were dutifully answered. Harry spoke of the storm.
They laughed about Fitz-Gilbert's blond hair and then
truly laughed about Mim's pontoon boat taking a lick.
Mim and that damned boat had caused more uproar
over the years—from crashing into the neighbors' docks
to nearly drowning Mim and the occupants. To be invited onto her "little yacht," as she mincingly called it,
was surely a siren call to disaster. Yet to refuse meant
banishment from the upper echelon of Crozet society.

As the laughter subsided, Fair, wearing his most ear-
nest face, said, "I wish you and Boom Boom could be
friends again. You all were friends once."

"I don't know as I'd say we were friends." Harry
warily put down her plastic fork. "We socialized together when Kelly was alive. We got along, I guess."

"She understands why you wouldn't want to be
friends with her but it hurts her. She talks tough but
she's very sensitive." He picked up the Styrofoam cup
and swallowed some hot coffee.

Harry wanted to reply that she was very sensitive
about herself and not others, and besides, what about
her feelings? Maybe he should talk to Boom Boom
about *her* sensitivities. She realized that Fair was
snagged, hook, line, and sinker. Boom Boom was reel-
ing him into her emotional demands, which, like her
material demands, were endless. Maybe men needed
women like Boom Boom to feel important. Until they
dropped from exhaustion.

As Harry kept quiet, Fair haltingly continued: "I wish
things had worked out differently and yet maybe I
don't. It was time for us."

"Guess so." Harry twiddled with her ballpoint pen.

"I don't hold grudges. I hope you don't." His blond eyebrows shielded his blue eyes.

Harry'd been looking into those eyes since kindergarten. "Easier said than done. Whenever women want to discuss emotions men become more rational, or at least you do. I can't just wipe out our marriage and say let's be friends, and I'm not without ego. I wish we had parted differently, but done is done. I'd rather think good of you than ill."

"Well, what about Boom Boom then?"

"Where is she?" Harry deflected the question for a moment.

"Bridge washed out."

"Oh, yeah, I forgot. Once the water goes down she'll find a place to ford."

"Least the phone lines are good. I spoke to her this morning. She has a terrible migraine. You know how low pressure affects her."

"To say nothing of garlic."

"Right." Fair remembered when Boom Boom was rushed to the hospital once after ingesting the forbidden garlic.

"And then we can't forget the rheumatism in her spine on these cold, dank days. Or her tendency to heat prostration, especially when any form of work befalls her." Harry smiled broadly, the smile of victory.

"Don't make fun of her. You know what a tough family life she had. I mean with that alcoholic father and her mother just having affair after affair."

"Well, she comes by it honestly then." Harry reached over with her ballpoint pen, jabbed a hole in the Styrofoam cup, and turned it around so the liquid dribbled onto Fair's cords. She got up and walked out, Mrs. Murphy and Tucker hastily following.

Fair, fuming, sat there and wiped the coffee off his pants with his left hand while trying to stem the flow from the cup with his right.

9

The creek swirled around the larger rocks, small whirlpools forming, then dispersing. Tucker paced the bank, slick with mud deposits. The waters had subsided and were back within their boundaries but remained high with a fast current. A mist hung over the meadows and the trees, now bare, since the pounding rains had knocked off most of the brilliant fall foliage.

High in the hayloft Mrs. Murphy watched her friend through a crack in the boards. When she lost sight of Tucker she gave up her conversation with Simon to hurry backward down the ladder. Cursing under her breath, she surrendered hope of keeping dry and ran across the fields. Water splashed up on her creamy beige belly, exacerbating her bad mood. Tucker could do the dumbest things. By the time Mrs. Murphy reached the creek the corgi was right in the middle of it, teetering on the tip of a huge rock.

"Get back here," Mrs. Murphy demanded.

"No," Tucker refused. *"Sniff."*

Mrs. Murphy held her nose up in the air. *"I smell mud, sap, and stale water."*

"It's the faintest whiff. Sweet and then it disappears. I've got to find it."

"What do you mean, sweet?" Mrs. Murphy swished her tail.

"Damn, I lost it."

"Tucker, you've got short little legs—swimming in this current isn't a smart idea."

"I've got to find that odor." With that she pushed off the rock, hit the water, and pulled with all her might. The muddy water swept over her head. She popped up again, swimming on an angle toward the far shore.

Mrs. Murphy screeched and screamed but Tucker paid no heed. By the time the corgi reached the bank she was so tired she had to rest for a moment. But the scent was slightly stronger now. Standing up on wobbly legs, she shook herself and laboriously climbed the mud-slide that was the creek bank.

"Are you all right?" the cat called.

"Yes."

"I'm staying right here until you come back."

"All right." Tucker scrambled over the bank and sniffed again. She got her bearings and trotted across Blair Bainbridge's land. The scent increased in power with each step. Tucker pulled up at the little cemetery.

The high winds had knocked over the tombstones Blair had righted, and the bad side of the wrought-iron fence had crashed down again. Carefully, the dog picked her way through the debris in the cemetery. The scent was now crystal clear and enticing, very enticing.

Nose to the ground, she walked over to the tomb-stone with the carved angel playing the harp. The fingers of a human hand pointed at the sky in front of the stone. The violence of the wind and rain had sheared off the loose topsoil; a section was rolled back like a tiny carpet. Tucker sniffed that too. When she and Mrs. Murphy passed the graveyard last week there was no enticing scent, no apparent change in the topsoil. The odor of decay, exhilarating to a dog, overcame her curiosity about the turf. She dug at the hand. Soon the whole hand was visible. She bit into the fleshy, swollen palm and tugged. The hand easily pulled out of the ground. Then she noticed that it had been severed at the wrist, a clean job of it, too, and the finger pads were missing.

Ecstatic with her booty, forgetting how tired she was, Tucker flew across the bog to the creek. She stopped because she was afraid to plunge into the creek. She didn't want to lose her pungent prize.

Mrs. Murphy, transfixed by the sight, was speechless.

Tucker delicately laid down the hand. *"I knew it! I knew I smelled something deliciously dead."*

"Tucker, don't chew on that." Mrs. Murphy was disgusted.

"Why not? I found it. I did the work. It's mine!" She barked, high-pitched because she was excited and upset.

"I don't want the hand, Tucker, but it's a bad omen."

"No, it's not. Remember the time Harry read to us about a dog bringing a hand to Vespasian when he was a general and the seers interpreting this to mean that he would be Emperor of Rome and he was? It's a good sign."

Mrs. Murphy dimly remembered Harry's reading aloud from one of her many history books but that was hardly her main concern. *"Listen to me. Humans put their dead in boxes. You know that if you found a hand it means the body wasn't packaged."*

"So what? It's my hand!" Tucker hollered at the top of her lungs, although with a moment to reflect she knew that Mrs. Murphy was right. Humans didn't cut up their dead.

"Tucker, if you destroy that hand then you've destroyed evidence. You're going to be in a shitload of trouble and you'll get Mother in trouble."

Dejected, Tucker squatted down next to the treasured hand, a gruesome sight. *"But it's mine."*

"I'm sorry. But something's wrong, don't you see?"

"No." Her voice was fainter now.

"A dead human not in a box means either he or she was ill and died far away from others or that he or she was murdered. The other humans have to know this. You know how they are, Tucker. Some of them kill for pleasure. It's dangerous for the others."

Tucker sat up. *"Why are they like that?"*

"I don't know and they don't know. It's some sickness in the species. You know, like dogs pass parvo. Please, Tucker, don't mess up that evidence. Let me go get Mother if I can. Promise me you'll wait."

"It might take her hours to figure out what you're telling her."

"I know. You've got to wait."

One miserable dog cocked her head and sighed. *"All right, Murphy."*

Mrs. Murphy skimmed across the pastures, her feet barely grazing the sodden earth. She found Harry in the bed of the truck. Nimbly Mrs. Murphy launched herself onto the truck bed. She meowed. She rubbed against Harry's leg. She meowed louder.

"Hey, little pussycat, I've got work to do."

The twilight was fading. Mrs. Murphy was getting desperate. *"Follow me, Mom. Come on. Right now."*

"What's gotten into you?" Harry was puzzled.

Mrs. Murphy hooted and hollered as much as she could. Finally she sprang up and dug her claws into Harry's jeans, climbing up her leg. Harry yelped and Mrs. Murphy jumped off her leg and ran a few paces. Harry rubbed her leg. Mrs. Murphy ran back and prepared to climb the other leg.

"Don't you dare!" Harry held out her hand.

"Then follow me, stupid." Mrs. Murphy moved away from her again.

Finally, Harry did. She didn't know what was going on but she'd lived with Mrs. Murphy for seven years, long enough and close enough to learn a little bit of cat ways.

The cat hurried across the meadow. When Harry slowed down, Mrs. Murphy would run back and then zip away again, encouraging her constantly. Harry picked up speed.

When Tucker saw them coming she started barking. Breathing hard, Harry stopped at the bank. "Oh, damn, Tucker, how'd you get over there."

"Look!" the cat shouted.

"Mommy, I found it and it's mine. If I have to give this up I want a knuckle bone," Tucker bargained. She picked up the hand in her mouth.

It took Harry a minute to focus in the fading light. At first, she couldn't believe her eyes. Then she did.

"Oh, my God."

10

Albemarle County Sheriff Rick Shaw bent down with his flashlight. Officer Cynthia Cooper, already hunkered down, gingerly lifted the digits with her pocket knife.

"Never seen anything like this," Shaw muttered. He reached in his pocket and pulled out a cigarette.

The sheriff battled his smoking addiction with disappointing results. Worse, Cooper had begun to sneak cigarettes herself.

Tucker sat staring at the hand. Blair Bainbridge, feeling a little queasy, and Harry stood beside Tucker. Mrs. Murphy rested across Harry's neck. Her feet were cold and she was tired, so Harry had slung her around her neck like a stole.

"Harry, any idea where this came from?"

"I know," Tucker volunteered.

"Like I said, the dog was sitting on the creek bank with this hand. I ran back home and called, then hopped in the truck to meet you. I don't know any more than that."

"What about you, uh . . ."

"Blair Bainbridge."

"Mr. Bainbridge, notice anything unusual? Before this, I mean?"

"No."

Rick grunted when he stood up. Cynthia Cooper wrapped the hand in a plastic bag.

"If you follow me, I can show you!" Tucker yapped and ran toward the cemetery.

"She's got a lot to say." Cynthia smiled. She loved the little dog and the cat.

Shaw inhaled, then exhaled a long blue line of smoke, which didn't curl upward. Most likely meant more rain.

Tucker sat by the graveyard and howled.

"I, for one, am going to see what she's about." Harry followed her dog.

"Me too." Cynthia followed, carrying the hand in its bag.

Rick grumbled but his curiosity was up. Blair stayed with him. When the humans reached the iron fence Tucker barked again and walked over to the angel with the harp tombstone. Cooper flung her flashlight beam over toward Tucker.

"Right here," Tucker instructed.

Harry squinted. "Coop, you'd better check this out."

Again Cynthia got down on her knees. Tucker dug in the dirt. She hit a pocket of air and the unmistakable odor of rotten flesh smacked Cynthia in the face. The young woman reeled backward and fought her gag reflex.

Rick Shaw, now beside her, turned his head aside. "Guess we've got work to do."

Blair, ashen-faced, said, "Would you like me to go back to the barn and get a spade?"

"No, thank you," the sheriff said. "I think we'll post a man out here tonight and start this in daylight. I don't want to take the chance of destroying evidence because we can't see."

As they walked back to the squad car Blair halted and turned to the sheriff, now on another cigarette. "I did see something. The night of the storm my transformer was hit by lightning. I didn't have any candles and I was standing by my kitchen window." He pointed to the window. "Another big bolt shot down and split that tree and for an instant I thought I saw someone standing up here in the cemetery. I dismissed it. It didn't seem possible."

Shaw wrote this down quickly in his small notebook as Coop called for a backup to watch the graveyard.

Harry wanted to make a crack about the graveyard shift but kept her mouth shut. Whenever things were grim her sense of humor kicked into high gear.

"Mr. Bainbridge, you're not planning on leaving anytime soon, are you?"

"No."

"Good. I might need to ask you more questions." Rick leaned against the car. "I'll call Herbie Jones. It's his cemetery. Harry, why don't you go home and eat something? It's past suppertime and you looked peaked."

"Lost my appetite," Harry replied.

"Yeah, me too. You never get used to this kind of thing, you know." The sheriff patted her on the back.

When Harry walked in the door she picked up the phone and called Susan. As soon as that conversation was finished she called Miranda Hogendobber. For Miranda, being the last to know would be almost as awful as finding the hand.

11

At first light a team of two men began carefully turning over the earth by the tombstone with the harp-playing angel. Larry Johnson, the retired elderly physician, acted as Crozet's coroner—an easy job, as there was generally precious little to do. He watched, as did Reverend Herbie Jones. Rick Shaw and Cynthia Cooper carefully sifted through the spadefuls of earth the men turned over. Harry and Blair stayed back at the fence. Miranda Hogendobber pulled up in her Falcon, bounded out of the car, and strode toward the graveyard.

"Harry, you called Miranda. Don't deny it, I know you did," Rick fussed.

"Well . . . she has an interesting turn of mind."

"Oh, please." Rick shook his head.

"Pay dirt." One of the diggers pulled his handkerchief up around his nose.

"I got it. I got it." The other digger reached down and gently extricated a leg.

Miranda Hogendobber reached the hill at that moment, took one look at the decaying leg, wearing torn pants and with the foot still in a sneaker, and passed out.

"She's your responsibility!" Rick pointed his forefinger at Harry.

Harry knew he was right. She hurried over to Mrs. Hogendobber and, assisted by Blair, hoisted her up. She began to come around. Not knowing what another look at the grisly specimen might do, they remonstrated with her. She resisted but then walked down to Blair's house supported by the two of them.

The police continued their work and discovered another hand, the fingertip pads also removed, and another leg, which, like its companion, had been cleaved where the thighbone joins the pelvis.

By noon, after sifting and digging for five hours, Rick called a halt to the proceedings.

"Want us to start in on these other graves?"

"As the ground is not disturbed I wish you wouldn't." Reverend Jones stepped in. "Let them rest in peace."

Rick wiped his forehead. "Reverend, I can appreciate the sentiment but if we need to come back up here . . . well, you know."

"I know, but you're standing on my mother." A hint of reproach crept into Herb's resonant voice. He was more upset than he realized.

"I'm sorry." Rick quickly moved. "Go back to work, Reverend. I'll be in touch."

"Who would do that?" Herbie pointed to the stinking evidence.

"Murder?" Cynthia Cooper opened her hands, palms

up, "Seemingly average people commit murder. Happens every day."

"No, who would cut up a human being like that?" The minister's eyes were moist.

"I don't know," Rick replied. "But whoever did it took great pains to remove identifying evidence."

After the good Reverend left, the four law enforcement officials walked a bit away from the smell and conferred among themselves. Where was the torso and where was the head?

They'd find out soon enough.

12

The starch in Tiffany Hayes's apron rattled as she approached the table. Little Marilyn, swathed in a full-length purple silk robe, sat across from Fitz-Gilbert, dressed for work. The pale-pink shirt and the suspenders completed a carefully thought-out ensemble.

Tiffany put down the eggs, bacon, grits, and various jams. "Will that be all, Miz Hamilton?"

Little Marilyn critically appraised the presentation. "Roberta forgot a sprig of parsley on the eggs."

Tiffany curtsied and repaired to the kitchen, where she informed Roberta of her heinous omission. At each meal there was some detail Little Marilyn found abrasive to her highly developed sense of decorum.

Hands on hips, Roberta replied to an appreciative Tiffany, "She can eat a pig's blister."

Back in the breakfast nook, husband and wife enjoyed a relaxing meal. The brief respite of sun was overtaken by clouds again.

"Isn't this the strangest weather?" Little Marilyn sighed.

"The changing seasons are full of surprises. And so are you." His voice dropped.

Little Marilyn smiled shyly. It had been her idea to attack her husband this morning during his shower. Those how-to-please sex books she devoured were paying off.

"Life is more exciting as a blond." He swept his hand across his forelock. His hair was meticulously cut with short sideburns, close cropped on the sides and back of the head, and longer on the top. "You really like it, don't you?"

"I do. And I like your suspenders too." She leaned across the table and snapped one.

"Braces, dear. Suspenders are for old men." He polished off his eggs. "Marilyn"—he paused—"would you love me if I weren't, well, if I weren't Andover-Princeton? A Hamilton? One of the Hamiltons?" He referred to his illustrious family, whose history in America reached back into the seventeenth century.

The Hamiltons, originally from England, first landed in the West Indies, where they amassed a fortune in sugar cane. A son, desirous of a larger theater for his talents, sailed to Philadelphia. From that ambitious sprig grew a long line of public servants, businessmen, and the occasional cad. Fitz-Gilbert's branch of the family, the New York branch, suffered many losses until only Fitz's immediate family remained. A fateful airplane crash carried away the New York Hamiltons the summer after Fitz's junior year in high school. At sixteen Fitz-Gilbert was an orphan.

Fitz appeared to withstand the shock and fight back.

He spent the summer working in a brokerage house as a messenger, just as his father had planned. Despite his blue-blood connections, his only real friend in those days was another boy at the brokerage house, a bright kid from Brooklyn, Tommy Norton. They escaped Wall Street on weekends, usually to the Hamptons or Cape Cod.

Fitz's stoicism impressed everyone, but Cabell Hall, his guardian and trust officer at Chase Manhattan, was troubled. Cracks had begun to show in Fitz's facade. He totaled a car but escaped unharmed. Cabell didn't blow up. He agreed that "boys will be boys." But then Fitz got a girl pregnant, and Cabell found a reputable doctor to take care of that. Finally, the second summer of Fitz's Wall Street apprenticeship, he and Tommy Norton were in a car accident on Cape Cod. Both boys were so drunk that, luckily for them, they sustained only facial lacerations and bruises when they went through the windshield. Fitz, since he was driving, paid all the medical bills, which meant they got the very best care. But Fitz's recovery was only physical. He had tempted fate and nearly killed not only himself but his best friend. The result was a nervous breakdown. Cabel checked him into an expensive, quiet clinic in Connecticut.

Fitz had related this history to Little Marilyn before they got married, but he hadn't mentioned it since.

She looked at him now and wondered what he was talking about. Fitz was high-born, rich, and so much fun. She didn't remember anywhere in her books being instructed that men need reassurance of their worth. The books concentrated on sexual pleasure and helping a husband through a business crisis and then dreaded male menopause, but, oh, they were years and years away from that. Probably he was playing a game. Fitz was inventive.

"I would love you if you were"—she thought for something déclassé, off the board—"Iraqi."

He laughed. "That is a stretch. Ah, yes, the Middle East, that lavatory of the human race."

"Wonder what they call us?"

"The Devil's seed." His voice became more menacing and he spoke with what he imagined was an Iraqi accent.

One of the fourteen phones in the overlarge house twittered. The harsh ring of the telephone was too cacophonous for Little Marilyn, who believed she had perfect pitch. So she paid bundles of money for phones that rang in bird calls. Consequently her house sounded like a metallic aviary.

Tiffany appeared. "I think it's your mother, Miz Mim, but I can't understand a word she's saying."

A flash of irritation crossed Marilyn Sanburne Hamilton's smooth white forehead. She reached over and picked up the phone, and her voice betrayed not a hint of it. "Mother, darling."

Mother darling ranted, raved, and emitted such strange noises that Fitz put down his napkin and rose to stand behind his wife, hands resting on her slender shoulders. She looked up at her husband and indicated that she also couldn't understand a word. Then her face changed; the voice through the earpiece had risen to raw hysteria.

"Mother, we'll be right over." The dutiful daughter hung up the receiver.

"What is it?"

"I don't know. She just screamed and hollered. Oh, Fitz, we'd better hurry."

"Where's your father?"

"In Richmond today, at a mayors' conference."

"Oh, Lord." If Mim's husband wasn't there it meant the burden of comfort and solution rested upon him. Small wonder that Jim Sanburne found so many opportunities to travel.

13

Those townspeople who weren't gathered in the post office were at Market Shiflett's. Harry frantically tried to sort the mail. She even called Susan Tucker to come down and help. Mrs. Hogendobber, positioned in front of the counter, told her gory tale to all, every putrid detail.

A hard scratching on the back door alerted Tucker, who barked. Susan rose and opened the door. Pewter walked in, tail to the vertical, whiskers swept forward.

"Hello, Pewter."

"Hello, Susan." She rubbed against Susan's leg and then against Tucker.

Mrs. Murphy was playing in the open post boxes.

Pewter looked up and spoke to the striped tail hanging out of Number 31. *"Fit to be tied over at the store. What about here?"*

"Same."

"I found the hand," Tucker bragged.

"Everybody knows, Tucker. You'll probably get your

name in the newspaper—again." Green jealousy swept through the fat gray body. *"Mrs. Murphy, turn around so I can talk to you."*

"I can't." She backed out of the box, hung for a moment by her paws, and then dropped lightly to the ground.

Usually Susan and Harry were amused by the athletic displays of the agile tiger cat but today no one paid much attention.

Blair called Harry to tell her Rick Shaw had elected not to tear up the cemetery just yet, and to thank her for being a good neighbor.

Naturally, with Blair being an outsider, suspicion immediately fell on him. After all, the severed hands and legs were found in his—well, Herbie's really—graveyard. And no one would ever suspect Reverend Jones.

The ideas and fantasies swirled up like a cloud of grasshoppers and then dropped to earth again. Harry listened to the people jammed into the post office even as she attempted to complete her tasks. Theories ranged from old-fashioned revenge to demonology. Since no one had any idea of who those body parts belonged to, the theories lacked the authenticity of personal connection.

One odd observation crossed Harry's mind. So much of the conjecture focused on establishing a motive. Why? As the voices of her friends, neighbors, and even her few enemies, or temporary enemies, rose and fell, the thrust was that in some way the victim must have brought this wretched fate upon himself. The true question formulating in Harry's mind was not motive but, Why is it so important for humans to blame the victim? Do they hope to ward off evil? If a woman is raped she is accused of dressing to entice. If a man is robbed, he should have had better sense than to walk the streets on that side of town. Are people incapable of accepting the randomness of evil? Apparently so.

As Rick Shaw sped by, siren splitting the air, the group fell silent to watch. Rick was followed closely by Cynthia Cooper in her squad car.

Fair Haristeen opened the door and stepped outside. He knew that Rick Shaw wasn't moving that fast just to dump off hands and legs; something else had happened. He walked over to Market's to see if anyone had fresher news. Being in Harry's presence wasn't that uncomfortable for him. Fair considered that women were irrational much of the time, a consideration reinforced by Boom Boom, who felt logic to be vulgar. He'd already forgiven Harry for punching a hole in his coffee cup. She chose to ignore him to his face, then watched him saunter next door. She breathed a sigh of relief. His presence rubbed like a pebble in her shoe.

"You know, I want my knuckle bone." Tucker started to pout. *"That was the deal."*

"Deal?" Pewter's long gray eyelashes fluttered.

Before Tucker could explain, the door flew open and Tiffany Hayes, still in her sparkling white apron, burst in. "Miz Sanburne's got a headless nekkid body in her boathouse!"

A split second of disbelief was followed by a roar of inquiry. How did she know? Who was it? Et cetera.

Tiffany cleared her throat and walked to the counter. Susan came up from the back. Mrs. Murphy and Pewter jumped on the counter and made circles to find papers to sit on, then did so. Tucker ran around front, ducking between legs to see Tiffany.

The Reverend Jones, a quick thinker, dashed next door to fetch the folks in the market. Soon the post office was over its fire code limit of people.

Once everyone was squeezed in, Tiffany gave the facts. "I was serving Little Marilyn and Mr. Fitz their eggs. She was complaining, naturally, but so what? I walked back into the kitchen and the phone rang. Roberta's hands were covered with flour, and Jack wasn't on duty yet so I picked it up. I recognized the voice as Miz Sanburne's, but lordy, I couldn't understand one word that woman was putting to me. She was crying and she was screaming and she was gasping and I just laid down that phone and left the kitchen to tell Little Marilyn her mother was on the phone and I couldn't understand her. I mean I couldn't say 'your mother is pitching a fit and falling in it,' now could I? So I waited while Little Marilyn picked up the phone and she couldn't understand her mother any better than I could. Well, the next thing I know she runs upstairs and starts to put on her makeup, and Mr. Fitz is waiting downstairs. He was so anxious he couldn't stand it no more so he bounded up those steps and told her in no uncertain terms that this was no time for makeup and to get a move on. So they left in that white Jeep thing of theirs. Not twenty minutes pass before the phone rings again and Jack, on duty now, picks up but Roberta and I couldn't help ourselves so we picked up too. It was Mr. Fitz. We could hear both Marilyns ascreaming in the background. Like banshees. Mr. Fitz, he was a little shaky, but he told Jack there was a headless corpse floating in Mim's boathouse. He told Jack to call and cancel all his business appointments for the day and all of Little Marilyn's social engagements. Then he told Jack to get hold of Mr. Sanburne in Richmond if in any way possible. The sheriff was on his way and not to worry. Nobody was in any danger. Jack asked a few questions and Mr. Fitz told him not to worry if he didn't get his chores done today. Thank God for Mr. Fitz."

She finished. This was possibly the only time in her life that Tiffany would be the center of attention. There was something touching about that.

What Tiffany didn't know was that the hands and legs had been dug up at Foxden. So now Miranda Hogendobber was able to tell *her* story again. Center stage was natural to Miranda.

Grateful to Mrs. Hogendobber for taking over the "entertainment" department, Harry returned to filling up the post boxes. She was glad she was behind the boxes because she was laughing silently, tears falling from her eyes. Susan came over, thinking she was upset.

Harry wiped her eyes and whispered, "Of all people, Mim! What will *Town and Country* think?"

Now Susan was laughing as hard as Harry. "Maybe whoever it was made the mistake of sailing in her pontoon boat."

This made them both break out in giggles again. Harry put her hand over her mouth to muffle her speech. "Mim has exhausted herself with accumulating possessions. Now she's got one that's a real original."

That did it. They nearly fell on the floor. Part of this explosion of mirth was from tension, of course. Yet part of it was directly attributable to Mim's character. Miranda said there was a good heart in there somewhere but no one wanted to find out. Maybe no one believed her. Mim had spent her life from the cradle onward tyrannizing people over bloodlines and money. The two are intertwined less frequently than Mim would wish. No matter what story you had, Mim could top it; if not, she would tip her head at an angle that made plain her distaste and social superiority.

Nobody would say it out loud but probably most people were delighted that a bloated corpse had found its way into her boathouse. More things stank over at the Sanburnes' than a rotten torso.

14

The deep glow from the firelit mahogany in Reverend Jones's library cast a youthful softening over his features. The light rain on the windowpane accentuated his mood, withdrawn and thoughtful, as well as exhausted. He had forgotten just how exhausting turmoil can be. His wife, Carol, her violet eyes sympathetic, entreated him to eat. When he refused she knew he was suffering.

"How about a cup of cocoa, then?"

"What? Oh, no, dear. You know I ran into Cabell at the bank and he thinks this is a nut case. Someone passing through, like a traveling serial killer. I don't think so, Carol. I think it's closer to home."

A loud crackle in the fireplace made him jump. He settled back down.

"Tell you what. I'll bring in the cocoa and if you don't want it, then the cat will drink it. It won't solve this horrible mess but it will make you feel better."

The doorbell rang and Carol answered it. Two cups

of cocoa. She invited Blair Bainbridge into the library. He also appeared exhausted.

Reverend Jones lifted himself out of his armchair to greet his impromptu guest.

"Oh, please stay seated, Reverend."

"You have a seat then."

Ella, the cat, joined them. Her full name was Elocution and she lived up to her name. Eating communion wafers was not her style, like that naughty Episcopalian cat, but Ella did once shred a sermon of Herbie's on a Sunday morning. For the first time in his life he gave a spontaneous sermon. The topic, "living with all God's creatures," was prompted, of course, by Ella's wanton destructiveness. It was the best sermon of his life. Parishioners begged for copies. As he had not one note, he thought he couldn't reproduce his sermon but Carol came to the rescue. She, too, moved by her husband's loving invocation of all life, remembered it word for word. The sermon, reprinted in many church magazines beyond even his own Lutheran denomination, made the Reverend something of an ecclesiastical celebrity.

Ella stared intently at Blair, since he was new to her. Once satisfied, she rested on her side before the fire as the men chatted and Carol brought in a large pot of cocoa. Carol excused herself and went upstairs to continue her own work.

"I apologize for dropping in like this without calling."

"Blair, this is the country. If you called first, people would think you were putting on airs." He poured his guest and himself a steaming cup each, the rich aroma filling the room.

"Well, I wanted to tell you how sorry I am that this,

this—I don't even know what to call it." Blair's eyebrows knitted together. "Well, that the awful discovery was made in your family plot. Since your back troubles you, I'm willing to make whatever repairs are necessary, once Sheriff Shaw allows me."

"Thank you." The Reverend meant it.

"How long before people start thinking that I've done it?" Blair blurted out.

"Oh, they've already gone through that possibility and most have dispensed with it, except for Rick, who never lets anyone off the hook and never rushes to judgment. Guess you have to be that way in his line of work."

"Dispensed . . . ?"

Herbie waved his right hand in the air, a friendly, dismissive gesture, while holding his cocoa cup and saucer in his left hand. "You haven't been here long enough to hate Marilyn Sanburne. You wouldn't have placed the body, or what was left of it, in her boathouse."

"I could have floated it in there."

"I spoke to Rick Shaw shortly after the discovery." Herb placed his cup on the table. Ella eyed it with interest. "From the condition of the body, he seriously doubted it could have floated into the boathouse without someone on the lake noticing its slow progress. Also, the boathouse doors were closed."

"It could have floated under them."

"The body was blown up to about three times normal size."

Blair fought an involuntary shudder. "That poor woman will have nightmares."

"She about had to be tranquilized with a dart gun. Little Marilyn was pretty shook up too. And I don't guess Fitz-Gilbert will have an appetite for some time either. For that matter, neither will I."

"Nor I." Blair watched as a log burned royal-blue from the bottom to crimson in the middle, releasing the bright-yellow flames to leap upward.

"What I dread are the reporters. The facts will be in the paper tomorrow. Cut and dried. But if this body is ever identified, those people will swarm over us like flies." Herb wished he hadn't said that because it reminded him of the legs and hands.

"Reverend Jones—"

"Herbie," came the interruption.

"Herbie. Why do people hate Marilyn Sanburne? I mean, I've only met her once and she carried on about pedigree but, well, everyone has a weakness."

"No one likes a snob, Blair. Not even another snob. Imagine living year in and year out being judged by Mim, being put in your place at her every opportunity. She works hard for her charities, undeniably, but she bullies others even in the performance of good works. Her son, Stafford, married a black woman and that brought out the worst in Mim and, I might add, the best in everyone else. She disowned him. He lives in New York with his wife. They made up, sort of, for Little Marilyn's wedding. I don't know, most people don't see below the surface when they look at others, and Mim's surface is cold and brittle."

"But you think otherwise, don't you?"

This young man was perceptive. Herb liked him more by the minute. "I do think otherwise." He pulled up a hassock for his feet, indicating to Blair that he should pull one up, too, then folded his hands across his chest. "You see, Marilyn Sanburne was born Marilyn

Urquhart Conrad. The Urquharts, of Scottish origin, were one of the earliest families to reach this far west. Hard to believe, but even during the time of the Revolutionary War this was a rough place, a frontier. Before that, the 1720's, the 1730's, you took your life in your hands to come to the Blue Ridge Mountains. Marilyn's mother, Isabelle Urquhart Conrad, filled all three of her children's heads with silly ideas about how they were royalty. The American version. Jimp Conrad, her husband, not of as august lineage as the Urquharts, was too busy buying up land to worry overmuch about how his children were being raised. A male problem, I would say. Anyway, her two brothers took this aristocracy stuff to heart and decided they didn't have to do anything so common as work for a living. James, Jr., became a steeplechase jockey and died in a freak accident up in Culpeper. That was right after World War Two. Horse dragged him to his death. I saw it with my own eyes. The younger brother, Theodore, a good horseman himself, quite simply drank himself to death. The heartbreak killed Jimp and made Isabelle bitter. She thought she was the only woman who'd ever lost sons. She quite forgot that hundreds of thousands of American mothers had recently lost sons in the mud of Europe and the sands of the South Pacific. Her mother's bitterness rubbed off on Mim. As she was the remaining child, the care of her mother became her burden as Isabelle aged. Social superiority became her refuge perhaps."

He rested a moment, then continued: "You know, I see people in crisis often. And over the years I have found that one of two things happens. Either people open up and grow, the pain allowing them to have compassion for others, to gain perspective on themselves, to feel God's love, if you will, or they shut down either through drink, drugs, promiscuity, or bitterness. Bitterness is an affront to God, as is any form of self-destructive behavior. Life is a gift, to be enjoyed and shared." He fell into silence.

Ella purred as she listened. She loved Herbie's voice, its deep, manly rumble, but she loved what he said too. Humans had such difficulty figuring out that life is a frolic as long as you have enough to eat, a warm bed, and plenty of catnip. She was very happy that Herb realized life was mostly wonderful.

For a long time the two men sat side by side in the quiet of understanding.

Blair spoke at last. "Herbie, I'm trying to open up. I don't have much practice."

Sensing that Blair would get around to telling his story sometime in the future, when he felt secure, Herb wisely didn't probe. Instead he reassured him with what he himself truly believed. "Trust in God. He will show you the way."

15

Although the sheriff and Officer Cooper knew little about the pieces of body that had been found, they did know that a vagrant, not an old man either, had been in town not long ago.

Relentless legwork, telephone calls, and questioning led the two to the Allied National Bank.

Marion Molnar remembered the bearded fellow vividly. His baseball jacket, royal blue, had an orange METS embroidered on it. As a devout Orioles fan, this upset Marion as much as the man's behavior.

She led Rick and Cynthia into Ben Seifert's office.

Beaming, shaking hands, Ben bade them sit down.

"Oh, yes, walked into my office big as day. Had some cockamamie story about his investments. Said he wanted to meet Cabell Hall right then and there."

"Did you call your president?" Rick asked.

"No. I said I'd take him down to our branch office at the downtown mall in Charlottesville. It was the only way I knew to get him out of here." Ben cracked his knuckles.

"Then what happened?" Cynthia inquired.

"I drove him to the outskirts of town on the east side. Finally talked him out of this crazy idea and he got out willingly. Last I saw of him."

"Thanks, Ben. We'll call you if we need you," Rick said.

"Glad to help." Ben accompanied them to the front door.

Once the squad car drove out of sight he shut his office door and picked up his phone. "Listen, asshole, the cops were here about that bum. I don't like it!" Ben, a country boy, had transformed himself over time, smoothing off his rough edges. Now he was a sleek glad-hander and a big deal in the Chamber of Commerce. There was scarcely any of the old Ben left in his oily new incarnation, but worry was resurrecting it.

16

The Harvest Fair committee, under the command of Miranda Hogendobber, met hastily to discuss their plans for the fair and the ball that immediately followed it. The glorious events of the Harvest Fair and Ball, crammed into Halloween day and night, were eagerly awaited by young and old. Everybody went to the Harvest Fair. The children competed for having the best costume and scariest costume, as well as in bobbing for apples, running races in costume, and other events that unfolded over the early evening hours. The advantage of this was that it kept the children off the streets, sparing everyone the trick-or-treat candy syndrome that caused adults to eat as much as the kids did. The children, gorged on good food as well as their treats, fell asleep at the Harvest Ball while the adults danced. There were as many sleeping bags as pumpkins.

The crisis confronting Mrs. Hogendobber, Taxi Hall, and their charges involved Harry Haristeen and Susan Tucker. Oh, not that the two had done anything wrong, but each year they appeared as Ichabod Crane and the Headless Horseman, Harry being the Horseman. Harry's Tomahawk was seal-brown but looked black at night, and his nostrils were always painted red. He was a fearsome sight. Harry struggled every year to see through the slits in her cape once the pumpkin head was hurled at the fleeing Ichabod. One year she lost her bearings and fell off, to the amusement of everyone but herself, although she did laugh about it later.

What could they do? This cherished tradition, ongoing in Crozet since Washington Irving first published his immortal tale, seemed in questionable taste this year. After all, a headless body had just been found.

After an agonizing debate the committee of worthies decided to cancel Ichabod Crane. As the ball was in a few days, they hadn't time to create another show. The librarian suggested she could find a story which could be read to the children. It wasn't perfect but it was something.

On her way to the post office, Miranda's steps dragged slower and slower. She reached the door. She stood there for a moment. She breathed deeply. She opened the front door.

"Harry!" she boomed.

"I'm right in front of you. You don't have to yell."

"So you are. I don't want to tell you this but the Harvest Ball committee has decided, wisely I think, to cancel the Headless Horseman reenactment."

Harry, obviously disappointed, saw the logic of it. "Don't feel bad, Mrs. H. We'll get back to it next year."

A sigh of relief escaped Miranda's red lips. "I'm so glad you see the point."

"I do and thank you for telling me. Would you like me to tell Susan?"

"No, I'll get over there. It's my responsibility."

As she left, Harry watched the squared shoulders, the straight back. Miranda could be a pain—couldn't we all —but she always knew the right thing to do and the manner in which to do it. Harry admired that.

17

Fitz-Gilbert could have used a secretary to make himself look like a functioning lawyer—which he wasn't.

It doesn't do for a man not to go to work, even a very wealthy man, so his office was mostly for show although it had developed into a welcome retreat from his mother-in-law and, occasionally, his wife.

He hadn't been to the office since the torso appeared in Mim's boathouse, two days ago.

He opened the door and beheld chaos. His chairs were overturned; papers were scattered everywhere; his file cabinet drawers sat askew.

He picked up the phone and dialed Sheriff Shaw.

18

Finding the remains of a human body, while unpleasant, wasn't rare. Every year in the state of Virginia hunters stumble across bodies picked clean by birds and scavengers, a few tatters of clothing left clinging to the bones. Occasionally the deceased has been killed by mistake by other hunters; other times an elderly person who suffered from disease or loss of memory simply wandered off in winter and died from exposure. Then, too, there were those tortured souls who walked into the woods to end it all. Murder, however, was not that common.

In the case of this cut-up corpse, Rick Shaw figured it had to be murder. The life of a county sheriff is usually clogged with serving subpoenas, testifying in poaching cases and land disputes, chasing speeders, and hauling drunks into the pokey. Murder added excitement. Not that he thought of it that way, exactly, but as he sat at his cluttered desk his mind moved faster; he concentrated fiercely. It took an unjust death to give him life.

"All right, Cooper." He wheeled around in his chair, pushing with the balls of his feet. "Give."

"Give what?"

"You know what." He stretched out his hand.

Irritated, Cynthia opened her long desk drawer, retrieved a pack of unfiltered Lucky Strikes, and smacked them in his hand. "You could at least smoke filtered cigarettes."

"Then I'd smoke two packs a day instead of one. What's the difference? And don't think I don't know that you're sneaking some."

When it was put that way, Cooper couldn't think of a difference. The surface of her desk shone, the grain of the old oak lending solidity to the piece. Papers, neatly stacked in piles, paperweights on top, provided a contrast to Rick's desk. Their minds contrasted too. She was logical, organized, and reserved. Rick was intuitive, disorganized, and as direct as he could be in his position. She liked the politics of the job. He didn't. As he was a good twenty years older than she, he'd remain sheriff and she'd be deputy. In time, barring accident, Cynthia Cooper could look forward to being the first woman sheriff of Albemarle County. Rick never thought of himself as a feminist. He hadn't wanted her in the first place but as the years rolled by her performance won him over. After a while he forgot she was a woman or maybe it didn't matter. He saw her as his right hand, and turning the department over to her someday was as it should be, not that he was ready to retire. He was too young for that.

The cigarette calmed him. The phones jangled. The small office enjoyed a secretary and a few part-time deputies. The department needed to expand but so far the county officials had passed no funds for that to their overworked sheriff.

One reporter from the local paper had showed up yesterday, and Rick had refused to dwell on the grisly details of the case. His low-key comments had satisfied the reporter for the moment, but Rick knew he'd be back. Rick and Coop hoped they'd have enough answers to forestall a panic or a squadron of reporters showing up from other papers, not to mention the TV.

"You've got a feeling about this case, boss?"

"The obvious. Destroying the identity of the corpse was paramount in the killer's mind. No fingerprints. No clothes on the torso. No head. Whoever this poor guy was, he knew too much. And we'd know too much if we knew who he was."

"I can't figure out why the killer would take the trouble to divide up the body. Lot of work. Then he or she would have to bag it so it wouldn't bleed all over everything, and *then* drive the parts around to dump them."

"Could be an undertaker, or someone with mortuary experience. Could have drained the body and then chopped it."

"Or a doctor," Cynthia added.

"Even a vet."

"Not Fair Haristeen. Poor guy, he was a suspect for a bit in Kelly Craycroft's murder."

"Well, he did wind up with Boom Boom, didn't he?"

"Yeah, poor sod." Cynthia burst out laughing.

Rick laughed too. "That woman, she's like to run him crazy. Pretty though."

"Men always say that." Cynthia smiled.

"Well, I don't see how you women can swoon over

Mel Gibson. What's so special about him?" Rick stubbed out his cigarette.

"If you knew, you and I would have a lot more to talk about," Cynthia cracked.

"Very funny." He reached in the pack to pull out another coffin nail.

"Come on, you just finished one!"

"Did I?" He picked up the ashtray and counted the butts. "Guess I did. This one's still smoking." He crushed it again.

"You're suffering one of your hunches. I know it. Come on, tell."

He lifted a shoulder and let it fall. He felt a little foolish when he had these hunches because he couldn't explain or defend them. Men are taught to back up what they say. He couldn't do that in this case but over time he had learned not to dismiss odd sensations or strange ideas. Often they led him to valuable evidence, valuable insights.

"Come on, boss. I can tell when you're catching the scent," Cynthia prodded.

He folded his hands on his desk. "Just this. Dividing up a body makes sense. That doesn't throw me. The hard rains worked against our killer. That and little Tucker. But really, the odds were that those legs and hands would never have been found. It's the boathouse that doesn't compute."

"He could have tossed the torso in the lake and, when it came up, gaffed it or something and dragged it into the boathouse." Cynthia stopped to think. "But everyone would have seen this person, male or female, unless it was the dead of night, and you can't schedule the appearance of waterlogged bodies, now can you?"

"Nope. That's why it doesn't compute. That piece of meat was *put* in the boathouse. No other explanation."

"Well, if the killer knows the community he would know or see Mim's pontoon boat at the dock. Nobody goes into the boathouse much unless she has one of her naval sorties planned. It's as good a place to hide a body as any other."

"Is it?"

They stared at each other. Then Cynthia spoke. "You think that head's going to show up?"

"I kinda hope it does and I kinda hope it doesn't." He couldn't fight temptation. He grabbed another cigarette but delayed lighting it. "See if there's a record for Blair Bainbridge in New York."

"Okay. Anyone else?"

"We know everyone else. Or we think we do."

19

The light frost crunched underfoot even though Mrs. Murphy trod lightly. The rain had finally stopped last night and she had risen early to hunt field mice. Tucker, flopped on her side on Harry's bed, was still sound asleep.

Although the cat's undercoat was thickening, the stiff wind sent a chill throughout her body. Another month and her coat would be more prepared for the cold. The prospect of running top speed after a rabbit or a mouse thrilled Mrs. Murphy, so what was a little cold? The mice ducked into their holes, which ended the chase, but the rabbits often ran across meadows and through woods. Occasionally she caught a rabbit, but more often a mouse. She'd come alongside and reach over to grab it at the base of the neck if she could. If not she'd bump and roll it. Mrs. Murphy dispatched her conquests rapidly; not for her the torture of batting her prey around until it was torn up and punch-drunk. A swift broken neck ended the business in a split second. Usually she brought the quarry back to Harry.

The frost held the scent. Even so it wasn't a good day for hunting. She growled once when she smelled a red vixen. Mrs. Murphy and fox competed for the same food, so the cat resented her rival. She also hotly resented that a fox had gotten into the henhouse years ago when she was a kitten and had killed every hen on the property. Feathers fluttered like snowflakes and the images of the pathetic bodies of ten hens and one rooster stayed in her mind. She couldn't have warned off the predator anyway, because of her youth, but Harry's dismay at the sight unnerved Mrs. Murphy. After that, Harry no longer kept chickens, which was a pity because, as a kitten, Mrs. Murphy had loved to flatten herself in the grass and watch the yellow chicks peep and run all over the place.

If Tucker wouldn't be so fussy, Harry could get a big dog, a dog that would live outside, to chase off foxes and those pesky raccoons. A puppy with big paws from the SPCA would grow up to fill the bill. The mere mention of it would send Tucker into a hissy fit.

"Would you tolerate another cat, I ask you?" Tucker would shriek.

"If we had a surplus of mice I guess I'd have to," Mrs. Murphy would usually reply.

Tucker declared that she could handle a fox. This was a patent lie. She could not. If a fox went to ground she might be able to dig it out but then what would she do with it? Tucker wasn't a good killer. Corgis were brave dogs—Mrs. Murphy had seen ample proof of that—but Tucker, at least, wasn't the hunter type. Corgis, bred to herd cattle, were low to the ground so that when a cow kicked, the small dog could easily duck the blow. Tough, resilient, and accustomed to animals much bigger than themselves, corgis could work with just about any large domesticated animal. But hunting wasn't in their blood, so Mrs. Murphy usually hunted alone.

A meow, deep and mellow in the distance, attracted Mrs. Murphy's attention. She tensed, and then relaxed when the splendidly handsome figure of her ex-husband slipped out of the woods. Paddy, as always, wore his black tuxedo; his white shirtfront was immaculate but the white spats were dirty. His gorgeous eyes glittered and he bounded up with unbridled enthusiasm to see his ex.

"Hunting, Sugar? Let's do it together."

"Thanks, Paddy. I'm better at it alone."

He sat down and flicked his tail. *"That's what you always say. You know, Murph, you won't be young and beautiful forever."*

"Neither will you," came the tart reply. *"Still hanging around that silver slut?"*

"Oh, her? She got very boring." Paddy referred to one of his many inamoratas, this one a silver Maine coon cat of extraordinary beauty. *"I hate it when they want to know where you've been every moment, as well as what you're thinking at every turn. Give it a rest."* His pink tongue accentuated his white fangs. *"You never did that."*

"I was too busy myself to worry about what you were doing." She changed the subject. *"Find anything?"*

"Hunting's not good. Let them get a little hungrier and then we'll catch a few. The field mice are fat and happy right now."

"Where'd you come from?"

"*Yellow Mountain. I left home in the middle of the night. I've got that door, you know—don't know why Harry doesn't put one in for you. Anyway, I was going to head toward the first railroad tunnel but it was too far away and the promise of hunting was already dim, so I trotted up the mountain instead.*"

"*Not much there either?*"

"*No,*" he replied.

"*Did you hear, Paddy, about those body parts in the graveyard?*"

"*Who cares? Humans kill one another and then pretend it's awful. If it's so awful, then why do they do it so much?*"

"*I don't know.*"

"*And think about it, Murphy. If the new guy is in his house, why would the killer drag those pieces of body down the driveway? Too risky.*"

"*Maybe he didn't know the new man had moved in.*"

"*In Crozet? You sneeze and your neighbor says God bless you. I think he, or she, parked somewhere within a mile—two legs and two hands aren't that heavy to carry. Came in off Yellow Mountain Road, up to the old logging road, and walked back through the woods into the pastures up to the cemetery. You wouldn't have seen the person from your place unless you were in the west meadows. You're usually out of the west meadows by sunset though, because the horses have been brought in, and this new guy, well, he was a risk but the cemetery is far enough away from the house that he might see someone up there but I doubt if he could have heard anything. Of course, the new guy could have done it himself.*"

Mrs. Murphy batted a soggy leaf. "*Got a point there, Paddy.*"

"*You know, people only kill for two reasons.*"

"What are they?"

"Love or money." His white whiskers shook with mirth. Both reasons seemed absurd to Paddy.

"Drugs."

"Still gets back to money," Paddy countered. *"Whatever this is, it will come to love or money. Harry's safe, since it hasn't a thing to do with her. You get so worried about Harry. She's pretty tough, you know."*

"You're right. I just wish her senses were sharper. She misses so much. You know, it takes her sometimes ten or twenty seconds longer to hear something and even then she can't recognize the difference in tire treads as they come down the driveway. She recognizes engine differences though. Her eyes are pretty good but I tell you she can't tell a field mouse five hundred yards away. Even though her eyes are better in daylight, she still misses the movement. It's so easy to hear if you just listen and let your eyes follow. At night, of course, she can't see that well and none of them can smell worth a damn. I just worry how she can function with such weak senses."

"If Harry were being stalked by a tiger, then I'd worry. Since one human's senses are about as bad as another's, they're equal. And since they seem to be their own worst enemies, they're well equipped to fight one another. Besides which, she has you and Tucker and you can give her the jump, if she'll listen."

"She listens to me—most of the time. She can be quite stubborn though. Selective hearing."

"They're all like that." Paddy nodded gravely. *"Hey, want to race across the front pasture, climb up the walnut by the creek, run across the limb, and then jump out to the other side? We can be at your back door in no time. Bet I get there first."*

"Deal!"

They ran like maniacs, arriving at the back porch door. Harry, coffeepot in hand and still sleepy, opened the back door. They both charged into the kitchen.

"Catting around?" She smiled and scratched Mrs. Murphy's head, and Paddy's too.

20

A crisp night dotted with bright stars like chunks of diamonds created the perfect Halloween. Each year the Harvest Fair was held at Crozet High. Before the high school was built in 1892, the fair was held in an open meadow across from the train station. The high school displayed the excesses of Victorian architecture. One either loved it or hated it. Since most everyone attending the Harvest Ball had graduated from Crozet High, they loved it.

Not Mim Sanburne, as she had graduated from Madeira, nor Little Marilyn, who had followed in her mother's spiked-heel steps. No, Crozet High smacked of the vulgate, the hoi polloi, the herd. Jim Sanburne, mayor of Crozet, had graduated from CHS in 1939. He carefully walked up and down rows of tables placed on the football field. Corn, squash, potatoes, wheat sheaves, and enormous pumpkins crowded the tables.

The mayor and his son-in-law had been cataloguing contestant entries that morning. In order to be impartial, Fitz wrote down all the produce entries. Since Jim was judging that category, it wouldn't do for him to see them early.

The crafts filled the halls inside the school. Mrs. Hogendobber would take a step or two, stop, study, rub her hand on her chin, remove her glasses, put them back on, and say, "Hmmn." This process was repeated for each display. Miranda took judging the crafts to new levels of seriousness.

The gym, decorated as a witches' lair, would welcome everyone after the awards. The dance attracted even the lame and the halt. If you breathed you showed up. Rick Shaw and Cynthia Cooper sat in the gym judging costumes. Children scampered about as Ninja Turtles, angels, devils, cowboys, and one little girl whose parents were dairy farmers came as a milk carton. The teenagers, also in costume, tended to stick together, but as the task of decorating for the Harvest Ball fell upon CHS's students, they heaped glory upon themselves. Every senior class was determined to top the class preceding it. The freshman, sophomore, and junior classes were pledged to help, and on Halloween Day classes were suspended so the decorating could proceed.

As Harry, Susan, and Blair strolled through the displays they admired the little flying witches overhead. The electronics wizards at the school had built intricate systems of wires, operating the witches by remote control. Ghosts and goblins also flew. The excitement mounted because if this was the warm-up, what would the dance be like? That was always the payoff.

Harry and Susan, in charge of the Harvest Ball for their class of 1976, ruefully admitted that these were the best decorations they'd seen since their time. No crepe paper for these kids. The orange and black colors snaked along the walls and the outside tables with Art Deco severity and sensuality. Susan, bursting with pride, accepted congratulations from other parents. Her son Danny was the freshman representative to the decorations committee and it was his idea to make the demons fly. He was determined to outdo his mother and was already well on his way to a chairmanship as a senior. His younger sister had proved a help too. Brookie was already worried about what would happen two years from now when she had the opportunity to be a Harvest Ball class representative. Could she top this? Susan and Ned had sent the kids to private school in Charlottesville for a couple of years, the result being that both were turning into horrid snobs. They had yanked the kids out of the private school, to everyone's eventual relief.

Blair observed it all in wonder and amusement. These young people displayed spirit and community involvement, something which had been missing at his prep school. He almost envied the students, although he knew he had been given the gift of a superb education as well as impeccable social contacts.

Boom Boom and Fair judged the livestock competition. Boom Boom was formally introduced to Blair by Harry. She took one look at this Apollo and audibly sucked in her breath. Fair, enraptured by a solid Holstein calf, elected not to notice. Boom Boom, far too intelligent to flirt openly, simply exuded radiance.

As they walked away Susan commented, "Well, she spared you the Boom Boom brush."

"What's that?" Blair smiled.

"In high school—on these very grounds, mind you—

Boom Boom would slide by a boy and gently brush him with her torpedoes. Naturally, the boy would die of embarrassment and joy."

"Yeah," Harry laughed. "Then she'd say, 'Damn the torpedoes and full speed ahead.' Boom Boom can be very funny when she puts her mind, or boobs, to it."

"You haven't told me what your theme was when you two co-chaired the Harvest Ball." Blair evidenced little curiosity about Boom Boom but plenty about Harry and Susan, which pleased them mightily.

"The Hound of the Baskervilles." Susan's voice lowered.

Harry's eyes lit up. "You wouldn't have believed it. I mean, we started working the day school started. The chair and co-chairs are elected the end of junior year. A really big deal—"

Susan interrupted. "Can you tell? I mean, we still remember everything. Sorry, Harry."

"That's okay. Well, Susan came up with the theme and we decorated the inside of the school like the inside of a Victorian mansion. Velvet drapes, old sofas—I mean, we hit up every junk shop in this state, I swear . . . that and what parents lent us. We took rolls and rolls of old butcher paper—Market Shiflett's dad donated it—and the art kids turned it into stone and we made fake walls with that outside."

"Don't forget the light."

"Oh, yeah, we had one of the boys up in the windows that are dark on the second floor going from room to room swinging a lantern. Boy, did that scare the little kids when they looked up. Painted his face too. We even got Mr. MacGregor—"

"My Mr. MacGregor?" Blair asked.

"The very one," Susan said.

"We got him to lend us his bloodhound, Charles the First, who emitted the most sorrowful cry."

"We walked him up and down the halls that were not in use and asked him to howl, which he did, dear dog. We really scared the poop out of them when we took him up on the second floor, opened a window, and his piercing howl floated over the grounds." Susan shivered with delight.

"The senior class dressed like characters from the story. God, it was fun."

By now they were outside. The Reverend Herbie and Carol Jones waved from among the wheat sheaves. A few people remarked that they'd miss Harry on Tomahawk this year. The local reporter roved around. Everyone was in a good mood. Naturally people talked about the grim discoveries but since it didn't touch anyone personally—the victim wasn't someone they knew—the talk soon dissolved into delicious personal gossip. Mim, Little Marilyn, and Fitz-Gilbert paraded around. Mim accepted everyone's sympathy with a nod and then asked them not to mention it again. Her nerves were raw, she said.

One stalwart soul was missing this year: old Fats Domino, the huge feline who had played the Halloween cat every year for the last fifteen. Fats had finally succumbed to old age, and Pewter had been pressed into service. Her dark-gray coat could almost pass for black in the night and she hadn't a speck of white on her. She gleefully padded over the tables, stopping to accept pats from her admirers.

Pewter grew expansive in the limelight. The more attention she received, the more she purred. Many people snapped photos of her, and she gladly paused for them. The newspaper photographer grabbed a few shots too. Well, that pesky Tucker had got her name in the papers once, the last time there'd been a murder in Crozet, but Pewter knew she'd be in color on the front page because the Harvest Festival always made the front page. Nor could she refrain from a major gloat over the fact that Mrs. Murphy and Tucker had to stay home, while she was the star of the occasion.

The craft and livestock prizes had been awarded, and now the harvest prizes were being announced. Miranda hurried over to stand behind her pumpkin. The gargantuan pumpkin next to hers was larger, indisputably larger, but Miranda hoped the competition's imperfect shape would sway Jim Sanburne her way. With so much milling about and chatting she didn't notice Pewter heading for the pumpkins. Mrs. Hogendobber felt no need to share this moment with the cat.

Mim, Little Marilyn, and Fitz-Gilbert stood off to the side. Mim noticed Harry and Blair.

"I know this Bainbridge fellow attended Yale and St. Paul's but we don't really know who he is. Harry ought to be more careful."

"You never minded Fair as her husband and he's not a stockbroker." Little Marilyn was simply making an observation, not trying to start an argument.

"At the time," Mim snapped, "I was relieved that Harry married, period. I feared she would go the way of Mildred Yost."

Mildred Yost, a pretty girl in Mim's class at Madeira, spurned so many beaus she finally ran out of them and spent her life as an old maid, a condition Mim found fearful. Single women just don't make it to the top of society. If a woman was manless she had better be a widow.

"Mother"—Fitz-Gilbert called Mim "Mother"—"Harry doesn't care about climbing to the top of society."

"Whether she cares or not, she shouldn't marry a person of low degree . . . I mean, once she's established the fact that she *can* get married."

Mim babbled on in this vein, making very little sense. Fitz-Gilbert heard her sniff that being a divorcée teetered on the brink of a shadowy status. Why was Mim so concerned with Harry and who she was dating? he wondered. No other reason than that she felt nothing could go on in Crozet without her express approval. As usual, Mim's conversation did not run a charitable course. She even complained that the little witches, ghosts, and goblins overhead whirred too much, giving her a headache. The shock of recent events was making her crabbier than usual. Fitz tuned her out.

Danny Tucker, as Hercule Poirot, scooted next to Mrs. Hogendobber. His was the enormous pumpkin.

"Danny, why didn't you inform me that you grew this . . . fruit?" Mrs. Hogendobber demanded.

"Well, Mom didn't want to upset you. We all know you want that blue ribbon."

Pewter arrived to sit between the two huge orange pumpkins, the finalists. Mrs. Hogendobber, talking to Danny, still didn't notice her. Pewter was insulted.

Jim picked up Miranda's pumpkin. He quickly put it back down. "These damn things get heavier every year." Miranda shot him a look. "Sorry, Miranda."

Pewter smelled pumpkin goo, as though the insides

had been removed for pumpkin pie. She sniffed Miranda's pumpkin.

"See, the cat likes my pumpkin." Miranda smiled to the crowd.

"I don't like any *pumpkins,"* Pewter replied.

"Do I want to pick this one up? I might fall over from the size of it." Jim smiled but put his large hands around Danny's pumpkin anyway. The enormous pumpkin was much heavier than the other pumpkin, oddly heavy. He replaced it. Puzzled, he lifted it up again.

Pewter, never able to control her curiosity, inspected the back of the pumpkin. A very neat, very large circle had been cut out and then glued back into place. If one wasn't searching for it, the tampering could easily be missed.

"Look," she said with forcefulness.

Danny Tucker was the only human who paid attention to her. He picked up his pumpkin. "Mayor Sanburne, I know my pumpkin's heavy, but not *this* heavy. Something's wrong."

"That *is* your pumpkin," Miranda stated.

"Yes, but it's too heavy." Danny picked it up again.

Pewter reached up and swatted the back of the orange globe. This led Danny's eyes, much sharper than Jim's or Miranda's, to the patch job in the back.

"Jim, we're waiting. We want a winner," Mim called out impatiently.

"Yes, dear, in a minute," he replied and the crowd laughed.

Danny pushed the circle and it wiggled. He reached into his jacket, retrieved a pocketknife, and slid it along the cutting line. The glue dislodged easily and he pried out the big circle. "Oh, wow!" Danny saw the back of a head. He assumed one of his buddies had done this as a joke. He reached in, grabbed the head by the hair, and pulled it out. A wave of sweet stink alerted him. This was no joke, no rubber or plastic head. Not quite knowing what to do he held the head away from him, giving the crowd a fine view of the loathsome sight. What was left of the eyes stared straight at them.

Danny, now realizing what he held, dropped the head. It hit the table with a sickening splat.

Pewter jumped away. She ran down to the squashes. If this was what the job of playing Halloween cat entailed, she was resigning.

People screamed. Jim Sanburne, almost by reflex, handed the ribbon to Miranda.

"I don't want it!" Miranda screamed.

Boom Boom Craycroft fainted dead away. The next thud heard was Blair Bainbridge hitting the ground.

Then Little Marilyn screeched, "I've seen that face before!"

21

Therapists in the county agreed to work with the students at Crozet High to help them through the trauma of what they'd seen.

Rick Shaw wondered if they could help him. He disliked the sight of the decayed head himself but not enough to have nightmares over it. When he and Cynthia Cooper collected the head, the first thing they did, apart from holding their noses, was check the open mouth. Not one tooth remained in the head. No dental records.

Cynthia led Little Marilyn away from the sight and asked her to clarify her statement.

"I don't know him but I think that's the vagrant who was wandering around maybe ten days ago. I'm not certain as to the date. You see, he passed the post office and I walked to the window and got a good look at him. That's all I can tell you." She was shaking.

"Thank you. You've had more than your share of this." Cynthia patted Little Marilyn on the back.

Fitz-Gilbert put his arms around her. "Come on, honey, let's go home."

"What about Mother?"

"Your father's taking care of her."

Meekly, Little Marilyn allowed Fitz to shepherd her to their Range Rover.

Cynthia stuck her notebook back in her pocket. As Rick was talking to other observers, the press photographer fired off some shots.

Cynthia took statements from Harry, Susan, Herb, Carol, Market, just everyone she could find. She would have interviewed Pewter if she could have. Market held the cat in his arms, each of them grateful for the reassuring warmth of the other.

Holding his wife's hand, Cabell Hall mentioned to Cynthia that she and Rick might want to call the video stores and have them pull their more gruesome horror movies until things settled down.

"Actually, Mr. Hall, I have no authority to do that but as a prominent citizen you could, or your wife could. People listen to you all."

"I'll do it then," Taxi Hall promised.

It took Cynthia more than an hour to get everyone out of there. Finally, Cynthia and Rick had a moment to themselves.

"Worse than I imagined." Rick slapped his thighs, a nervous gesture.

"Yeah, I thought we'd find the head, if we found it at all, back in the woods somewhere. It would be something someone would stumble on."

"You know what we got, Coop?" Rick breathed in the cool night air. "We got us a killer with a sick sense of humor."

22

Firelight casts shadows, which, depending on one's mood, can either be friendly highlights on the wall or misshapen monsters. Susan, Harry, and Blair sat before Harry's fireplace. The best friends had decided that Blair needed some company before he returned to his empty house.

The Harvest Fair had rattled everyone and Harry found another surprise when she opened the door to her house. Tucker, in a fit of pique at being left behind, had demolished Harry's favorite slippers. Mrs. Murphy told her not to do it but Tucker, when furious, was not a reasonable creature. The dog's punishment was that she had to remain locked in the kitchen while the adults talked in the living room. To make matters worse, Mrs. Murphy was allowed in the living room with them. Tucker laid her head between her paws and howled.

"Come on, Harry, let her in," Susan chided.

"Easy for you to say—they weren't your slippers."

"Actually, you should have taken her. She finds more

clues than anyone." Susan cast a glance at the alert Mrs. Murphy perched on Harry's armchair. "And Murphy, of course."

"Is anyone hungry?" Harry remembered to be a hostess.

"No." Blair shook his head.

"Me neither," Susan agreed. "Poor you." She indicated Blair. "You moved here for peace and quiet and you landed in the middle of murder."

The muscles in Blair's handsome face tightened. "There's no escaping human nature. Remember the men put off the H.M.S. *Bounty* on Pitcairn Island?"

"I remember the great movie with Charles Laughton as Captain Bligh," Susan said.

"Well, in real life those Englishmen stranded on that paradise soon created their own version of hell. The sickness was within. The natives—by then they were mostly women, since the whites had killed the men— slit the Englishmen's throats in the middle of the night while they slept. Or at least historians think they did. No one really knows how the mutineers died, except that years later, when a European ship stopped by, the 'civilized' men were gone."

"Is that by way of saying that Crozet is a smaller version of Manhattan?" Harry reached over and poked the fire with one of the brass utensils left her by her parents.

"Big Marilyn as Brooke Astor." Susan then added, "Actually, Brooke Astor is a great lady. Mim's a wannabe."

"In the main, Crozet is a kinder place than Manhattan, but whatever is wrong with us shows up wherever we may be—on a more reduced scale. Passions are passions, regardless of century and geography." Blair stared into the fire.

"True enough." Harry sank back into her seat. "How about Little Marilyn saying she recognized that head?" The memory of the head made Harry queasy.

"A hobo she saw walking down the tracks while she was inside the post office." Blair added, "I vaguely remember him too. He was wearing old jeans and a baseball jacket. I wasn't that interested. Did you get a look at him?"

Harry nodded. "I noticed the Mets jacket. That's about it. However, even if these body parts belong to the fellow, we still don't know who he is."

"A student at U.V.A.?"

"God, Susan, I hope not." Harry allowed Mrs. Murphy to crawl into her lap.

"Too old." Blair folded his hands.

"It's a little hard to tell." Susan also called up the grisly sight.

"Ladies, I think I'll go home. I'm exhausted and I'm embarrassed that I passed out. This is getting to me, I suppose."

Harry walked him to the door and bade him goodnight before returning to Susan. Mrs. Murphy had taken over her chair. She lifted up the cat, who protested and then settled down again.

"He was distant tonight," Susan observed. "Guess it has been right much of a shock. He doesn't have a stick of furniture in his house, he doesn't know any of us, and then they find pieces of a body on his land. Now this. There goes his bucolic dream."

"The only good thing about tonight was getting to see Boom Boom faint."

"Aren't you ugly?" Susan laughed at her.

"You have to admit it was funny."

"Kind of. Fair had the pleasure of reviving her, digging in her voluminous purse for her tranquilizers, and then taking her home. If she gets too difficult I guess he could hit her up with a cc of Ace."

The thought of Boom Boom dosed with a horse tranquilizer struck Susan as amusing. "I'd say that Boom Boom wasn't an easy keeper," she said, using an equine term—quite accurate, too, because Boom Boom was anything but an easy keeper.

"I suppose we have to laugh at something. This is so macabre, what else can we do?" Harry scratched Mrs. Murphy behind the ears.

"I don't know."

"Are you afraid?"

"Are you?" Susan shot back.

"I asked you first."

"Not for myself," Susan replied.

"Me neither, because I don't think it had anything to do with me, but what if I fall into it? For all I know the killer might have buried those body parts in my cemetery."

"I think we're all right if we don't get in the way," Susan said.

"But what's 'in the way'? What's this all about?"

Mrs. Murphy opened one eye and said, *"Love or money."*

23

Sunday dawned frosty but clear. The day's high might reach into the low fifties but not much more. Harry loved Sundays. She could work from sunup to sundown without interruption. Today she was planning to strip stalls, put down lime, and then cover and bank the sides with wood shavings. Physical labor limbered up her mind. Out in the stable she popped a soothing tape into the boom box and proceeded to fill up the wheelbarrow. The manure spreader was pulled up under a small earthen bank. That way Harry could roll the wheelbarrow to the top of the bank and tip the contents over into the wagon. She and her father had built the ramp in the late sixties. Harry was twelve. She worked so hard and with so much enthusiasm that as a reward her father bought her a pair of fitted chaps. The ramp had lasted these many years and so did the memory of the chaps.

Both of Harry's parents thought that idle hands did the Devil's work. True to her roots, Harry couldn't sit still. She was happiest when working and found it a cure for most ills. After her divorce she couldn't sleep much, so she would work sometimes sixteen or eighteen hours a day. The farm reflected this intensity. So did Harry. Her weight dropped to 110, too low for a woman of five foot six. Finally, Susan and Mrs. Hogendobber tricked her into going to the doctor. Hayden McIntire, forewarned, slammed shut his office door as they dragged her through it. A shot of B_{12} and a severe tongue-lashing convinced her that she'd better eat more. He also prescribed a mild sedative so she could sleep. She took it for a week and then threw it out. Harry hated drugs of any sort but her body accepted sleep and food again, so whatever Hayden did worked.

Each year with the repetition of the seasons, the cycle of planting, weeding, harvesting, and winter repairs, it was brought home to Harry that life was finite. Perhaps LIFE in capital letters wasn't finite but her life was. There would be a beginning, a middle, and an end. She wasn't quite at the middle yet, but she endured hints that she wasn't fifteen either. Injuries took longer to heal. Actually, she enjoyed more energy than she'd had as a teenager but what had changed the most was her mind. She'd lived just long enough to be seeing events and human personality types for the second and third time. She wasn't easily impressed or fooled. Most movies bored her to death, for that reason as well. She'd seen versions of those plots long before. They enthralled a new generation of fifteen-year-olds but there wasn't anything for her. What enthralled Harry was a job well done, laughter with her friends, a quiet ride on one of the horses. She'd withdrawn from the social whirl after her divorce—no great loss, but she was shocked to find out how little a single woman was valued. A single man was a plus. A single woman, a liability. The married women, Susan excepted, feared you.

Although Fair lacked money he didn't lack prestige in his field and Harry had been dragged along to banquets, boring dinners at the homes of thoroughbred breeders, and even more boring dinners at Saratoga. It was the same old parade of excellent facelifts, good bourbon, and tired stories. She was glad to be out of it. Boom Boom could have it all. Boom Boom could have Fair too. Harry didn't know why she'd gotten so mad at Fair the other day. She didn't love him anymore but she liked him. How could you not like a man you've known since you were in grade school and liked at first sight? The sheer folly of his attachment to Boom Boom irritated her though. If he found a sensible woman like Susan she'd be relieved. Boom Boom would suck up so much of his energy and money that eventually his work would suffer. He'd spent years building his practice. Boom Boom could wreck it in one circle of the seasons if he didn't wake up.

The sweet smell of pine shavings caressed her senses. For an instant Harry picked up the wall-phone receiver. She was going to call Fair and tell him what she really thought. Then she hung it up. How could she? He wouldn't listen. No one ever does in that situation. They wake up when they can.

She spread fresh shavings in the stalls.

Mrs. Murphy checked out the hayloft. Simon, sound asleep, never heard her tiptoe around him. He'd dragged up an old T-shirt of Harry's and then hollowed out part of a hay bale. He was curled up in the hollow on the shirt. She then walked over to the south side of the loft.

The snake was hibernating. Nothing would wake her up until spring. Overhead the owl also slept. Satisfied that everything was as it should be, Mrs. Murphy climbed back down the ladder.

"Tucker," she called.

"What?" Tucker lounged around in the tack room.

"Want to go for a walk?"

"Where?"

"Foxden pastures off Yellow Mountain Road."

"Why there?"

"Paddy gave me an idea the other day and this is the first time I've had a chance to look in the daylight."

"Okay." Tucker stood up, shook herself, and then trotted out into the brisk air with her companion.

Mrs. Murphy told Tucker Paddy's idea about someone parking off Yellow Mountain Road on the old logging road and carrying the body parts to the cemetery in a plastic bag or something.

Once in the pastures Tucker put her nose down. Too much rain and too much time had elapsed. She smelled field mice, deer, fox, lots of wild turkeys, raccoons, and even the faint scent of bobcat.

While Tucker kept her nose to the ground Mrs. Murphy cast her sharp eyes around for a glint of metal, a piece of flesh, but there was nothing, nothing at all.

"Find anything?"

"No, too late." Tucker lifted her head. *"How else could the body get to the cemetery? If the murderer didn't walk through these pastures, then he or she had to go right down Blair's driveway in front of God and Blair, anyway. Paddy's right. He came through here. Unless it's Blair."*

Mrs. Murphy jerked her head around to view her friend full in the face. *"You don't think that, do you?"*

"I hope not. Who knows?"

The cat fluffed out her fur and then let it settle down. She headed for home. *"You know what I think?"*

"No."

"I think tomorrow at work will be impossible. Lardguts will go on and on and on about the head in the pumpkin. She got her name and her picture in the paper. God help us." Mrs. Murphy laughed.

24

". . . *and the maggots had a field day, I can tell you that.*" Pewter perched on the hood of Harry's truck, parked behind the post office.

Mrs. Murphy, seated next to her, listened to the unending paean of self-praise. Tucker sat on the ground.

"*I heard you ran into the squashes,*" Tucker called up.

"*Of course I did, nitwit. I didn't want to injure the evidence,*" Pewter bragged. "*Boy, you should have heard people scream once they realized it was real. A few even puked. Now I watched everyone—everyone—from my vantage point. Mrs. Hogendobber was horrified but has a cast-iron stomach. Poor Danny, was he grossed out! Susan and Ned rushed up to him but he wanted to go to his friends instead. That age, you know. Oh, Big Marilyn, she wasn't grossed out at all. She was outraged. I thought she'd flip her lid after the corpse in the boathouse but no, she was mad, bullshit mad, I tell you. Fitz stood there with his mouth hanging open. Little Marilyn hollered that she recognized the face, what there was of it. Harry didn't move a muscle. Stood there like a stone taking it all in. You know how she gets when things are awful. Real quiet and still. Oh, Boom Boom dropped, tits into the sand, and Blair keeled over too. What a night. I knew something was wrong with that pumpkin. I sat next to it. It takes humans so long to see the obvious.*" Pewter sighed a superior sigh.

"*You were a teeny weeny bit disgusted.*" Mrs. Murphy flicked her tail.

Pewter turned her head. She puffed out her chest, refusing to be baited by her dearest friend, who was also a source of torment. "*Certainly not.*"

A door closed in the near distance. The animals turned, observing Mrs. Hogendobber striding up the alleyway. As she drew near the animals she opened her mouth to speak to them but closed it again. She felt vaguely foolish carrying on a conversation with animals. This didn't prevent her from talking to herself, however. She smiled at the creatures and walked into the post office.

"*Why'd Harry bring the truck?*" Pewter asked.

"*Wore herself out yesterday,*" Tucker replied.

Mrs. Murphy licked the side of her right front paw and rubbed it over her ears. "*Pewter, do you have any theories about this?*"

"*Yeah, we got a real nut case on the loose.*"

"*I don't think so.*" Mrs. Murphy washed the other paw.

"*What makes you so smart?*" Pewter snapped.

Mrs. Murphy let that go by. "*If a human being has the time to think about a murder he can often make it look like an accident or natural death. If one of them kills in the heat of passion it's a bullet wound or a knife wound. Right?*"

"Right," Tucker echoed, while Pewter's eyes narrowed to slits.

"Murphy, we all know that."

"Then we know it was a hurry-up job and it wasn't passion. Someone in Crozet was surprised by the dead person."

"A nasty surprise." Tucker followed her friend's thinking. *"But who? And what could be so terrible about the victim that he should have had to die for it?"*

"When we know that, we'll know everything," the cat said in a low voice.

25

The coroner's conclusions, neatly typed, rested on Rick Shaw's desk. The deceased was a white male in his early thirties. Identity remained unknown but what was known was that this fellow, who should have been in the prime of life, was suffering from malnutrition and liver damage. Larry Johnson, meticulous in the performance of his duties, added in his bold vertical handwriting that while alcohol abuse might have contributed to the liver damage, the organ could have been diseased for reasons other than alcohol abuse. Then, too, certain medications taken over many years could also have caused liver damage.

Cooper charged into the office. She tossed more paperwork onto the sheriff's desk. "More reports from Saturday night."

Rick grunted and shoved them aside. "You haven't said anything about the coroner's report."

"Died of a blow to the head. A child can kill someone

with a blow to the head if it's done right. We're still in the dark."

"What about a revenge motive?"

She was tired of kicking around ideas. Dead ends frustrated her. The fax machine hummed. She walked over to it almost absent-mindedly. "Boss, come over here."

Rick joined her and watched as the pages slowly rolled out of the machine. It was Blair Bainbridge's record.

He had been a suspect in the murder of his lover, an actress. However, he wasn't a suspect for long. The killer, an obsessed fan, was picked up by the police and confessed. The eerie thing was that the beautiful woman's corpse had been dismembered.

"Shit," was Cynthia's response.

"Let's go," was Rick's.

26

Heavy work gloves protected his hands as Blair righted tombstones, replaced the sod, and rolled it flat. The trees, now barren, surrounded the little cemetery like mournful sentinels. He stopped his labors when he saw the squad car roll down the driveway. He swung open the iron gate and headed down the hill to meet them.

A cool breeze eased off Yellow Mountain. Blair asked Rick Shaw and Cynthia Cooper inside. A couple of orange crates doubled as chairs.

"You know, there are wonderful auctions this time of year," Coop volunteered. "Check in the classifieds. I furnished my house, thanks to those auctions."

"I'll check it out."

Rick noticed that Blair was growing a thin military moustache. "Another modeling job coming up?"

"How'd you guess?" Blair smiled.

Rick rubbed under his nose. "Well, I'll get to the point. This isn't a social call, as I'm sure you've surmised. Your records indicate an actress with whom you were involved was brutally murdered and dismembered. What do you have to say?"

Blair blanched. "It was horrible. I thought when the police caught the murderer I'd feel some comfort. Well, I guess I did, in that I knew he wouldn't kill anyone else, but it didn't fill the . . . void."

"Is there anyone in Crozet or Charlottesville who might know of this incident?"

"Not that I know of. I mean, a few people recognized my face from magazines but no one knows me here. Guess that doesn't look so good for me, huh?"

"Let's just say you're an unknown factor." Rick shifted his weight. The orange crate wasn't comfortable.

"I didn't kill anybody. I think I could kill in self-defense or to protect someone I love, but other than that, I don't think I could do it."

"What one person defines as self-defense another might define as murder." Cynthia watched Blair's handsome features.

"I am willing to cooperate with you in any way. And I've refused to talk to the press. They'll only muck it up."

"Why don't you tell me what happened in New York?" Rick's voice was steady, unemotional.

Blair ran his hands through his hair. "You know, Sheriff, I'd like to forget that. I came here to forget that. Can you imagine what it was like to see that head pulled out of a pumpkin?"

The sheriff softened. "Not pretty for any of us."

Blair took a deep breath. "I knew Robin Mangione from a shoot we did for Baker and Reeves, the big New York department store. I guess that was three years ago. One thing led to another and, well, we stopped dating other people and got involved. Our work schedules often took us out of town but whenever we were in New York we were together."

"You didn't live together?" Rick asked.

"No. It's a little different in New York than here. In a place like this people get married. In New York, people can be as good as married and yet live in separate apartments for their entire lives. Maybe because of the millions of people, one needs a sense of privacy, of separate space, more than you do here. Anyway, living together wasn't a goal."

"What about her goals?" Cooper was suspicious about this living-apart stuff.

"She was more independent than I was, truthfully. Anyway, Robin inspired devotion from men. She could stop traffic. Fame, any kind of fame really, brings good and bad. The flotsam and jetsam of fame is how I think of it, and Robin was sometimes hassled by male admirers. Usually a sharp word from her, or if need be from me, took care of the problem. Except for the guy who killed her."

"Know anything about him?" Rick asked.

"What you know, except that I watched him at the trial. He's short, balding, one of those men you could pass on the street and never notice. He sent letters. He called. She changed her number. He'd wait for her outside the theater. I got in the habit of picking her up because he was such a nuisance. He began to threaten. We told the police. With predictable results." Rick dropped his gaze for a moment while Blair continued: "And one day when I was out of town on a shoot he broke the locks and got into her apartment. She was alone. The rest you know."

Indeed they did. Stanley Richards, the crazed fan, panicked after he killed Robin. Disposing of a body in New York City would try the imagination of a far more intelligent man than Stanley. So he put her in the bathtub, cut her throat and wrists and ankles, and tried to drain most of the blood out of the body. Then he dismembered her with the help of a meat cleaver. He fed pieces of the body to the disposal but it jammed up on the bone. Finally, desperate, he spent the rest of the night hauling out little bits of body and dumping her east, west, north, and south. The head he saved for the Sheep Meadow, in the middle of Central Park, where in exhaustion he put it down on the grass. A dawn jogger saw him and reported him as soon as he found a cop.

Neither Rick nor Cynthia felt the need to rehash those details.

"Don't you find it curious that—"

"*Curious?!*" Blair erupted, cutting off Rick. "It's sick!"

"Do you have any enemies?" Cynthia inquired.

Blair lapsed into silence. "My agent, occasionally."

"What's his name?" Rick had a pencil and pad out.

"Her name. Gwendolyn Blackwell. She's not my enemy but she broods if I don't take every job that comes down the pike. That woman would work me into an early grave if I let her."

"That's it? No irate husbands? No jilted ladies? No jealous competitor?"

"Sheriff, modeling isn't as glamorous as you might suppose."

"I thought all you guys were gay," Rick blurted out.

"Fifty-fifty, I'd say." Blair had heard this so many times it didn't rock his boat.

"Is there anyone you can think of—the wildest connection doesn't matter—*any*one who would know enough to duplicate what happened to Robin?"

Blair cast his deep eyes on Cynthia. It made her heart flutter. "Not one person. I really do think this is a grim coincidence."

Rick and Cynthia left as baffled as they were when they arrived. They'd keep an eye on Blair, but then they'd keep an eye on everyone.

27

The western half of Albemarle County would soon feel the blade of the bulldozer. The great state of Virginia and its Department of Highways, a little fiefdom, decided to create a bypass through much of the best land in the county. Businesses would be obliterated, pastures uprooted, property values crunched, and dreams strangled. The western bypass, as it came to be known, had the distinction of being outmoded before it was even begun. That and the fact that it imperiled the watershed meant little to the highway department. They wanted the western bypass and they were going to have it no matter who they displaced and no matter how they scarred the environment.

The uproar caused by this high-handed tactic obscured the follow-up story about the head in the pumpkin. Since no one could identify the corpse, interest fizzled. It would remain a good story for Halloweens to come.

The respite was appreciated by Jim Sanburne, mayor,

and the civic worthies of Crozet. Big Marilyn refused to discuss the subject, so it withered in her social circle, which was to say the six or seven ladies as snobbish as herself.

Little Marilyn recovered sufficiently to call her brother, Stafford, and invite him home for a weekend. This upset Mim more than the sum of the body parts. It meant she'd have to be sociable with his wife, Brenda.

This projected discomfort, awarded to Little Marilyn in lavish proportions by her mother, almost made the young woman back down and uninvite her brother and his wife. But it was opening hunt, such a pretty sight, and Stafford loved to photograph such events. She kept her nerve. Stafford would be home next weekend.

Weary of the swirl of tempestuous egos, Fitz-Gilbert decided to stay out late that night. First he stopped at Charley's, where he bumped into Ben Seifert on his way out. Fitz tossed back one beer and then hit the road again. He ran into Fair Haristeen at Sloan's and pulled up the barstool next to the vet.

"A night of freedom?"

Fair signaled for a beer for Fitz. "You might call it that. What about you?"

"It's been a hell of a week. You know my office was ransacked. Doesn't appear to have anything to do with the . . . murder . . . but it was upsetting on top of everything else. The sheriff and his deputy came out, took notes and so forth. Some money was missing, and a CD player, but obviously it's not at the top of their list. Then Cabell Hall called me to tell me to watch my stock market investments, since the market is on a one-way trip these days—down—and my mother-in-law—oh, well, why talk about her? Oh, I just ran into Ben

Seifert at Charley's. He's an okay guy, but he's just
burning to succeed Cabell some day. The thought of
Ben Seifert running Allied National gives me pause.
And then of course there's my father-in-law. He wants
to call out the National Guard.

"Those are my problems. What are yours?" Fitz
asked.

"I don't know." Fair was puzzled. "Boom Boom's
out with that model guy. She says he asked her to the
Cancer Fund Ball but I don't know. He didn't seem
that interested in her when I met him. I kind of thought
he liked Harry."

"Here's to women." Fitz-Gilbert smiled. "I don't
know anything about them but I've got one." He
clinked glasses with Fair.

Fair laughed. "My daddy used to say, 'You can't live
with them and you can't live without them.' I didn't
know what he was talking about. I do now."

"Marilyn is great by herself. It's when she's in the
company of her mother . . ." Fitz-Gilbert wiped froth
off his lips. "My mother-in-law can be a whistling bitch.
I feel guilty just being here . . . like I slipped my
leash. But I'm glad I didn't get dragged to the Cancer
Ball. Marilyn says she can only do but so many a year,
and she wanted to get things ready for Stafford and
Brenda. Thank God. I need the break."

Fair changed the subject. "Do you think this new guy
likes Harry? I thought guys like that wanted leggy
blondes or other guys."

"Can't speak for his preferences, but Harry's a good-
looking woman. Natural. Outdoorsy. I'll never know
why you guys broke up, buddy."

Fair, unaccustomed to exchanging much personal information, sat quietly and then signaled for another beer. "She's a good person. We grew up together. We dated in high school. We, well, she was more like my sister than my wife."

"Yeah, but you knew Boom Boom since you were yay-high," Fitz countered.

"Not the same."

"That's the truth."

"Just what do you mean by that?" Fair felt prickly anxiety creeping up his spine.

"Uh . . . well, I mean that they are so totally different from one another. One's a quarter horse and the other's a racehorse." What he wanted to say was, "One's a quarter horse and the other's a jackass," but he didn't. "Boom Boom puts lead in your pencil. I've seen her start motors that have been stalled for years."

Fair smiled broadly. "She is attractive."

"Dynamite, buddy, dynamite." Fitz, less inhibited than usual, kept on. "But I'd take Harry any day of the week. She's funny. She's a partner. She's a friend. That other stuff—hey, Fair, it gets old."

"You're certainly forthcoming," came the dry reply.

"Nothing's preventing you from telling me to keep my mouth shut."

"While we're on the subject, tell me what you see in Little Marilyn. She's a miniature of her mother, on her way to being as cold as a wedge, and near as I can tell she's even slacking off on the charity work. What's the—"

"Attraction?" Fitz decided not to take offense. After all, he was handing it out so he'd better take it. "The truth? The truth is that I married her because it was the thing to do. Two respectable family fortunes. Two great family names. My parents, had they lived, would have been proud. Superficial stuff, when you get right down to it. And I was kind of wild as a kid. I was ready to settle down. I needed to settle down. What's strange is that I've come to love Marilyn. You don't know the real Marilyn. When she's not knocking herself out trying to be superior she's pretty wonderful. She's a shy little bug and underneath it there's a good heart. And what's so funny is that I think she likes me too. I don't think she married me for love, any more than I married her for it. She went along with the merger orchestrated by that *harridan*"—he sputtered the word—"of a mother. Maybe Mim knew more than we did. Whatever the reason, I have learned to love my wife. And someday I hope I can tear her away from this place. We'll go someplace where the names Sanburne and Hamilton don't mean diddly."

Fair stared at Fitz, and Fitz returned the stare. Then they burst out laughing.

"Another beer for my buddy." Fitz slapped money on the counter.

Fair eagerly grabbed the cold glass. "We might as well get shitfaced."

"My sentiments exactly."

By the time Fitz reached home, supper was cold and his wife was not amused. He cajoled her with the tidbit about Boom Boom and Blair attending the Cancer Fund Ball and then poured them each a delicious sherry for a nightcap, a ritual of theirs. By the time they crawled into bed, Little Marilyn had forgiven her husband.

28

Two men argued at the end of an old country road. Heavy cloud cover added to the tension and gloom. Way up in the distance beckoned the sealed cavern of Claudius Crozet's first tunnel through the Blue Ridge Mountains.

One man clenched his fists and shook them in the face of the other. "You goddamned bloodsucker. I'm not giving you another cent. How was I to know he'd show up? He's been locked away for years!"

Ben Seifert, being threatened, just laughed. "He showed up in my office, not yours, asshole, and I want something for my pains—a bonus!"

The next thing he knew a brightly colored climbing rope was flipped over his neck and the word *bonus* was choked right out of him. Strangulation took less than two minutes.

Still furious, the killer viciously kicked the body, breaking some ribs. Then he shook his head, collected his wits, and bent down to pick up the limp corpse.

This was an unpleasant task, since the dead man had voided himself.

Cursing, he tossed the body over his shoulder, for he was a strong man, and carried him up to the tunnel. Although it had been sealed after World War II, there was an opening of loose stones which had been dug out by a former Crozet resident. The railroad had overlooked resealing the tunnel.

His brain worked clearly now. He removed the stones with care so as not to tear up his hands and then dragged the body into the tunnel. He could hear the click of little claws as he slammed his unwanted burden on the ground. He walked outside and replaced the stones. Then he picked his way down the hillside, composing himself, brushing off his clothes. People rarely hiked up to the tunnels. With luck it would be months before they found that bastard, if they found him at all.

The problem was Seifert's car. He searched the seats, trunk, and glove compartment to make certain no note existed, no clue to their meeting. Then he started the engine and drove to the outskirts of town, leaving the car at a gas station. He wiped off the steering wheel, the door handle, everything he'd touched. The car shone when he finished with it. Shrewdly, he'd left his own car three miles away, where the victim had picked him up on Three Chopt Road. That was at one o'clock this morning. It was now four-thirty and darkness would soon enough give way to light.

He jogged the three miles to his own car, parked behind one of the cement trucks at Craycroft Cement. Unless someone walked around the mixer they'd never have seen his car.

He had figured killing his unwanted partner was a

possibility, hence the preparation. Not that he had wanted to kill the dumb son of a bitch, but he'd gotten so greedy. He kept bleeding him. That left little choice.

Blackmail rarely ended with both parties wreathed in smiles.

29

The mail slid into the boxes but the magazines had to be folded. Ned Tucker received more magazines than anyone in Crozet. What was even more amazing was that he read them. Susan said it was like living with an encyclopedia.

The morning temperature hovered at thirty-nine degrees Fahrenheit, so Harry, Mrs. Murphy, and Tucker hopped to work at a brisk pace. Harry brought the blue truck only when the weather was filthy or she had errands to run. As she'd done her grocery shopping yesterday, the blue bomb reposed by the barn.

Harry cherished the quiet of her walk and the early hour alone in the post office after Rob Collier dropped off the mail. The repetition of chores soothed her, like a labor's liturgy. There was comfort in consistency.

The back door opened and closed. Mrs. Murphy, Tucker, and even Harry could tell by the tread that it was Mrs. Hogendobber.

"Harry."

"Mrs. H."

"Missed you at the Cancer Ball."

"Wasn't invited."

"You could have gone alone. I do sometimes."

"Not at a hundred and fifty dollars a ticket I can't."

"I forgot about that part. Larry Johnson paid for my ticket. He's quite a good dancer."

"Who all was there?"

"Susan and Ned. She wore her peach organdy dress. Very becoming. Herbie and Carol. She wore the ice-blue gown with the ostrich feather ruff. You should have seen Mim. She had on one of those gowns Bob Mackie designs for *Dynasty*."

"Did she really?"

"I am here to tell you, girl, she did, and that dress must have cost her as much as a Toyota. There isn't a bugle bead left in Los Angeles, I am sure of it. Why, if you dropped her in that lake of hers she'd attract every fish in it."

Harry giggled. "Maybe she'd get along better with the fish than she does with people."

"Let's see, I said Ned and Susan. Fair wasn't there. Little Marilyn and Fitz weren't there either—must be taking a break from the black-tie circuit. Most of the Keswick and Farmington Hunt Clubs showed up, and the country club set too. Wall to wall." Mrs. Hogendobber picked up a handful of mail and helped to sort.

Mrs. Murphy sat in a mail bin. She had sat so long waiting for a push that she fell asleep. Mrs. Hogendobber's arrival woke her up.

"What did you wear?"

"You know that emerald-green satin dress I wear at Christmas?"

"Uh-huh."

"I had it copied in black with gold accents. I don't look so fat in black."

"You're not fat," Harry reassured her. It was true. She wasn't fat but she was, well, ample.

"Ha. If I eat any more I'm going to resemble a heifer."

"How come you haven't told me that Blair escorted Boom Boom to the ball?"

"If you know it why should I tell you?" Mrs. Hogendobber liked to stand behind the post boxes and shoot the letters in. "Well, he did. Actually, I think she asked him, because the tickets were in her name. The hussy."

"Did he have a good time?"

"He just looked so handsome in his tuxedo and I like his new moustache. Reminds me of Ronald Colman. Boom Boom dragged him to meet everyone. She was wearing her party face. I guess he had a good time."

"No dread disease?"

"No. She danced so much I doubt she even had time to tell him of the sorrows of her youth and how awful her parents were." Miranda didn't crack a smile when she relayed this observation but her eyes twinkled.

"My, my, doesn't he have something to look forward to: 'The Life and Times of Boom Boom Craycroft.' "

"Don't worry about her."

"I'm not."

"Harry, I've known you since you were born. Don't lie to me. I remember the day you insisted we call you Harry instead of Mary. Funny that you later married Fair Haristeen."

"You remember everything."

"I do indeed. You were four years old and you loved your kitty—now let me see, her name was Skippy. You wanted to be furry like Skippy, so you asked us to call you Hairy, which became Harry. You thought if we called you that, you'd get furry and turn into a kitty. Name stuck."

"What a great cat Skippy was."

This aroused Mrs. Murphy from her half-slumberous state. *"Not as great as the Murphy!"*

"Ha!" Tucker laughed.

"Shut up, Tucker. There was a dog before you, you know. A German shepherd. His photo is on the desk at home, for your information."

"Big deal."

"Playtime." Harry heard the meows and thought Mrs. Murphy wanted a push in the mail bin. Although it wasn't what the cat was talking about, she happily rolled around in the canvas-bottomed cart.

Mrs. Hogendobber unlocked the front door. She no sooner turned the key than Blair appeared, wearing a heavy red Buffalo-checked jacket over a flannel shirt. He rubbed his boots over the scraper.

"Good morning, Mrs. Hogendobber. I enjoyed our dance last night. You float over the floor."

Mrs. Hogendobber blushed. "Why, what a sweet thing to say."

Blair stepped right up to the counter. "Harry."

"No packages."

"I don't want any packages. I want your attention."

He got Mrs. Hogendobber's too.

"Okay." Harry leaned over the other side of the counter. "My full attention."

"I've been told there are furniture and antique auctions on the weekends. Will you tell me which are the good ones and will you go along with me? I'm getting tired of sitting on the floor."

"Of course." Harry liked to help out.

Mrs. Murphy grumbled and then jumped out of the mail bin, sending it clattering across the floor. She hopped up on the counter.

"The other request I have is that you accompany me to a dinner party Little Marilyn is giving for Stafford and Brenda tomorrow night. I know it's short notice but she called this morning to ask me."

"What's the dress?" Harry couldn't believe her ears.

"I'm going to wear a yellow shirt, a teal tie, and a brown herringbone jacket. Does that help?"

"Yes." Mrs. Hogendobber answered because she knew Harry was hopeless in these matters.

"I've never seen you dressed up, Harry." Blair smiled. "I'll pick you up tomorrow night at seven." He paused. "I looked for you at the Cancer Ball last night."

Harry started to say that she wasn't invited but Mrs. Hogendobber leapt into this breach. "Harry had another engagement. She's kept so busy."

"Oh. Well, I wanted to dance with you." He jammed his hands in his pockets. "That Craycroft woman is a real motor-mouth. Never stopped talking about herself. I know it isn't gallant of me to criticize someone who made such an effort to have me meet people, but jeez" —he let out his breath—"she likes to party."

Both Harry and Mrs. Hogendobber tried to conceal their delight at this comment.

"Boom Boom knows you're rich," Mrs. Murphy piped up. *"Plus you're single, good-looking, and she's not above driving Fair crazy with you, either."*

"She has a lot to say this morning, doesn't she?" Blair patted Mrs. Murphy's head.

"You bet, buster. Stick with me, I'll give you the scoop on everybody."

Blair laughed. "Now, Murphy—I mean, Mrs. Murphy; how rude of me—you promised to help me find a friend exactly like you."

"I'm going to throw up," Tucker mumbled from the floor.

Blair picked up his mail, got to the door, and stopped. "Harry?"

"What?"

He held up his hands in entreaty. Mrs. Hogendobber kicked Harry behind the counter. Blair couldn't see this.

"Oh, yes, I'd love to go."

"Seven tomorrow." He left, whistling.

"That hurt. I'll have a bruised ankle tomorrow."

"You have no sense when it comes to men!" Miranda exclaimed.

"I wonder what got into him?" Harry's gaze followed him to his truck.

"Yours is not to reason why. Yours is but to do and die."

Just then Susan sauntered in through the back door. " 'Into the valley of Death rode the six hundred.' "

"Blair Bainbridge just asked her to a dinner party at the Hamiltons' tomorrow night and he wants her to take him to some auctions."

"Yahoo!" Susan clapped her hands together. "Good work, girl."

"I didn't do anything."

"Susan, help me with her. She nearly told him she didn't have a date for the Cancer Ball. She's going to iron her jeans for the dinner party and think she's dressed. This calls for action."

Miranda and Susan looked at each other and then both looked at Harry. Before she knew it, each one grabbed an arm and she was propelled out the back door and thrown into Susan's car.

"Hey, hey, I can't leave work."

"I'll take care of everything, dear." Miranda slammed shut the door as Susan cranked the motor.

30

The Allied National Bank overlooked Benjamin Seifert's tardiness. No one called Cabell Hall to report Ben's absence. If Ben had found out about such a call the perpetrator wouldn't have kept his job for long. Often on the run and not the most organized man in the office, Benjamin might have made morning appointments without notifying the secretary. Ben, a bright light at Allied, could look forward to taking over the huge new branch being built on Route 29N in Charlottesville, so no one wanted to get on his bad side. The more astute workers realized that his ambitions extended beyond the new branch at 29N.

When he didn't phone in after lunch the little group thought it odd. By three, Marion Molnar was worried enough to call his home. No answer. Benjamin, divorced, often stayed out into the wee hours. No hangover lasted this long.

By five, everyone expressed concern. They dialed Rick Shaw, who said he'd check around. Just about the time

Marion called, so did Yancey Mills, owner of the little gas station. He recognized Benjamin's car. He'd figured something was wrong with it and that Benjamin would call in. But it was near to closing time and he hadn't heard anything and there was no answer at Ben's house.

Rick sent Cynthia Cooper over to the gas station. She checked out the car. Seemed fine. Neither she nor Rick pressed the panic button but they routinely called around. Cynthia called Ben's parents. By now she was getting a bit alarmed. If they found no trace of him by morning they'd start looking for him. What if Ben had refused a loan, or the bank had foreclosed, and someone had it in for him? It seemed far-fetched, but then nothing was normal anymore.

31

It was her face reflecting back from the mirror, but Harry needed time to get used to it. The new haircut revealed those high cheekbones, full lips, and strong jaw so reminiscent of her mother's family, the Hepworths. The clear brown Minor eyes looked back at her too. Like everyone else in Crozet, Harry combined the traits of her parents, a genetic testimony to the roulette of human breeding. The luck held in her case. For others, some of them friends, this wasn't true. Multiple sclerosis haunted generation after generation of one Crozet family; others never escaped the snares of cancer; still others inherited a marked tendency to drink or drugs. The older she got the luckier she felt.

As she focused on the mirror she recalled her mother seated before this very mirror, paint pots out, lipsticks marshaled like stubby soldiers, powder puffs lurking like peach-colored land mines. Much as Grace Hepworth Minor had harassed, wheedled, and bribed her sole child, Harry steadfastly refused the lure of feminine artifice. She was too young then to articulate her steely rejection of the commercialization of womanness. All she knew was that she didn't want to do it, and no one could make her. As years sped by, this instinctual rejection was examined. Harry realized that she thought she was clean and neat in appearance, healthy, and outgoing. If a man needed that fake stuff, in her opinion he wasn't much of a man. She was determined to be loved for herself and not because she'd paid out good money to fit the current definition of femininity. Then again, Harry never felt the need to prove that she was feminine. She felt feminine and that was enough for her. It ought to be enough for him. In the case of Fair it turned out to be enough for a while.

In this respect Boom Boom and Harry represented the two poles of female philosophy. Maybe it was why they never could get along. Boom Boom averaged one thousand dollars each month on her upkeep. She was waxed, dyed, massaged. She was awash in nutrients which took into account her special hormonal needs. At least that's what the bottles said. She dieted constantly. She thought nothing of flying to New York to shop. Then the bills truly rolled in. One pair of crocodile shoes from Gucci was $1,200. Sleek, up-to-date, and careful to cover any flaws, real or imagined, Boom Boom represented a triumph of American cosmetics, fashion, and elective surgery. Her self-centeredness, fed by this culture, blossomed into solipsism of the highest degree. Boom Boom marketed herself as an ornament. In time she became one. Many men chased after that ornament.

When Harry inspected the new Harry, courtesy of the strong-arm tactics of Miranda and Susan, she was relieved to see a lot of the old Harry. Okay, blusher highlighted those cheeks, lipstick warmed her mouth, but nothing too extreme. No nasty eyeshadow covered her lids. The mascara only accentuated her already long black lashes. She looked like herself, only maybe more so. She was trying to make sense of it, trying to like the simple suede skirt and silk shirt that Susan had forced her to buy upon pain of death. Spending is worse than pain, she thought; it lasts longer.

Too late now. The check had been written, the merchandise carried home. No more time to fret over it anyway because Blair was knocking at the front door.

She opened it.

He studied Harry. "You're the only woman I know who looks as good in jeans as in a skirt. Come on."

Mrs. Murphy and Tucker stood on the back of the sofa and watched the humans motor down the driveway.

"What do you think?" Tucker asked the cat.

"She looks hot." Mrs. Murphy batted Tucker. *"Aren't you glad we don't have to wear clothes? Wouldn't you look adorable in a little gingham dress?"*

"And you'd have to wear four bras." Tucker nudged Mrs. Murphy in the ribs, nearly knocking her off the sofa.

That appealed to Mrs. Murphy's demented sense of humor. She rocketed off the back of the sofa, calling for the dog to chase her. She dashed straight for the wall, enticing Tucker to think that she was trapped, and then hit the wall with all fours, banking off it, sailing right over Tucker's head while the dog skidded into the wall with a hard bump. Mrs. Murphy performed this maneuver with a demonic sense of purpose. Enraged,

Tucker's feet spun so fast under her that she shook like a speeded-up movie. Around and around they ripped and tore until finally, as Tucker charged under an end table and Mrs. Murphy pranced on top of it, the lamp on the table teetered and tottered, only to wobble on its base and smash onto the floor. The crash scared them and they flew into the kitchen. After a few moments of quiet they ventured out.

"*Uh-oh,*" Tucker said.

"*Well, she needed a new lamp anyway. This one had gray hairs.*"

"*She'll blame me for it.*" Tucker already felt persecuted.

"*As soon as we hear the truck, we'll hide under the bed. That way she can rant and rave and get it out of her system. She'll be over it by tomorrow morning.*"

"*Good idea.*"

32

"The meringue tarts." Little Marilyn triumphantly nodded to Tiffany to serve the dessert.

Little Marilyn practiced nouvelle cuisine. Big Marilyn followed suit, which was the first time mother had imitated daughter. Jim Sanburne complained that nouvelle cuisine was a way to feed people less. Bird food, he called it. Fortunately, Big Marilyn and Jim weren't invited to the small dinner tonight. Cabell Hall was, though. Fitz continually flattered the important banker, his justification being that three years ago Cabell had introduced him to Marilyn. Little Marilyn's septic personality had been somewhat sweetened by the absence of her maternal unit, so she, too, showered attention on Cabell and Taxi.

"Tell Blair how you were nicknamed Taxi." Little Marilyn beamed at the older woman.

"Oh, that. He doesn't want to hear that." Taxi smiled.

"Yes, I do." Blair encouraged her as Cabby watched with affection his wife of nearly three decades.

"Cabell is called Cabby. Fine and good but when the children were little I hauled them to school. I picked them up from school. I carried them to the doctor, the dentist, Little League, dance lessons, piano lessons, and tennis lessons. One day I came home dog tired and ready to bite. My husband, just home from his own hard day, wanted to know how I could be so worn out from doing my duties as a housewife. I explained in vivid terms what I'd been doing all day and he said I should start a local taxi service, as I already ran one for my own children. The name stuck. It's sexier than Florence."

"Honey, you'd be sexy if your name were Amanda," Cabby praised her.

"What's wrong with the name Amanda?" Brenda Sanburne asked.

"Miss Amanda Westover was the feared history teacher at my prep school," her husband told her. "She taught Cabell, me—she may have even taught Grandfather. *Mean.*" Stafford Sanburne and Cabell Hall were both Choate graduates.

"Not as mean as my predecessor at the bank." Cabell winked.

"Artie Schubert." Little Marilyn tried to recall a face. "Wasn't it Artie Schubert?"

"You were too young to remember." Taxi patted Little Marilyn's bejeweled hand. "He made getting a loan a most unpleasant process, or so I heard. Cabby and I were still in Manhattan at the time and he was approached by a board member of Allied National to take over the bank. Well, Richmond seemed like the end of the earth—"

Cabby interrupted: "It wasn't that bad."

"What happened was that we fell in love with central Virginia, so we bought a house here and Cabby commuted to work every day."

"Still do. Mondays, Wednesdays, and Fridays. Tuesdays and Thursdays I'm at the branch in the downtown mall in Charlottesville. Do you know that in the last ten years or so our growth rate has exceeded that of every other bank in the state of Virginia—by percentage, of course. We're still a small bank when compared to Central Fidelity, or Crestar, or Nations Bank."

"Darling, this is a dinner party, not a stockholders' meeting." Taxi laughed. "Is it obvious how much my husband loves his job?"

As the guests agreed with Taxi and speculated on how people find the work that suits them, Fitz-Gilbert asked Blair, "Will you be attending opening hunt?"

Blair turned to Harry. "Will I be attending opening hunt?"

Stafford leaned toward Blair. "If she won't take you, I will. You see, Harry will probably be riding tomorrow."

"Why don't you help me get ready in the morning and then you can meet everyone there?" Harry's voice registered nothing but innocence.

This drew peals of laughter from the others, even Brenda Sanburne, who knew enough to realize that getting ready for a fox hunt can be a nerve-racking experience.

"Nice try, Harry." Fitz-Gilbert toasted in her direction.

"Now my curiosity's got the better of me. What time do I have to be at your barn?"

Harry twirled her fork. "Seven-thirty."

"That's not so bad," Blair rejoined.

"If you drink enough tonight it will be," Stafford promised.

"Don't even mention it." Fitz-Gilbert put his hand to his forehead.

"I'll say. You've been getting snookered lately. This morning when I woke up, what a sorry face I saw." Little Marilyn pursed her lips.

"Did you know, Blair, that Virginia is home to more fox-hunting clubs than any other state in the Union? Nineteen in all—two in Albemarle County," Cabell informed him. "Keswick on the east side and Farmington on the west side."

"No, I didn't know that. I guess there are a lot of foxes. What's the difference between the two clubs here? Why don't they have just one large club?"

Harry answered, a wicked smile on her face, "Well, you see, Blair, Keswick Hunt Club is old, old, old Virginia money living in old, old, old Virginia homes. Farmington Hunt Club is old, old, old Virginia money that's subdivided."

This caused a whoop and a shout. Stafford nearly choked on his dessert.

Once recovered from this barb, the small group discussed New York, the demise of the theater, a topic creating lively debate, since Blair didn't think theater was pooping out and Brenda did. Blair told some funny modeling stories which were enlivened by his talent for mimicry. Everyone decided the stock market was dismal so they'd wait out the bad times.

After dessert, the women moved over to the window seat in the living room. Brenda liked Harry. Many white people were likable but you couldn't really trust them. Even though she knew her but slightly, Brenda felt she could trust Harry. In her odd way, the postmistress was color blind. What you saw with Harry was what you got and Brenda truly appreciated that. Whenever a white person said, "I'm not prejudiced myself . . . ," you knew you were in trouble.

The men retired to the library for brandy and Cuban cigars. Fitz-Gilbert prided himself on the contraband and wouldn't divulge his source. Once you smoked a Montecristo, well, there was no looking back.

"One day you'll spill the beans." Stafford passed the cigar under his nose, thrilling to the beguiling scent of the tobacco.

Cabell laughed. "When hell freezes over. Fitz can keep a secret."

"The only reason you guys are nice to me is because of my cigars."

"That and the fact that you were first oar for Andover." Stafford puffed away.

"You look more like a wrestler than a first oar." Blair, too, surrendered to the languor the cigar produced.

"I was skinny as a rail when I was a kid." Fitz patted his small potbelly. "Not anymore."

"Ever know Binky Colfax when you were at Andover? My class at Yale."

"Binky Colfax. Valedictorian." Fitz-Gilbert flipped through his yearbook and handed it to Blair.

"God, it's a good thing Binky was an academic." Blair laughed. "You know, he's in the administration now. An undersecretary in the State Department. When you remember what a wuss the guy was, it makes me fear for our government. I mean, think of it, all those guys we knew at Yale and Harvard and Princeton and . . ."

"Stanford," Stafford chipped in.

"Do I have to?" Blair asked.

"Uh-huh." Stafford nodded.

". . . Stanford. Well, the nerds went into government or research. In ten years' time those guys will be the bureaucracy serving the guys that will be elected." Blair shook his head.

"Do you think every generation goes through this? You pick up the paper one day or you watch the six o'clock news and there's one of the wieners." Fitz-Gilbert laughed.

"My father—he was Yale '49—said it used to scare him to death. Then he got used to it," Blair said.

Cabby chimed in: "Everyone muddles through. Think how I feel. The guys in my class at Dartmouth are starting to retire. Retire? I remember when all we thought about was getting . . ."

He stopped, as his hostess had stuck her head into the library, hand curled around the door frame. "Are you fellows finished yet? I mean, we've solved the problems of the world in the last forty-five minutes."

"Lonesome, honey?" Fitz called to her.

"Oh, an eensie-weensie bit."

"We'll be out in a minute."

"You know, Fitz, I think we must know a lot of people in common since so many of your schoolmates came to Yale. Someday we'll have to compare notes," Blair said.

"Yes, I'd like that." Fitz, distracted by Little Marilyn, wasn't paying much attention.

"Yale and Princeton. Yeck." Stafford made a thumbs-down sign.

"And you went to Stanford?" Blair quizzed him.

"Yes. Finance."

"Ah." Blair nodded. No wonder Stafford was making so much money as an investment banker, and no wonder Cabell shone smiles upon him. No doubt these two would talk business over the weekend.

"You were smart not to become a lawyer." Fitz twirled his cigar, the beautiful, understated band announcing MONTECRISTO. "A lawyer is a hired gun, even if it's tax law. I'll never know how I passed the bar, I was so bored."

"There are worse jobs." Cabell squinted his eyes from the smoke. "You could be a proctologist."

The men laughed.

The phone rang. Tiffany called out from the kitchen, "Mr. Hamilton."

"Excuse me."

As Fitz picked up the phone, Stafford, Cabell, and Blair joined the ladies in the living room. In a few minutes Fitz-Gilbert joined them too.

"Has anyone seen or heard from Benjamin Seifert?"

"No. Why?" Little Marilyn asked.

"He didn't go to work today. That was Cynthia Cooper. She's spent the evening calling his business associates and family. Now she's calling friends and acquaintances. I told them you were here, Cabby. They'd like to talk to you."

Cabell left the room to pick up the phone.

"He's out of the office as much as he's in it," Harry volunteered, now that Ben's boss was out of earshot.

"I told him just last week to watch his step, but you know Ben." Fitz pulled up a chair. "He'll show up and I bet the story will be a doozie."

Harry opened her mouth but closed it. She wanted to say "What if this has something to do with the vagrant's murder?" What if Ben was the killer and skipped town? Realizing Little Marilyn's sensitivity to the topic, she said nothing.

Harry had forgotten all about Ben Seifert when Blair dropped her at her door. He promised he'd be there at seven-thirty in the morning. She opened the door and turned on the lights. Only one came on. She walked over to the debris on the floor, the lamp cord yanked out of the wall.

"Tucker! Mrs. Murphy!"

The two animals giggled under the bed but they stayed put. Harry walked into the bedroom, knelt down and looked under the bed, and beheld two luminous pairs of eyes staring back at her.

"I know you two did this."

"Prove it," was all Mrs. Murphy would say, her tail swaying back and forth.

"I had a wonderful time tonight and I'm not going to let you spoil it."

It was good that Harry had that attitude. Events would spoil things soon enough.

33

The earth glittered silvery and beige under its cloak of frost. The sun, pale and low in the sky, turned the ground fog into champagne mist. Mrs. Murphy and Tucker curled up in a horse blanket in the tack room and watched Harry groom Tomahawk.

Blair arrived at seven forty-five. As Harry had already brushed and braided Tomahawk, painted his feet with hoof dressing, and brushed him again, she was ready for a clean-up.

"What time did you get up?" Blair admired her handiwork.

"Five-thirty. Same time I always get up. Wish I could sleep past it but I can't, even if I go to bed at one in the morning."

"What can I do?"

Harry shed her garage mechanic overalls to reveal her buff breeches. A heavy sweater covered her good white shirt. Her worn boots, polished, leaned against the tack room wall. Her derby, brushed, hung on a tack hook.

Harry had earned her colors with the hunt while she was in high school and her ancient black melton coat with its Belgian-blue collar was carefully hung on the other side of the tack hook.

Harry placed a heavy wool cooler over Tomahawk and tied it at the front. Unhooking the crossties, she led him to his stall. "Don't even think about rubbing your braids, Tommy, and don't get tangled up in your cooler." She gave her horse a pat on the neck. "Tommy'll be good but I always remind him, just in case," she said to Blair. "Come on, everything's done. Let's get some coffee."

After a light breakfast, Blair watched Harry replace Tomahawk's square cooler with a fitted wool dress sheet, put on his leather shipping halter, and load him into her two-horse gooseneck, which, like the truck, was showing its age but still serviceable. He hopped in the cab, camera in his coat pocket, ready for the meet.

He was beginning to appreciate Harry's make-do attitude as he perceived how little money she really had. False pride about possessions wasn't one of her faults but pride about making her own way was. She wouldn't ask for help, and as the blue bomb chugged along he realized what a simple gift it would have been for him to offer the use of his dually to pull her rig. If he had asked politely she might even have let him. Harry was funny. She feared favors, maybe because she lacked the resources to return them, but by Blair's reckoning she kept her accounts even in her own way.

Opening meet of the hunt brought out everyone who had ever thrown a leg over a horse. Blair couldn't believe his eyes as Harry pulled into the flat pasture. Horse trailers littered the landscape. There were little tagalongs, two-horse goosenecks, four-horse goosenecks. There were a few semis pulling rigs a family could live in, Imperatore vans with the box built onto the back of the truck, and there was even one of the new Mitsubishi vans, its snub nose exciting both admiration and derision.

Horses, unloaded and tied to the sides of these conveyances, provided splashes of color. Each stable sported its own colors and these were displayed both in the paint jobs of the rigs and on the horses themselves, blanketed in their own special uniforms, the sheets or blankets indicating their allegiances. Harry's colors were royal-blue and gold, so Tomahawk's blue wool dress sheet was trimmed in gold and had a braided gold tail cord on the hindquarters. There were coolers and blankets in a myriad of color combinations: hunter-green and red, red and gold, black and red, blue and green, tan and blue, tan and hunter-green, silver and green, sky-blue and white, white and every color, and one cooler was even purple and pink. The purple and pink one belonged to Mrs. Annabelle Milliken, who had ordered a purple and white cooler years ago but the clerk wrote down the wrong colors and Mrs. Milliken was too polite to correct her. After a time everyone became accustomed to the purple and pink combination. Even Mrs. Milliken.

Big Marilyn's colors were red and gold. Her horse, a shining seal-brown, could have galloped out of a Ben Marshall painting, just as Little Marilyn's bold chestnut might have trotted out of a George Stubbs.

Harry put on her stock tie, her canary vest, her coat, derby, and deerskin gloves. Using the trailer fender as a mounting block, she swung into the saddle. Blair asked her if she wanted a leg up but she said that she and Tomahawk were used to the do-it-yourself method. Good old Tommy, in a D-ring snaffle, stood quietly, ears pricked. He loved hunting. Blair handed Harry her hunting crop with its long thong and lash just as Jock Fiery rode by and wished her "good hunting."

As Harry trotted off to hear the words of wisdom from the Joint Masters, Jill Summers and Tim Bishop, Blair found Mrs. Hogendobber. Together they watched the tableau as the Huntsman, Jack Eicher, brought the hounds to the far side of the gathering. Horse, hounds, staff, and field glistened in the soft light. Susan joined the group. She was still struggling with her hairnet, which she dropped. Gloria Fennel, Master of the Hilltoppers, reached in her pocket and gave Susan another hairnet.

Blair turned to Mrs. Hogendobber. "Does everyone ride?"

"I don't, obviously." She nodded in the direction of Stafford and Brenda, both of them madly snapping photos. "He used to."

"Guess I'd better take some lessons."

"Lynne Beegle." Mrs. Hogendobber pointed out a petite young lady on a gloriously built thoroughbred. "Whole family rides. She's a wonderful teacher."

Before Blair could ask more questions, the staff, which consisted of three Whippers-In, the Huntsman, and the Masters, moved the hounds down to where the pasture dropped off. The field followed.

"The Huntsman will cast the hounds."

Blair heard a high-pitched "Whooe, whoop whoop, whooe." The sounds made no sense to him but the hounds knew what to do. They fanned out, noses to the ground, sterns to heaven. Soon a deep-throated bitch named Streisand gave tongue. Another joined her and then another. The chorus sent a chill down Blair's spine. The animal in him overrode his overdeveloped brain. He wanted to hunt too.

So did Mrs. Hogendobber, as she motioned for him to follow on foot. Mrs. H. knew every inch of the western part of the county. An avid beagler, she could divine where the hounds would go and could often find the best place to watch. Mrs. H. explained to Blair that beagling was much like fox hunting except that the quarry was rabbits and the field followed on foot. Blair gained a new respect for Mrs. Hogendobber. Rough terrain barely slowed her down.

They reached a large hill from which they could see a long, low valley. The hounds, following the fox's line, streaked across the meadow. The Field Master, the staff member in charge of maintaining order and directing the field, led the hunt over the first of a series of coops —a two-sided, slanted panel, jumpable from both directions. It was a solidly imposing three feet three inches high.

"Is that Harry?" Blair pointed to a relaxed figure floating over the coop.

"Yes. Susan's in her pocket and Mim isn't far behind."

"Hard to believe Mim would endure the discomforts of fox hunting."

"For all her fussiness that woman is tough as nails. She can ride." Mrs. Hogendobber folded her arms in front of her. Big Marilyn's seal-brown gelding seemed to step over the coop. The obstacle presented no challenge.

As the pace increased, Harry smiled. She loved a good

run but she was grateful for the first check. They held up and the Huntsman recast the hounds so they could regain the line. Joining her in the first flight were the Reverend Herbert Jones, dazzling in his scarlet frock coat, or "pinks"; Carol, looking like an enchantress in her black jacket with its Belgian-blue collar and hunt cap; Big Marilyn and Little Marilyn, both in shadbelly coats and top hats, the hunt's colors emblazoned on the collars of their tailed cutaways; and Fitz-Gilbert in his black frock coat and derby. Fitz had not yet earned his colors, so he did not have the privilege of festooning himself in pinks. The group behind them ran up and someone yelled, "Hold hard!" and the followers came to a halt. As Harry glanced around her she felt a surge of affection for these people. On foot she could have boxed Mim's ears but on a horse the social tyrant didn't have the time to tell everyone what to do.

Within moments the hounds had again found the line, and giving tongue, they soon trotted off toward the rough lands formerly owned by the first Joneses to settle in these parts.

A steep bank followed a bold creek. Harry heard the hounds splashing through the water. The Field Master located the best place to ford, which, although steep, provided good footing. It was either that or slide down rocks or get stuck in a bog. The horses picked their way down to the creek. Harry, one of the first to the creek, saw a staff member's horse suddenly plunge in up to his belly. She quickly pulled her feet up onto the skirts of her saddle, just in the nick of time. A few curses behind her indicated that Fitz-Gilbert hadn't been so quick and now suffered from wet feet.

No time to worry, for once on the other side the field

tore after the hounds. Susan, right behind Harry, called out, "The fence ahead. Turn sharp right, Harry."

Harry had forgotten how evil that fence was. It was like an airplane landing strip but without the strip. You touched down and you turned, or else you crashed into the trees. Tomahawk easily soared over the fence. In the air and as she landed Harry pressed hard with her left leg and opened her right rein, holding her hand away from and to the side of Tommy's neck. He turned like a charm and so did Susan's horse right on her heels. Mim boldly took the fence at an angle so she didn't have to maneuver as much. Little Marilyn and Fitz made it. Harry didn't look over her shoulder to see who made it after that because she was moving so fast that tears were filling her eyes.

They thundered along the wood's edge and then found a deer path through the thick growth. Harry hated galloping through woods. She always feared losing a kneecap but the pace was too good and there wasn't time to worry about it. Also, Tomahawk was handy at weaving in and out through the trees and did a pretty good job keeping his sides, and Harry's legs, away from the trunks. The field wove its way through the oaks, sweet gums, and maples to emerge on a meadow, undulating toward the mountains. Harry dropped the reins on Tomahawk's neck and the old boy flew. His joy mingled with her joy. Susan drew alongside, her dappled gray running with his ears back. He always did that. Didn't mean much except it sometimes scared people who didn't know Susan or the horse.

A three-board fence, interrupted by a three-foot-six coop, hove into view. Before she knew it Harry had landed on the other side. The pace and the cold morning air burned her lungs. She could see Big Marilyn out of the corner of her left eye. Standing in her stirrup irons with her hands well up her gelding's neck, Mim urged on her steed. She was determined to overtake Harry. A horse race, and what a place for it! Harry glanced over at Mim, who glanced back. Clods of earth spewed into the air. Susan, not one to drop back, stayed right with them. A big jump with a drop on the other side beckoned ahead. The Field Master cleared it. Mim's horse inched in front of Tomahawk. Harry carefully dropped behind Mim's thoroughbred. It wouldn't do to take a jump in tandem unplanned. Mim soared over with plenty of daylight showing underneath her horse's belly. Harry let the weight sink into her heels, preparing to absorb the shock of the drop on the other side, and flew over it, though her heart was in her mouth. Those jumps with a drop on the other side made you feel as if you were airborne forever and the landing often came as a jarring surprise.

A steep hill rose before them and they rode up it, little stones clattering underneath. They pulled up at the crest. The hounds had lost the line again.

"Good run." Mim smiled. "Good run, Harry."

Mrs. Hogendobber and Blair drove in her Falcon to where she thought the run would go. The old car nosed into a turnaround. She sprang out of the vehicle. "Hurry up!"

Blair, breathing hard, followed her up another large hill, this one with a commanding view of the Blue Ridge Mountains. His eyes moved in the direction of her pointing finger.

"That's the first of Crozet's tunnels, way up there. This is the very edge of Farmington's territory."

"What do you mean by that?"

"Well, there's a national association that divides up the territory. No one can hunt up in the mountains, too rough really, but on the other side the territory belongs to another hunt, Glenmore, I think. To our north it's Rappahannock, then Old Dominion; to the east, Keswick and then Deep Run. Think of it like states."

"I don't know when I've ever seen anything so beautiful. Did the hounds lose the scent?"

"Yes. They've checked while the Huntsman casts the hounds. Think of it like casting a net with a nose for fox. Good pack too. As fleet as sound."

Far, far in the distance she heard the strange cry of a hound.

Down at the check, all heads turned.

Fitz, now winded, whispered to Little Marilyn, "Honey, can we go in soon?"

"You can."

"This terrain is really pretty rugged. I don't want to leave you alone."

"I'm not alone and I'm a better rider than you are," Little Marilyn informed him, somewhat haughtily but still in a whisper.

The Huntsman followed the cry of his lone hound. The pack moved toward the call. The Field Master waited for a moment, then motioned for the field to move off. The sweet roll of earth crunched up. More rock outcroppings challenged the sure-footedness of the horses.

"We're about out of real estate," Harry said to Susan. She kept her voice low. It was irritating to strain to hear the hounds and have someone chattering behind you. She didn't want to bother any of the others.

"Yeah, he'll have to pull the hounds back."

"We're heading toward the tunnel," Mim stated.

"Can't go there. And we shouldn't. Who knows what's up there? That's all we need, for a bear or something to jump out of the tunnel and scare the bejesus out of these horses." Little Marilyn wasn't thrilled at the prospect.

"Well, we can't go up there, that's for sure. Anyway, the Chesapeake and Ohio sealed up the tunnel," Fitz-Gilbert added.

"Yes, but Kelly Craycroft opened it up again." Susan referred to Kelly Craycroft's clever reopening and camouflaging of the tunnel. "Wonder if the railroad did seal it back up?"

"I don't want to find out." Fitz's horse was getting restive.

The cry of the lone hound soon found answers. The pack worked its way toward the tunnel. The Field Master held back the field. The Huntsman stopped. He blew his horn but only some of the hounds returned as they were bidden. The stray hound cried and cried. A few others now joined in this throaty song.

"Letting me down. Those hounds are letting me down," the Huntsman, shamed by their disobedience, moaned to a Whipper-In who rode along with him to get the hounds back in line.

The Whipper-In flicked the lash at the end of his whip after a straggler, who shuttled back to the pack. "Deer? But they haven't run deer. Except for Big Lou."

"That's not Big Lou up there though." The Huntsman moved toward the sound. "Well, come along with me and we'll see if we can't get those babies back down before they ruin a good day's hunting."

The two staff horses picked their way through the unforgiving terrain. They could now see the tunnel. The hounds sniffed and worried at the entrance. A huge turkey vulture flew above them, swooped down on an air current, bold as brass, and disappeared into the tunnel.

"Damn," the Whip exclaimed.

The Huntsman blew his horn. The Whipper-In made good use of his whip but the animals kept speaking. They weren't confused; they were upset.

As this had never happened before to the Huntsman in his more than thirty years of hunting, he dismounted and handed his reins to the Whip. He walked toward the entrance. The vulture emerged, another in its wake. The Huntsman noticed hunks of rancid meat dangling from their beaks. He caught a whiff of it too. As he neared the tunnel entrance he caught another blast, much stronger. The hounds whined now. One even rolled over and showed its belly. The Huntsman noticed that some stones had fallen away from the entrance. The odor of decay, one he knew well from life in the country, seeped out of the hole full bore. He kicked at the stones and a section rolled away. The railroad had neglected to reclose the entrance after all. He squinted, trying to see into the darkness, but his nose told him plenty. It was a second or two before he recognized that the dead creature was a human being. He involuntarily stepped back. The hounds whined pitifully. He called them away from the tunnel, swaying a bit as he came out into the light.

"It's Benjamin Seifert."

$$\boxed{34}$$

A sensuous Georgian tea service glowed on the long mahogany sideboard. Exquisite blue and white teacups, which had been brought over from England in the late seventeenth century, surrounded the service. A Hepplewhite table, loaded with ham biscuits, cheese omelettes, artichoke salad, hard cheeses, shepherd's pie, and fresh breads commanded the center of the dining room. Brownies and pound cake rounded out the offerings.

Susan had knocked herself out for the hunt breakfast. The excited hum of voices, ordinarily the sign of a successful hunt, meant something different today.

After the Huntsman identified Ben Seifert he rode with the Whip down to the Masters, the Field Master, and the other Whips. They decided to lift the hounds and return to the kennels. Not until everyone was safely away from the tunnel and had arrived at the breakfast did the Masters break the news.

After caring for the hounds, the Huntsman and the Whip who'd accompanied him to the grisly site returned to the tunnel to help Rick Shaw and Cynthia Cooper.

Despite the dolorous news, appetites drove the riders and their audience to the table. The food disappeared and Susan filled up the plates and bowls again. Her husband, Ned, presided over the bar.

Big Marilyn, seated in an apricot-colored wing chair, balanced her plate on her knees. She hated buffets for that very reason. Mim wanted to sit at the table. Herbie and Carol sat on the floor along with Harry, Blair, and Boom Boom, who was making a point of being charming.

Cabell and Taxi arrived late and were told the news by a well-meaning person. They were so shocked they left for home.

Fair hung back at the food table. He noticed the gathering on the floor and brought desserts for everyone, including his ex-wife. Fitz-Gilbert and Little Marilyn joined Mim. Mrs. Hogendobber wouldn't sit on the floor in her skirt so she grabbed the other wing chair, a soothing mint-green.

"Miranda." Big Marilyn speared some omelette. "Your views."

"Shall we judge society by its malcontents?"

"And what do you mean by that?" Big Marilyn demanded before Mrs. Hogendobber could take another breath.

"I mean Crozet will be in the papers again. Our shortcomings will be trumpeted hither and yon. We'll be judged by these murders instead of by our good citizens."

"That's not what I was asking." Mim zeroed in. "Who do you think killed Ben Seifert?"

"We don't know that he was murdered yet." Fitz-Gilbert spoke up.

"Well, you don't think he walked up to that tunnel and killed himself, do you? He'd be the last person to commit suicide."

"What do you think, Mim?" Susan knew her guest was bursting to give her views.

"I think when money passes hands it sometimes sticks to fingers. We all know that Ben Seifert and the work ethic were unacquainted with one another. Yet he lived extremely well. Didn't he?" Heads nodded in agreement. "The only person who would have wanted to kill him is his ex-wife and she's not that stupid. No, he fiddled in someone's trust. He was the type."

"Mother, that's a harsh judgment."

"I see no need to pussyfoot."

"He handled many of our trusts, or at least Allied did, so he knew who had what." Fitz gobbled a brownie. "But Cabell would have had his hide if he thought for an instant that Ben was dishonest."

"Maybe someone's trust was running out." Carol Jones thought out loud. "And maybe that person expected a favor from Ben. What if he didn't deliver?"

"Or someone caught him with his hand in the till." The Reverend Jones added his thoughts.

"I don't think this has anything to do with Ben and sticky fingers." Harry crossed her legs underneath her. "Ben's death is tied to that unidentified body."

"Oh, Harry, that's a stretch." Fitz reached for his Bloody Mary.

"It's a feeling. I can't explain it." Harry's quiet conviction was unsettling.

"You stick to your feelings. I'll stick to facts," Fitz-Gilbert jabbed.

Fair spoke up, defending Harry. "I used to think that way, too, but life with Harry taught me to listen to, well, feelings."

"Well, what do your deeper voices tell you now?" Mim said "deeper" with an impertinent edge.

"That we don't know much at all," Harry said firmly. "That now one of us has been killed and we can't feel so safe in our sleep anymore because we haven't one clue, one single idea as to motive. Is this a nut who comes out at the full moon? Is it someone with a grudge finally settling the score? Is this a cover-up for something else? Something we can't begin to imagine? My deeper voice tells me to keep eyes in the back of my head."

That shut up the room for a moment.

"You're right." Herbie placed his plate on the coffee table. "And I am not unconvinced that there may be some satanic element to this. I've not spoken of it before because it's so disturbing. But certain cults do practice ritual killings and how they dispatch their victims is part of the ritual. We have one corpse dismembered, and, well, we don't know how Ben died."

"Do we know how the other fellow died?" Little Marilyn asked.

"Blow to the head," Ned Tucker informed them. "Larry Johnson performed the autopsy and I ran into him after that. I don't believe, Herbie, that satanic cults usually bash in heads."

"No, most don't."

"So, we're back to square one." Fitz got up for another dessert. "We're not in danger. I bet you when the authorities examine Ben's books they'll find discrepancies, or another set of books."

"Even if this is over misallocation of funds, that doesn't tell us who killed him or who killed that other man," Susan stated.

"These murders do have something to do with Satan." Mrs. Hogendobber's clear alto voice rang out. "The Devil has sunk his deep claws into someone, and forgive the old expression, but there will be hell to pay."

35

Long shadows spilled over the graves of Grace and Cliff Minor. The sun was setting, a golden oracle sending tongues of flame up from the Blue Ridge Mountains. The scarlet streaks climbed heavenward and then changed to gold, golden pink, lavender, deep purple, and finally deep Prussian-blue, Night's first kiss.

Harry wrapped her scarf around her neck as she watched the sun's last shout on this day. Mrs. Murphy and Tucker sat at her feet. The aching melancholy of the sunset ripped through her with needles of sorrow. She mourned the loss of the sun; she wanted to bathe in rivers of light. Each twilight she would suspend her chores for a moment, to trust that the sun would return tomorrow like a new birth. And this evening that same hope tugged but with a sharper pull. The future is ever blind. The sun would rise but would she?

No one believes she will die; neither her mother nor her father did. Like a game of tag, Death is "it," and around he chases, touching people who fall to earth.

Surely she would get up at dawn; another day would unfold like an opening rose. But hadn't Ben Seifert believed that also? Losing a parent, wrenching and profound, felt very different to Harry than losing a peer. Benjamin Seifert graduated from Crozet High School one year ahead of Harry. This time Death had tagged someone close to her—at least close in age.

A terrible loneliness gnawed at Harry. Those tombstones covered the two people who gave her life. She remembered their teachings, she remembered their voices, and she remembered their laughter. Who would remember them when she was gone, and who would hold the memory of her life? Century after century the human race lurched two steps forward and one step back, but always there were good people, funny people, strong people, and their memories washed away with the ages. Kings and queens received a mention in the chronicles, but what about the horse trainers, the farmers, the seamstresses? What about the postmistresses and stagecoach drivers? Who would hold the memory of their lives?

The loneliness filled her. If she could have, she would have embraced every life and cherished it. As it was, she was struggling on with her own.

Harry began to fear the coming years. Formerly, time was her ally. Now she wasn't so sure. If death could snatch you in an instant, then life had better be lived to the fullest. The worst thing would be to go down in the grave without having lived.

The bite of the night's air made her fingertips tingle and her toes hurt. She whistled to Tucker and Mrs. Murphy and started back for the house.

Harry was not by nature an introspective person. She

liked to work. She liked to see the results of her work. Deeper thoughts and philosophic worries were for other people. But after today's jolt Harry turned inward, if only for a brief moment, and was suffused with life's sadness and harmony.

36

A terrible rumpus outside awoke Mrs. Murphy and Tucker. Mrs. Murphy ran to the window.

"It's Simon and the raccoons."

Tucker barked to wake up Harry, because now that it was cold Harry made sure to shut the back door tight, and they couldn't get out to the screened-in porch. That door was easy to open, so if Harry would just open the back door they could get outside.

"Go away, Tucker," Harry groaned.

"Wake up, Mom. Come on."

"Goddammit." Harry's feet hit the cold floor. She thought the dog was barking at an animal or had to go to the bathroom. She tramped downstairs and opened the back door and both creatures zoomed out. "Go on out and freeze your asses. I'm not letting you back in."

The cat and dog didn't have time to reply. They streaked toward Simon, backed up against the barn by two masked raccoons.

"Beat it!" Tucker barked.

Mrs. Murphy, fur puffed up to the max, ears flat back, spit and howled, *"I'll rip your eyes out!"*

The raccoons decided they didn't want to fight, so they waddled off.

"Thanks," Simon puffed, his flanks heaving.

"What was all that about?" Mrs. Murphy asked.

"Marshmallows. Blair put out marshmallows and I love them. Unfortunately, so do those creeps. They chased me all the way back here." A trickle of blood oozed from Simon's pink nose. His left ear was also bleeding.

"You got the worst of the fight. Why don't we go up to the loft?" Mrs. Murphy suggested.

"I'm still hungry. Did Harry put out leftovers?"

"No. She had a bad day," Tucker answered. *"The humans found another body today."*

"In pieces?" Simon was curious.

"No, except that the vultures got at it." Mrs. Murphy quivered as the wind kicked up. It felt like zero degrees.

"I've always wondered why birds like the eyes. First thing they'll go for: the eyes and the head." Simon rubbed his ear, which had begun to sting.

"Let's go inside. Come on. It's vile out here."

They wiggled under the big barn doors. Simon paused to pick up bits of grain that Tomahawk and Gin Fizz had dropped. As the horses were sloppy eaters, Simon could enjoy the gleanings.

"That ought to hold me until tomorrow." The gray possum sat down and wrapped his pink tail around him. *"If you come upstairs it's warm in the hay."*

"I can't climb the ladder," Tucker whimpered.

"Oh, yeah, I forgot about that." Simon rubbed his nose.

"Let's go into the tack room. That old, heavy horse blan-

*ket is in there, the one Gin Fizz ripped up. The lining is
fleecy and we could curl up in that."*

"It's hanging over the saddle rack," Tucker called.

"So? I'll push it down." Mrs. Murphy was already
hooking her claws under the door bottom. The door,
old and warped, wavered a little and she wedged her
paw behind it while Tucker stuck her nose down to see
if she could help. In a minute the door squeaked open.

The cat leapt onto the saddle rack, dug her claws in
the blanket, and leaned over with it. She came down
with the blanket. The three snuggled next to one another in the fleece.

When Harry hurried into the barn the next morning
she felt guilty for leaving her pets outside. She knew
she'd find them in the barn but she was quite surprised
to find them curled up with a possum in the tack room.
Simon was surprised, too, so surprised that he pretended
to be dead.

Tucker licked Harry's gloved hands while Mrs. Murphy rubbed against her legs.

"This little guy's been in the ring." Harry noticed
Simon's torn ear and scratched nose.

"Simon, wake up. We know you're not dead." Mrs.
Murphy patted his rump.

Harry reached for a tube of ointment and while Simon squeezed his eyes more tightly shut she rubbed
salve on his wounds. He couldn't stand it. He opened
one eye.

Mrs. Murphy patted his rump again. "See, she's not so
bad. She's a good human."

Simon, who didn't trust humans, kept silent, but

Tucker piped up, *"Look grateful, Simon, and maybe she'll give you some food. Let her pick you up. She'll love that."*

Harry petted Simon's funny little head. "You'll be all right, fella. You stay here if you want and I'll do my chores."

She left the animals and climbed into the hayloft.

Simon panicked for a moment. *"She won't steal my treasures, will she? I think I'd better see."* Simon walked out of the tack room and grabbed the lowest ladder rung. He moved quickly. Mrs. Murphy followed. Tucker stayed where she was and looked up. She could hear the hay moving around as Harry prepared to toss it through the holes in the loft floor over the stalls.

Harry turned around to see Simon and Mrs. Murphy hurrying toward the back. She put down her bale and followed them.

"You two certainly are chummy."

The T-shirt made Harry laugh. Simon's nest was much improved since Mrs. Murphy had last visited.

"Shut up, down there," the owl called out.

"Shut up, yourself, flatface," Mrs. Murphy snarled.

Harry knelt down as Simon darted into his half-cave. He'd brought up some excess yarn Harry had used to braid Tomahawk for opening hunt. He also had shredded the sweet feed bag and brought it up in strips. Simon's nest was now very cozy and the T-shirt had been lovingly placed over his homemade insulation. One ballpoint pen, two pennies, and the tassled end of an old longe line were artfully arranged in one corner.

"This is quite a house." Harry admired the possum's work.

A shiny glint caught Mrs. Murphy's sharp eye. *"What's that?"*

"Found it over at Foxden."

"I didn't think possums were pack rats." Harry smiled at the display.

"I operate on the principle that it is better to have something and not need it than need it and not have it. I am not a pack rat," Simon stated with dignity.

"Where at Foxden did you find this?" Mrs. Murphy reached out and grabbed the shiny object. As she drew it toward her she saw that it was a misshapen earring.

"I like pretty things." Simon watched with apprehension as Harry took the earring from her cat. *"I found it on the old logging road in the woods—out in the middle of nowhere."*

"Gold." Harry placed the earring in her palm. It seemed to her that she had seen this earring before. It was clearly expensive. She couldn't make out the goldstamp, as it appeared the earring had been run over or stepped on. She was able to make out the T-I-F of TIFFANY. She turned the earring over and over.

"She's going to give it back to me, isn't she?" Simon nervously asked. *"I mean, she isn't a thief, is she?"*

"No, she's not a thief, but if you found it over at Foxden she ought to take it. It might be a clue."

"Who cares? Humans kill one another all the time. You catch one, and somebody else starts killing."

"It's not as bad as that."

The owl called out again, *"Keep it down!"*

Harry loved the sound of an owl hooting but she detected the crabby note. She placed the earring back in Simon's nest. "Well, kiddo, it looks like you're part of the family. I'll set out the scraps."

Simon, visibly relieved, stuck his nose out of his nest

and regarded Harry with his bright eyes. Then he spoke to Mrs. Murphy. *"I'm glad she's not going to kill me."*

"Harry doesn't kill animals."

"She goes fox hunting," came the stout reply.

As Harry returned to dropping the hay down to the horses, the cat and the possum discussed this.

"Simon, they only kill the old foxes or the sick ones. Healthy ones are too smart to get caught."

"What about that fox last year that ran into Posy Dent's garage? He was young."

"And that exception proves the rule. He was dumb." Mrs. Murphy laughed. *"I feel about foxes the way you feel about raccoons. Well, Harry's going back down, so I'll follow her. Now that she knows where you live she'll probably want to talk to you. She's like that, so try and be nice to her. She's a good egg. She put stuff on your scratches."*

Simon thought about it. *"I'll try."*

"Good." Mrs. Murphy scampered down the ladder.

As she and Tucker trotted back to the house for breakfast the cat told the dog about the earring. The more they talked, the more questions they raised. Neither animal was sure the earring was important to the case but if Simon found it in a suspicious place, its value couldn't be overlooked. All this time they'd assumed the killer was a man but it could be a woman. The body was cut up and stashed in different places. The parts weren't heavy by themselves. As to dragging Ben Seifert into the tunnel, that would be hard, but maybe the two deaths weren't connected.

Mrs. Murphy stopped. *"Tucker, maybe we're barking up the wrong tree. Maybe the killer is a man but he's killing for a woman."*

"Getting rid of competitors?"

"Could be. Or maybe she's directing him—maybe she's the brains behind the brawn. I wish we could get Mom to see how important that earring is, but she doesn't know where it came from and we can't tell her."

"Murphy, what if we took it from Simon and put it where he found it?"

"Even if he'd part with it, how are we going to get her over there?"

Inside now, they waited for their breakfasts.

Tucker thought of something: *"What if a man is killing for a woman, killing to keep her? What if he knows something she doesn't?"*

Mrs. Murphy leaned her head on Tucker's shoulder for a moment. *"I hope we can find out, because I've got a bad feeling about this."*

37

Not only had Larry Johnson taken the precaution of sending tissue samples to Richmond, he wisely kept the head of the unidentified corpse rather than turning it over to the sheriff. After contacting a forensics expert, the elderly doctor sent the head to a reconstruction team in Washington, D.C. Since Crozet did not have a potter's field, a burial ground for the indigent, the Reverend Jones secured a burial plot in a commercial cemetery on Route 29 in Charlottesville. When he asked his congregation for contributions they were forthcoming, and to his pleasant surprise, the Sanburnes, the Hamiltons, and Blair Bainbridge made up the balance. So the unknown man was put to rest under a nameless but numbered brass marker.

Larry never dreamed he would have a second corpse on his hands. Ben's family arranged for interment in the Seifert vault, but Cabell Hall handled all the funeral details, which was a tremendous help to the distraught couple. Larry's examination determined that Ben had been strangled with a rope and that death had occurred approximately three days before discovery. The temperature fluctuated so much between day and night, he felt he could not pinpoint the exact time of death based on the condition of the corpse. Also, the animal damage added to the difficulty. Larry insisted on sparing Ben's mother and father the ordeal of identifying the corpse. He knew Ben; that was identification enough. For once, Rick Shaw agreed with him and relented.

Rick did put up a fight about shipping off the head of the original victim. He was loath to part with this one piece of evidence. Damaged as the head was, it was his only hope. Someone had to have known the victim. Larry patiently showed him the work of the reconstructive artists. Cynthia Cooper helped, too, as she was impressed with what could be done.

After carefully studying the head in its present condition, the team would strip the skull of the remaining flesh and then build a new face, teeth, hair, everything. Drawings would be made to assist in the rebuilding. Once complete, drawings and photographs of the head would be sent to Rick Shaw. They would also be sent to other police stations and sheriff's offices. Long shots do come in. Someone, somewhere, might identify the face.

Since a second murder had followed closely on the heels of the first, Larry Johnson called Washington and asked them to hurry.

This they did. Rick Shaw walked into the post office with a large white envelope in his hand.

"Sheriff, want me to weigh that?" Harry offered.

"No. This just arrived Federal Express." Rick pulled out the photograph and slid it over the counter to Harry. "This is a reconstruction of the head of the dismembered victim. Looks like an all right guy, wouldn't you say?"

Harry stared at the photograph. The face was pleasant, not handsome but attractive. Sandy hair, combed to one side, gave the face a clean-cut appearance. The man had a prominent, jutting chin. "He could be anybody."

"Put it on the wall. Let's hope somebody here recognizes him. Triggers a memory."

"Or a mistake."

"Harry, you'll know before I do." Rick tapped the counter twice. It was his way of saying "Be careful."

She pinned the photograph by the counter. No one could miss it. Mrs. Murphy stared at it. The man was no one she knew, and she saw people from a vastly different angle than did Harry.

Brookie and Danny Tucker stopped by after school. Harry explained to them who the photograph was. Danny couldn't believe that it was a likeness of the head he'd plucked out of his pumpkin. The photographed head lacked a beard, which made the man appear younger.

Mim came in later. She also studied the photograph. "Don't you think this will upset people?"

"Better upset than dead."

Those ice-blue eyes peered into Harry's own. "You think we've got a serial killer on the loose? That's jumping to conclusions. *Any*thing could have happened to this man." A long, frosted fingernail pointed at the bland face. "How do we know he wasn't killed in some sort of bizarre sexual episode? A homeless person, no one to care, he's offered a meal and a shower. Who's to know?"

How interesting that a sliver of Mim's fantasies was showing. Harry replied, "I can't think of one woman who would go to bed with a man and then kill him and cut him up."

"Insects do it all the time."

"We're mammals."

And poor excuses at that. Tucker chuckled.

Mim went on. "Maybe it was a group of people."

"In my wildest imaginings I can't think of any group here in town that would do that. Wife swapping, yes. Sex murders, no."

Mim's eyes brightened. "Wife swapping? What do you know that I don't?"

"The postmistress knows everything in a small town," Harry teased.

"Not everything or you'd know who the killer is. I still think it's some group thing and Ben was in on it. Or it was about money. But I spoke with Cabell Hall today and he's had a team scouring the books, just going over them with a fine-tooth comb, and everything is in order. Very, very strange."

Boom Boom, Fair, Fitz-Gilbert, and Little Marilyn crowded in at once. They, too, examined the photo.

"Makes me nauseated to think about that." Boom Boom held her stomach. "I wasn't right for days. I thought I'd seen everything when my husband was killed."

Fair put his arm around her. "I wonder what Kelly would have made of this?"

"He would have found humor in it somewhere." Little Marilyn had liked Boom Boom's deceased husband.

Fitz-Gilbert nearly put his nose on the photograph. "Isn't it something what these guys can do? Imagine putting together a face, given the condition of that head. It's just amazing. He looks better than he did in life, I bet."

"The organization behind something like this is amazing, too," Harry said. "Rick told me that this photograph will be in every police station in the country. He's hoping it will pay off."

"So do we," Mim announced.

Mrs. Hogendobber let herself in through the back door. She bustled over to see what was going on and was drawn to the photograph. "He was young. Thirty, early thirties, I should say. What a shame. What a shame for a life to end so young and so violently and we don't even know who he was."

"He was a no-count. We do know that." Fitz-Gilbert referred to the man's vagabond existence.

"No one's a no-count. Something must have happened to him, perhaps something awful. Perhaps an illness." Mrs. Hogendobber folded her arms across her chest.

"I bet he was one of those people who used to live in halfway houses," Little Marilyn put in. "So many of these places have been shut down, now that the programs have been cut off. They say that flophouses in big cities are full of those people—low normals, you'd call them, or people who aren't a hundred percent functional. Anyway, the state pays hotels to give them lodging because they can't work. I bet he was one of those people. Just thrown out into a world where he couldn't cope." Little Marilyn's high-pitched voice lowered a trifle.

"Then what in the world was he doing in Crozet?" Mim never could give her daughter credit for anything.

"On his way to Miami?" Fitz-Gilbert posited. "The homeless who can leave the northern cities in winter try to get to the Sunbelt cities. He could have hopped on a freight at Penn Station."

"What could he have in common with Ben Seifert?" Boom Boom wondered.

"Bad luck." Fitz smiled.

"If these murders are connected, there is one interesting thing." Harry stroked Mrs. Murphy, lounging on the counter. "The killer didn't want us to know the dismembered victim, yet he or she didn't care at all if we recognized Ben Seifert."

"Identify the dismembered man and you'll identify the killer." Fair's clear voice seemed to echo in the room.

"We'd at least be halfway home," Mrs. Hogendobber added.

"That's what worries me," Mim confessed. "We are home. These murders are happening here."

38

Layers of sweaters, winter golf gloves, and heavy socks protected Cabby and Taxi Hall from the cold. Avid golfers, they tried to squeeze in nine holes after Cabell's work hours when the season permitted, and they never missed a weekend.

Taxi's relaxed swing off the tee placed her ball squarely in the fairway. "Good shot if I do say so myself."

She stepped aside as Cabell stuck his orange tee into the ground. He placed a bright-yellow ball on the tee, stepped back, shifted around a little, and fired. The ball soared into the air and then drifted right, into the woods. He said nothing, just climbed back into the cart. Taxi joined him. They reached the woods. As the ball was such a bright color they easily located it, even though it had plopped into the leaves.

Cabell studied his position. Then he pulled out a five iron. This was a risky shot, since he'd have to shoot through the trees or go over them. He planted his feet, took a deep breath, and blasted away.

"What a shot!" Taxi exclaimed as the ball miraculously cleared the trees.

Cabby smiled his first genuine smile since Ben was discovered dead. "Not bad for an old man."

They headed back to the cart. "Honey," Taxi said, "what's wrong, other than the obvious?"

"Nothing," he lied.

"Don't shut me out." Her voice carried both firmness and reproach.

"Florence, sugar, I'm plain tired. Between worried employees, the sheriff's investigation, and a constant stream of questions from our customers, I am beat, crabby—you name it."

"I will. You're preoccupied. I've seen you handle bank problems and people problems before. This is different. Are the books cooked? Was Ben a thief?"

"I told you as soon as we had that audit, around the clock—can't wait for the bill on that one—no. Ben's books look okay."

"Is someone running through his trust fund? Fitz-Gilbert spends like there's no tomorrow."

Cabby shook his head. "For him there *is* no tomorrow. He's got more money than God. I tried to instill some restraint in him when he was a boy but I obviously failed. Combine his fortune with the Sanburnes' and, well"—Cabell swung his club—"what's the purpose in restraint?"

"It's not right for a man not to work, no matter how much money he has. He could do charity work." Taxi got in the driver's seat of the cart. Cabell hopped in.

"See"—she pointed—"you've got a good lie. I don't know how you made that shot."

"Neither do I."

"Cab . . . are we in trouble?"

"No, dear. Our investments are sound. I've put enough away. I'm just puzzled. I can't imagine what Ben got himself into. I mean, he was my anointed. I trusted him. How does this look to the board of directors?"

Taxi cast a sharp glance at her husband. "You never really liked Ben."

Cabell sighed. "No. He was a smarmy little bastard, impressed with money and bloodlines, but he worked harder than people gave him credit for, he had very good ideas, and I felt he could run Allied when I stepped down."

"In other words, you don't have to like the chicken to enjoy the omelette."

"I never said I didn't like Ben. Not once in his eight years at the bank have I said that."

Taxi pulled up by the bright-yellow ball. "We've been married twenty-seven years."

"Oh." Cabby sat for a moment, then got out and fussed over which iron to use.

"The seven," Taxi advised.

"Well"—he took a look at the green—"well, you might be right."

As they continued play, Cabell Hall thought about the differences between women and men, or perhaps between his wife and himself. Taxi always knew more about him than he realized. He wasn't sure that he knew his wife as well as she knew him: his likes, dislikes, hidden fears. True, he kept much of his business life from her, but then she didn't share every moment of her day either. He didn't care if the washer repairman came on time any more than she cared whether one of the tellers had a bad cold.

Still, it was a curious thing to be reminded that his life partner could see into him and possibly through him.

"Cabell," Taxi interrupted his reverie, "I'm serious about Fitz. A man needs a real life, real responsibilities. I know Fitz seems happy enough, but he's so aimless. I'm sure it all goes back to losing his parents when he was so young. You did all you could for him, but—"

"Honey, you aren't going to improve Fitz. Nobody is. He's going to drift through life surrounded by things. Besides, if he did something useful like, say, taking over the Easter Seal drive, it would mean he couldn't play with his wife. Work might conflict with deep-sea fishing in Florida and skiing in Aspen."

"Just an idea." Taxi chipped onto the green.

He waited, then spoke: "Do you have any idea who killed Ben?"

"Not one."

Cabell let out a long, low breath, shook his head, snatched what he thought was his putter out of a bag. "I swear I'm going to put all of this out of my mind and concentrate on golf."

"Then I suggest you replace my putter and use your own."

39

Late that night Harry's telephone rang.

Susan's excited voice apologized. "I know you're asleep but I had to wake you."

"You okay?" came the foggy reply.

"I am. Ned got home from his office about fifteen minutes ago. He was Ben's lawyer, you know. Anyway, Rick Shaw was at the office asking him a lot of questions, none of which Ned could answer, since all he ever did for Ben was real estate closings. It turns out that after the sheriff and the bank inspected their books they checked over Ben's personal accounts. Spread among the bank, the brokerage house, and the commodities market, Ben Seifert had amassed seven hundred and fifty thousand dollars. Even Cabell Hall was amazed at how sophisticated Ben was."

That woke up Harry. "Seven hundred and fifty thousand dollars? Susan, he couldn't have made more than forty-five thousand a year at the bank, if he made that. Banks are notoriously cheap."

"I know. They also called in his accountant and double-checked his IRS returns. He was clever as to how he declared the money. Mostly he identified the gains as stock market wins, I guess you'd say. Well, the accountant reported that Ben said he'd get his records to him but he never did. He figured he'd alerted Ben plenty of times. If the materials weren't there, it was Ben's problem come audit day. Assuming that day ever came."

"Funny."

"What's funny?"

"He didn't cheat on his income taxes but he must have been cheating somewhere. Actually, it doesn't sound like cheating. It sounds like payoffs or money-laundering."

"I never thought Ben was that smart."

"He wasn't," Harry agreed. "But whoever was in this with him was, or is."

"Smart people don't kill."

"They do when they're cornered."

"Why don't you come into town and stay with me?"

"Why?"

"You know what Cynthia Cooper told us about Blair. I mean, about his girlfriend."

"Yes."

"He seems awfully smart to me."

"Does your gut tell you he's a murderer?"

"I don't know what to think or feel anymore."

Harry sat up in the bed. "Susan, I just thought of something. Listen, will you come over here tomorrow morning before I go to work? This sounds crazy but I found a little possum—"

"No more of your charity cases, Harry! I took the

squirrel with the broken leg, remember? She ate my dresses."

"No, no. This little guy had an earring in his nest. It's kind of bent up, but well, I don't know. It's a very expensive earring, and he could have picked it up anywhere. What if it has something to do with these deaths?"

"Okay, I'll see you in the morning. Lock your doors."

"I did." Harry hung up the phone.

Mrs. Murphy remarked to Tucker, also on the bed, *"Sometimes she's smarter than I think she is."*

40

Simon heard Harry climbing the ladder. He anticipated her arrival, since she'd put out delicious chicken bones, stale crackers, and Hershey's chocolate kisses last night.

Mrs. Murphy sank her claws into the wood alongside the ladder and pulled herself into the loft before the humans could get there. *"Don't fret, Simon. Harry's bringing a friend."*

"One human's all I can stand." Simon shuttled farther back in the timothy and alfalfa bales.

Harry and Susan sat down in front of Simon's nest.

"Do you charge him for all this?" Susan cracked.

"If it isn't nailed down, he takes it." Mrs. Murphy laughed.

"I only take the good stuff," the possum said under his breath.

"See." Harry reached in and retrieved the earring.

Susan held the object in her palm. "Good piece. Tiffany."

"That's what I thought." Harry took the earring, holding it to the light. "This isn't yours and it isn't mine. Nor is it Elizabeth MacGregor's."

"What's Mrs. MacGregor got to do with it?"

"The only women out here on this part of Yellow Mountain Road are me, you when you're visiting me, and formerly Elizabeth MacGregor. Oh, and Miranda drops by sometimes but this isn't her type of earring. It's more youthful."

"True, but we have no way of knowing where this came from."

"In a way we do. We know that this nest is home base. At the largest, a possum's territory is generally a rough circle a mile and a half in diameter. If we walk north, east, south, and west to the limit of that perimeter, we'll have a pretty good idea of where this earring might have come from."

"I can tell her," Simon called out from his hiding place.

"She can't understand but she'll figure it out," Mrs. Murphy said.

"Is that other one okay, really?"

"Yes," the cat reassured him.

Simon peeped his head up over the alfalfa bale and then cautiously walked toward the two women. Harry held out a big peanut butter cookie. He approached, sat down, and reached for the cookie. He put it in his nest.

"What a cute fellow," Susan whispered. "You've always had a way with animals."

" 'Cept for men."

"They don't count."

Simon shocked them. He reached up, grabbing the

earring out of Harry's hand, and then dashed into his nest. *"Mine!"*

"Maybe he's a drag queen." Harry laughed at Simon, then remembered one of those odd tidbits from reading history books. During Elizabeth I's reign in England only the most masculine men wore earrings.

They were still laughing as they climbed down the ladder.

"Well?" Tucker demanded.

"We're going to have to make a circle following the possum's territory." Harry thought out loud.

"Let's run over to the graveyard and see if they follow," Tucker sensibly proposed.

"You know Harry—she's going to be thorough." The cat walked out the barn door and Tucker followed.

The two women, accompanied by the animals, walked the limits of the possum's turf. By the time they swept by the cemetery, both considered that it was possible, just possible, that the earring came from there.

Susan stopped by the iron fence. "How do we know the earring doesn't belong to Blair? It could have been his girlfriend's. There could be a woman now that we don't know about."

"I'll ask him."

"That might not be wise."

Harry considered that. "Well, I don't agree but I'll do it your way." She paused. "What's your way?"

"To casually ask our women friends if anyone has lost an earring, and what does it look like?"

"Well, Jesus, Susan, if a woman is the killer or is in on this, that's going to get—"

Susan held up her hands. "You're right. You're right. Next plan. We get into the jewelry boxes of our friends."

"Easier said than done."

"But it can be done."

41

Frost coated the windowpanes, creating a crystalline kaleidoscope. The lamplight reflected off the silver swirls. Outside it was black as pitch.

Little Marilyn and Fitz-Gilbert, snug in Porthault sheets and a goose-down comforter, studied their Christmas lists.

Little Marilyn checked off Carol Jones's name.

Fitz looked over her list. "What did you get Carol?"

"This wonderful book of photographs which create a biography of a Montana woman. What a life, and it's pure serendipity that the old photos were saved."

Fitz pointed to a name on her list. "Scratch that."

Little Marilyn, Xeroxing last year's Christmas list as a guide, had forgotten to remove Ben Seifert's name. She grimaced.

They returned to their lists and after a bit she interrupted Fitz. "Ben had access to our records."

"Uh-huh." Fitz wasn't exactly paying attention.

"Did you check our investments?"

"Yes." Fitz remained uninterested.

She jabbed him with her elbow.

"Ow." He turned toward her. "What?"

"And? Our investments?!"

"First of all, Ben Seifert was a banker, not a stockbroker. There's little he could have done to our investments. Cabby double-checked our accounts just to make sure. Everything's okay."

"You never liked Ben, did you?"

"Did you?" Fitz's eyebrow rose.

"No."

"Then why are you asking me what you already know?"

"Well, it's curious how you get feelings about people. You didn't like him. I didn't like him. Yet we were nice to him."

"We're nice to everybody." Fitz thought that was true, although he knew his wife could sometimes be a pale imitation of her imperious mother.

They went back to work on their lists. Little Marilyn interrupted again. "What if it was Ben who ransacked your office?"

Surrendering to the interruption, Fitz put down his list. "Where on earth do you get these ideas?"

"I don't know. Just popped into my head. But then what would you have that he wanted? Unless he was siphoning off our accounts, but both you and Cabby say all is well."

"All *is* well. I don't know who violated my office. Rick Shaw doesn't have a clue and since the computer and Xerox machine were unmolested, he's treating it as an unrelated vandalism. Kid stuff, most likely."

"Like whoever is knocking over mailboxes with base-ball bats in Earlysville?"

"When did that happen?" Fitz's eyes widened in curi-osity.

"Don't you read the 'Crime Report' in the Sunday paper?" He shook his head, so Little Marilyn continued. "For the last six or seven months someone's been driv-ing around in the late afternoon, smashing up mailboxes with baseball bats."

"You don't miss much, do you, honey?" Fitz put his arm around her.

She smiled back. "Once things settle down around here . . ."

"You mean, once they downshift from chaos to a dull roar?"

"Yes . . . let's go to the Homestead. I need a break from all this. And I need a break from Mother."

"Amen."

42

Weeks passed, and the frenzy of Christmas preparations clouded over the recent bizarre events until they were virtually obscured by holiday cheer. Virginia plunged into winter, skies alternating between steel-gray and brilliant blue. The mountains, moody with the weather, changed colors hourly. The spots of color remaining were the bright-red holly berries and the orange pyracantha berries. Fields lapsed into brown; the less well-cared-for fields waved with bright broomstraw. The ground thawed and froze, thawed and froze, so fox hunting was never a sure thing. Harry called before each scheduled meet.

The post office, awash in tons of mail, provided Harry with a slant on Christmas different from other people's. Surely the Devil invented the Christmas card. Volume, staggering this year, caused her to call in Mrs. Hogendobber for the entire month of December, and she wangled good pay for her friend too.

So far, Susan had rummaged through Boom Boom's

jewelry, an easy task, since Boom Boom loved showing off her goodies. Harry picked over Miranda's earrings, not such an easy task, since Miranda kept asking "Why?" and Harry lied by saying that it had to do with Christmas. The result was that she had to buy Miranda a pair of earrings to put under her Christmas tree. Biff McGuire and Pat Harlan found the perfect pair for Mrs. H., large ovals of beaten gold. They were a bit more than Harry could comfortably afford, but what the hell —Miranda had been a port in a storm at the post office. She also splurged and bought Susan a pair of big gold balls. That exhausted her budget except for presents for Mrs. Murphy and Tucker.

Fair and Boom Boom were holding and eroding. She asked Blair to accompany her to a Piedmont Environmental Council meeting under the guise of acquainting him with the area's progressive people. This she did but she also performed at her best and Blair began to revise somewhat his opinion of Boom Boom, enough, at least, to invite her to a gala fund-raiser in New York City.

Harry and Miranda were up to their knees in Christmas cards when Fair Haristeen pushed open the front door.

"Hi," Harry called to him. "Fair, we're behind. I know you've got more mail than is in your box but I don't know when I'll find it. As you can see, we're hard pressed."

"Didn't come in for that. Morning, Mrs. Hogendobber."

"Morning, Fair."

"Guess you know that Boom Boom left this morning for New York. Her Christmas shopping spree."

"Yes." Harry didn't know how much Fair knew, so she kept mum.

"Guess you know, too, that Blair Bainbridge is taking her to the Knickerbocker Christmas Ball at the Waldorf. I hear princes and dukes will be there."

So he did know. "Sounds very glamorous."

"Eurotrash," Mrs. Hogendobber pronounced.

"Miranda, you've been reading the tabloids again while you're in line at the supermarket."

Mrs. Hogendobber tossed another empty mail bag into the bin, just missing Mrs. Murphy. "What if I have? I have also become an expert on the marriage of Charles and Diana. In case anyone wants to know." She smiled.

"What I want to know"—Fair spoke to Mrs. Hogendobber—"is what is going on with Blair and Boom Boom."

"Now, how would I know that?"

"You know Boom Boom."

"Fair, forgive the pun but this isn't fair," Harry interjected.

"I bet you're just laughing up your sleeve, Harry. I've got egg all over my face."

"You think I'm that vindictive?"

"In a word, yes." He spun on his heel and stormed out.

Miranda came up next to Harry. "Overlook it. It will pass. And he does have egg on his face."

"Lots of yolk, I'd say." Harry started to giggle.

"Don't gloat, Mary Minor Haristeen. The Lord doesn't smile on gloaters. And as I recall, you like Blair Bainbridge."

That sobered Harry up in a jiffy. "Sure, I like him, but I'm not mooning about over him."

"*Ha!*" Tucker snorted.

"You do like him though." Miranda stuck to her guns.

"Okay, okay, so I like him. Why is it that a single person is an affront to everyone in Crozet? Just because I like my neighbor doesn't mean I want to go out with him, doesn't mean I want to go to bed with him, and doesn't mean I want to marry him. Everyone's got the cart before the horse. I actually like living alone. I don't have to pick up Fair's clothes, I don't have to wash and iron them, and I don't have to worry about what to make for supper. I don't have to pick up the phone at seven and hear that he's got a foaling mare in trouble and he won't be home. And I suspect some of those mares were Boom Boom Craycroft. My nightmare. I am not taking care of another man."

"Now, now, marriage is a fifty-fifty proposition."

"Oh, balls, Miranda. You show me any marriage in this town and I'll show you the wives doing seventy-five percent of the work, both physical and emotional. Hell, half of the men around here don't even mow their lawns. Their wives do it."

The grain of truth in this outburst caused Miranda to think it over. Once she took a position it was quite difficult for her to reverse it—modify it perhaps, but not reverse. "Well, dear, don't you think that the men are exhausted from their work?"

"Who's rich enough to keep a wife that doesn't work? The women are exhausted too. I'd come home and the housework would land in my lap. He wouldn't do it, and I think I worked pretty damn hard myself."

Little Marilyn came in. "Are you two having a fight?"

"No!" Harry yelled at her.

"Christmas." Miranda smiled as if to explain the tension.

"Take Valium. That's what Mother does. Her shopping list contains close to three hundred names. You can imagine what a tizz she's in. Can't say that I enjoy this either. But you know we have a position to maintain, and we can't let down the little people."

That toasted Harry, pushed her right over the edge. "Well, Marilyn, allow me to relieve you and your mother of one little person!" Harry walked out the back door and slammed it hard.

"She never has liked me, even when we were children." Little Marilyn pouted.

Miranda, inviolate in her social position, spoke directly. "Marilyn, you don't make it easy."

"And what do you mean by that?"

"You've got your nose so far up in the air that if it rains, you'll drown. Stop imitating your mother and be yourself. Yes, be yourself. It's the one thing you can do better than anyone else. You'll be a lot happier and so will everyone around you."

This bracing breeze of honesty so stunned the younger woman that she blinked but didn't move. Mrs. Murphy, hanging out of the mail bin, observed the stricken Little Marilyn.

"Tucker, go on around the counter. Little Marilyn's either going to faint or pitch a hissy."

Tucker eagerly snuck around the door, her claws clicking on the wooden floorboards.

Little Marilyn caught her breath. "Mrs. Hogendobber, you have no right to speak to me like that."

"I have every right. I'm one of the few people who sees beneath your veneer and I'm one of the few people who actually likes you despite all."

"If this is your idea of friendship I find it most peculiar." The color returned to Little Marilyn's narrow face.

"Child, go home and think about it. Who tells you the truth? Who would you call at three in the morning if you were feeling low? Your mother? I think not. Are you doing anything with your life that makes you truly happy? How many bracelets and necklaces and cars can you buy? Do they make you happy? You know, Marilyn, life is like an aircraft carrier. If there's a mistake in navigation, it takes one mile just to turn the ship around."

"I am not an aircraft carrier." Little Marilyn recovered enough to turn and leave.

Miranda slapped letters on the counter. "It's going to be that kind of day." She said this to the cat and dog, then realized who she was talking to and shook her head. "What am I doing?"

"Having an intelligent conversation," Mrs. Murphy purred.

Harry sheepishly opened the back door. "Sorry."

"I know." Miranda opened another sack of mail.

"I hate Christmas."

"Oh, don't let work get to you."

"It isn't just that. I can't wipe the murders out of my mind and I suppose I am more upset than I realized about Blair taking Boom Boom to that stupid ball. But why would he ask me? I can't afford to travel to New York and I don't have anything to wear. I'm not an impressive specimen on a man's arm. Still . . ." Her voice trailed off. "And I can't believe Fair can be taken in by that woman." She paused. "And I miss Mom and Dad the most at Christmas."

Tucker sat beside Harry's feet and Mrs. Murphy walked over to her too.

Miranda understood. She, too, lived with her losses. "I'm sorry, Harry. Because you're young I sometimes think that everything's wonderful. But I know what it's like to hear the carols and wish those old familiar voices were singing with us. Nothing is ever quite the same again." She went over and patted Harry on the back, for Mrs. Hogendobber wasn't a physically demonstrative woman. "God never closes one door that he doesn't open another. You try and remember that."

43

Resplendent sashes swept across the men's chests; medals dangled over hearts. Those in military dress caused the women to breathe harder. Such handsome men, such beautiful women laden with jewelry, the aggregate sum of which was more than the gross national product of Bolivia.

Boom Boom's head spun. Blair, in white tie and tails, squired her around the dance floor, one of the best in America. What was Crozet compared to this? Boom Boom felt she had arrived. If she couldn't turn Blair's head, and he was attentive but not physically attracted to her—she could tell—she knew she'd snare someone else before the night surrendered to dawn.

A coral dress accentuated her dark coloring, the low-cut bodice calling attention to her glories. When she and Blair returned to their table after dancing, a college friend of his joined them. After the introductions, Orlando Heguay pulled up a chair.

"How's life in the boonies?"

"Interesting."

Orlando smiled at Boom Boom. "If this lovely lady is proof, I should say so."

Boom Boom smiled back. Her teeth glistened; she'd had them cleaned the day before. "You flatter me."

"Quite the contrary. My vocabulary fails me."

Blair smiled indulgently. "Come visit for New Year's. I might even have furniture by then."

"Blair, that's a deal."

"Orlando, refresh my memory. Were you at Exeter or Andover?"

"Andover. Carlos was Exeter. Mother and Dad thought we should go to separate schools, since we were so competitive. And now we're in business together. I suppose they were right."

"And what is your business, Mr. Heguay?"

"Oh, please call me Orlando." He smiled again. He was a fine-looking man. "Carlos and I own The Atlantic Company. We provide architects and interior designers to various clients, many of whom reside in South America as well as North America. I was the original architect and Carlos was the original interior designer, but now we have a team of fifteen employees."

"You sound as though you love it," Boom Boom cooed.

"I do."

Blair, amused by Boom Boom's obvious interest—an interest reflected by Orlando—asked, "Didn't you go to school with Fitz-Gilbert Hamilton?"

"Year behind me. Poor guy."

"What do you mean?"

"His parents were killed in a small plane crash one

summer. Then he and a buddy were in a car wreck. Messed them up pretty badly. I heard he'd had kind of a breakdown. People were surprised when he made it to Princeton in the fall, 'cause there'd been so much talk about him his senior year. People thought he was definitely on the skids."

"He lives in Crozet, too . . . seems to be perfectly fine."

"How about that. Remember Izzy Diamond?"

"I remember that he wanted to make Pen and Scroll so badly at Yale that I thought he'd die if he didn't. Didn't make it either."

"Just got arrested for an investment scam."

"Izzy Diamond?"

"Yes." Orlando's eyebrows darted upward, then he gazed at Boom Boom. "How rude of us to reminisce about college. Mademoiselle, may I have this dance?" He turned to Blair. "You're going to have to find yourself another girl."

Blair smiled and waved them off. He felt grateful to Boom Boom for easing his social passage into Central Virginia. In an odd way he liked her, although her need to be the center of attention bored him the more he was around her. Asking her to the Knickerbocker Ball was more of a payback than anything else. He couldn't have been happier that Orlando found her tremendously attractive. Many of the men there cast admiring glances at Boom Boom. Blair was off women for a while, although he found himself thinking of Harry at the oddest times. He wondered what she'd do at a ball. Not that she'd be awkward but he couldn't imagine her in a ball gown. Her natural element was boots, jeans, and a shirt. Given

Harry's small rear end, her natural element illuminated her physical charms. She was so practical, so down to earth. Suddenly Blair wished she were with him. Wouldn't she find some funny things to say about this crowd?

44

"Who'll start at fifteen thousand? Do I hear fifteen thousand? Now you can't buy this new for under thirty-five. Who'll bid fifteen thousand?"

As the auctioneer sang, insulted, joked, and carried on, Harry and Blair stood at the edge of the auction ground. A light rain dampened the attendance, and as temperatures were dropping, the rain could quite possibly turn to snow. People stamped their feet and rubbed their hands together. Even though she wore silk long johns, a T-shirt, a heavy sweater, and her down jacket, the cold nipped at Harry's nose, hands, and feet. She could always keep her body warm but the extremities proved difficult.

Blair shifted from foot to foot. "Now you're sure I need a seventy-horsepower tractor?"

"You can get along with forty-five or so, but if you have seventy you can do everything you'll ever want to do. You want to turn up that back field of yours and fertilize it, right? You'll want to bush-hog. You've got a lot to do at Foxden. I know that John Deere is old but it's been well maintained and if you have a tiny bit of mechanical ability you can keep it humming."

"Do I need a blade?"

"To scrape the driveway? You could get through the winter without one. It doesn't usually snow much in Virginia. Let's concentrate on the essentials."

Life in the country was proving more complicated and expensive than Blair had imagined. Fortunately, he had resources, and fortunately, he had Harry. Otherwise he would have walked into a dealer and paid top dollar for a piece of new equipment, plus oodles of attachments he didn't need immediately and might never even use.

The green and yellow John Deere tractor beckoned to more folks than Blair. Bidding was lively but he finally prevailed at twenty-two thousand five hundred, which was a whopping good buy. Harry did the bidding.

Harry, thrilled with his purchase, crawled up into the tractor, started her up, and chugged over in first gear to her gooseneck, a step-up. She'd brought along a wooden ramp, which weighed a ton. She kept the tractor running, put it in neutral, and locked the brake.

"Blair, this might take another man."

He lifted one end. "How'd you get this thing on in the first place?"

"I keep it on the old hay wagon and when I need it I take it to the earthen ramp and then shove it off into the trailer, backed up to the ramp. I expand my vocabulary of abuse too." She noticed Mr. Tapscott, who had purchased a dump truck. "Hey, Stuart, give me a hand."

Mr. Tapscott ambled over, a tall man with gorgeous

gray hair. " 'Bout time you replenished your tractor, and you got the best deal today."

"Blair bought it. I just did the bidding." Harry introduced them.

Mr. Tapscott eyed Blair. As he liked Harry his eye was critical. He didn't want any man hanging around who didn't have some backbone.

"Harry showed me the roadwork you did out at Reverend Jones'. That was quite a job."

"Enjoyed it." Mr. Tapscott smiled. "Well, you feeling strong?"

To assist in this maneuver, Travis, Stuart's son, joined in. The men easily positioned the heavy ramp, and Harry, in the driver's seat, rolled the tractor into the gooseneck. Then the men slid the ramp into the trailer, leaning it against the tractor.

"Thank you, Mr. Tapscott." Blair held out his hand.

"Glad to help the friend of a friend." He smiled and wished them good day.

Once in her truck, Harry drove slowly because she wanted the ramp to bang up against the tractor only so much.

"I'm going to take this to my place, because we can drive the tractor straight off. Then you can help me slide off the wooden ramp. Wish they made an aluminum ramp that I could use, but no luck."

"At the hunt meets I've seen trailers with ramps."

"Sure, but those kinds of trailers cost so much—especially the aluminum ones, which are the best. My stock trailer is serviceable but nothing fancy like a ramp comes with it."

She backed up to the earthen ramp. Took two tries. They could hear Tucker barking in the house. They rolled off the tractor, after which they pushed and pulled on the wooden ramp.

"Well, how are we going to get it off the bank?" Blair was puzzled, as the heavy wooden ramp was precariously perched on the earthen rampart.

"Watch." Harry pulled the gooseneck away, hopped out of the truck, and unhitched it. Then she climbed back in the truck and backed it over to the old hay wagon. A chain hung from the wagon's long shaft, a leftover from the days when it was drawn by horses. She dropped the chain over the ball hitch on her bumper. Harry wisely had both hitches on her trailer: the steel plate and ball bolted into the bed of her truck for the gooseneck and another hitch welded onto the frame under the bed of the truck, with its adjustable ball mount. Then she drove the hay wagon alongside the embankment.

"Okay, now we push the ramp onto the wagon."

Blair, sweating now despite the temperature, pushed the heavy wooden ramp onto the beckoning platform. "Presto."

Harry cut the motor, rolled up her windows, and got out of the truck. "Blair, I spoke too soon. I think it's going to snow. We can put the tractor in my barn or you can drive it over to yours and I'll follow you in your truck."

As if on cue the first snowflake lazed out of the darkening sky.

"Let's leave it here. I don't know how to work one of these contraptions yet. You still gonna teach me?"

"Yeah, it's easy."

The heavens seemed to have opened a zipper then; snow poured out of the sky. The two of them walked into the house after Harry parked the tractor in the barn. The animals joyously greeted their mother. She put on coffee and dug out lunch meat to make sandwiches.

"Harry, your truck isn't four-wheel drive, is it?"

"No."

"Hold those sandwiches for about twenty minutes. I'll run down to the market and get food, because this looks like a real snowstorm. Your pantry is low and I know mine is."

Before she could protest he was gone. An hour later he returned with eight bags of groceries. He'd bought a frying chicken, a pork roast, potatoes, potato chips, Cokes, lettuce, an assortment of cheese, vegetables, apples, and some for the horses too. Pancake mix, milk, real butter, brownie mix, a six-pack of Mexican beer, expensive coffee beans, a coffee grinder, and two whole bags of cat and dog food. He truly astounded Harry by putting the food away and making a fire in the kitchen fireplace, using a starter log and some of the split wood she had stacked on the porch. Her protests were ignored.

"Now we can eat."

"Blair, I don't know how to make a pork roast."

"You make a good sandwich. If this keeps up like the weather report says, there'll be two feet of snow on the ground by tomorrow noon. I'll come over and show you how to cook a pork roast. Can you make waffles?"

"I watched Mother do it. I bet I can."

"You make breakfast and I'll make dinner. In between we'll paint your tack room."

"You bought paint too?"

"It's in the back of the truck."

"Blair, it'll freeze." Harry jumped up and ran outside, followed by Blair. They laughed as they hauled the paint into the kitchen, their hair dotted with snowflakes, their feet wet. They finished eating, took off their shoes, and sat back down with their feet toward the fire.

Mrs. Murphy sprawled before the fire, as did Tucker.

"How come you haven't asked me about taking Boom Boom to the Knickerbocker Ball?"

"It's none of my business."

"I apologize for not asking you, but Boom Boom has been helpful and for two seconds there I found her intriguing, so I thought I'd take her to the Waldorf as sort of a thank you."

"Like buying the groceries?"

He pondered this. "Yes and no. I don't like to take advantage of people and you've both been helpful. She met someone there that I went to college with, Orlando Heguay. A big hit." He wiggled his toes.

"Rich?"

"Um, and handsome too."

Harry smiled. As the twilight deepened, a soft purple cast over the snow like a melancholy net. Blair told her about his continuing struggles with his father, who had wanted him either to be a doctor like himself or go into business. He talked about his two sisters, his mother, and finally he got to the story about his murdered girlfriend. Blair confessed that although it had happened about a year and a half ago he was just now beginning to feel human again.

Harry sympathized and when he asked her about her life she told him that she had studied art history at Smith, never quite found her career direction, and fell into the job at the post office which, truthfully, she enjoyed. Her marriage had been like a second job and when it ended she was amazed at the free time she had. She was casting about for something to do in addition to the post office. She was thinking of being an agent for equine art but she didn't know enough about the market. And she was in no hurry. She, too, was beginning to feel as if she was waking up.

She wondered whether to ask him to stay. His house was so barren, but it didn't seem right to ask him just yet. Harry was never one to rush things.

When he got up to go home, she hugged him good-bye, thanked him for the groceries, and said she'd see him in the morning.

She watched his lights as he drove down the curving driveway. Then she put on her jacket and took out scraps for the possum.

45

Tucked into bed with the latest Susan Isaacs novel, Harry was surprised when the phone rang.

Fair's voice crackled over the line. "Can you hear me?"

"Yes, kind of."

"The lines are icing up. You might lose your power and your phone. Are you alone?"

"What kind of question is that? Are you?"

"Yes. I'm worried about you, Harry. Who knows what will happen if you're cut off from the world?"

"I'm in no danger."

"You don't know that. Just because nothing has happened recently doesn't mean that you might not be in danger."

"Maybe you're in danger." Harry sighed. "Fair, is this your way of apologizing?"

"Uh . . . well, yes."

"Is the bloom off the rose with Boom Boom?"

A long silence filled with static was finally broken. "I don't know."

"Fair, I was your wife and before that I was one of your best friends. Maybe we'll get back to being best friends over time. So take that into consideration when I ask this next question. Have you spent a lot of money on her?"

This time the silence was agonizing. "I suppose I have, by my standards. Harry, it's never enough. I buy her something beautiful—you know, an English bridle, and those things aren't cheap. But anyway, for example, an English bridle, and she's all over me, she's so happy. Two hours later she's in a funk and I'm not sensitive to her needs. Does she ever run out of needs? Is she this way with women or is this something reserved for men?"

"She's that way with women. Remember her sob story to Mrs. MacGregor and how Mrs. MacGregor helped her out and lent her horses—this was way back before she married Kelly. Mrs. MacGregor wearied of it before long. She'd have to clean the tack and the horse for Boom Boom, who showed up late for their rides. She's just, oh, I don't know. She's just not reliable. The best thing that ever happened to her was marrying Kelly Craycroft. He could afford her."

"Well, that's just it, Harry. We know Kelly left a respectable estate and she's crying poor."

"Pity gets more money out of people than other emotions, I guess. Are you strapped? Did you spend . . . a lot?"

"Well . . . more than I could afford."

"Can you pay your rent on the house and the office?"

"That's about all I can pay for."

Harry thought awhile. "You know, if you owe on equipment you can ask for smaller payments until you're back on your feet. And if your hunt club dues are a problem, Jock couldn't be more understanding. He'll work with you."

"Harry"—Fair's words nearly choked him—"I was a fool. I wish I'd given the money to you."

Tears rolled down Harry's cheeks. "Honey, it's water over the dam. Just get back on your feet and take a break from women, a sabbatical."

"Do you hate me?"

"I did. I'm over that, I hope. I wish things had turned out differently. My ego took a sound beating, which I didn't appreciate, but who would? It's amazing how the most reasonable people become unreasonable and, well, not very bright, when love or sex appears. Does it even appear? I don't know what it is anymore."

"Me, neither." He swallowed. "But I know you loved me. You never lied to me. You worked alongside me and you didn't ask for things. How we lost the fire, I don't know. One day it was gone."

Now it was Harry's turn to be quiet. "Who knows, Fair, who knows? Can people get that feeling back? Maybe some can but I don't think we could have. It doesn't mean we're bad people. It slipped away somehow. Over time we'll come back to that place where we can appreciate—I guess that's the word—the good things about each other and the years we had. Most of Crozet doesn't believe that's possible between a man and a woman but I hope we prove them wrong."

"Me too."

After he hung up Harry dialed Susan and told all. By now she was working on a good cry. Susan consoled her and felt happy that perhaps she and Fair could be friends. Once Harry purged herself she returned to her primary focus these days, a focus she shared only with Susan: the murders.

"No leads on that money in Ben's portfolio?"

"Not that I know of, and I pumped Cynthia Cooper at the supermarket too," Susan replied. "And Ned has worked with Cabell, who's taking this hard."

"And nothing is missing from the bank?"

"No. And they've checked and double-checked. Everyone asks that same question. It's driving Cabell crazy."

"Did you get into any more jewel boxes?"

"Very funny. My idea wasn't so good after all."

"I felt positively guilty asking Miranda to go through her stuff. She's in her Christmas mood. Even the mail doesn't stop her. Did you see her tree? I think it's bigger than the one at the White House."

"It's the Christmas-tree pin that kills me, all those little twinkling lights on her bosom. She must have a mile of wire under her blouse and skirt," Susan laughed.

"You going to Mim's party?"

"I didn't know we were allowed to miss it."

"I'm going to wear the earring. It's our only chance."

"Harry, don't do that."

"I'm doing it."

"Then I'm telling Rick Shaw."

"Tell him afterwards. Otherwise he'll come and take the earring. Which reminds me, do you have an earring without a mate . . . ?"

"Thanks a lot, pal!"

"No, no, I don't mean that. I have so few earrings I

was hoping you'd have one I could have, preferably a
big one."

"Why?"

"So I can trade with the possum."

"Harry, for heaven's sake, it's an animal. Take it some
food."

"I do that. This little guy likes shiny things. I have to
trade."

Susan sighed dramatically. "I'll find something.
You're looney-tunes."

"What's that say about you? You're my best friend."

On this note they hung up.

Mrs. Murphy asked Tucker, *"Did you know that cats
wore golden earrings in ancient Egypt?"*

"I don't care. Go to sleep." Tucker rolled over.

"What a crab," the cat thought to herself before she
crawled under the covers. She liked to sleep with her
head on the pillow next to Harry's.

46

All through the night heavy snow fell over Central Virginia. A slight rise in the temperature at dawn changed the snow to freezing rain, and soon the beautiful white blanket was encased in thick ice. By seven the temperature plunged again, creating more snow. Driving was treacherous because the ice was hidden. State police blared warnings over the TV and radio for people to stay home.

Blair spun around in front of the barn when he tried to get his dually down the driveway. He grabbed his skis and poles and slid cross-country to the creek between his property and Harry's. The edges of the creek were caked with ice; icicles hung down from bushes, and tree branches sparkled even in the gray light and the continued snow. Blair removed his skis, threw them to the other side of the creek, and then used his poles to help him get across. Any stepping stone he could find was slick as a cue ball. What normally took a minute or two took fifteen. By the time he arrived at Harry's back door he was panting and red in the face. The waffles returned his vigor.

When Harry and Blair reached the tack room it was warm enough to paint, because Harry had set up a space heater in the middle of the room. They painted all day. Blair cooked his pork roast as promised. Over dessert they sat talking. He borrowed a strong flashlight, strapped on his skis, and left for home early, at 8:30 P.M. He called Harry at close to 9:00 P.M. to let her know he'd finally made it. They agreed it had been a great day and then they hung up.

47

The snow continued to fall off and on through Sunday. Monday morning Susan Tucker slowly chugged out to Harry's to pick her up for work. The ancient Jeep, sporting chains, was packed with Harry, Mrs. Murphy, and Tucker. As they drove back to town Harry was astonished at the number of vehicles left by the side of the road or that had slipped off and now reposed at the bottom of an embankment. She knew the owners of most of the cars too.

"What a boon to the body shop," Harry remarked.

"And what a boon to Art Bushey. Most of those people will be so furious they'll tow the car out as soon as possible and take it over to him for a trade. Four-wheel drive is more expensive to run but you gotta have it in these parts."

"I know." Harry sounded mournful.

Susan, well-acquainted with her best friend's impecunious state, smiled. "A friend with four-wheel drive is as good as owning it yourself."

Harry shifted Tucker's weight on her lap as the little dog's hind foot dug into her bladder. "I need to come up with a sideline. Really. I can't make it on the post office salary."

"Bad time to start a business."

"Do you think we're on the verge of a depression? Forget this recession garbage. Politicians create a euphemism for everything."

"You can always tell when a politician is lying. It's whenever his mouth is moving." Susan slowed down even more as they reached the outskirts of town. Although the roads had been plowed and plowed again, the ice underneath would not yield. "Yes, I think we're in for it. We're going to pay for the scandals on Wall Street, and even worse, we're going to pay for the savings and loan disaster for the rest of our natural lives. The party's over."

"Then I'd better come up with a party clean-up business." Harry was glum.

Susan slowly slid into the wooden guard rails in front of the post office when she applied her brakes. The Jeep was four-wheel drive but not four-wheel stop. She could see Miranda already at work. "I've got to get back home. Oh, here, I almost forgot." She reached into her purse and retrieved a large gold earring.

"This isn't real gold, is it? I can't take it if it is."

"Gold plate. And I go on record as being opposed to your plan."

"I hear you but I'm not listening." Harry opened the door. Tucker leapt out and sank into the snow over her head.

Mrs. Murphy laughed. *"Swim, Tucker."*

"Very funny." Tucker pushed through the snow, leap-

ing upward every step to get her head above the white froth.

The cat remained on Harry's shoulder. Harry helped Tucker along and Mrs. Hogendobber opened the door.

"I've got something to show you." Mrs. Hogendobber shut the door and locked it again. "Come here."

As Harry removed her coat and extra layers, Miranda plunked a handful of cards on the counter. They appeared to be sale postcards sent out at regular intervals by businesses wanting to save the additional postage on a regular letter. Until Harry read one.

" 'Don't stick your nose where it don't belong,' " she read aloud. "What is this?"

"I don't know what it is, apart from incorrect grammar, but Herbie and Carol have received one. So have the Sanburnes, the Hamiltons, Fair Haristeen, Boom Boom, Cabby and Taxi—in fact, nearly everyone we know."

"Who hasn't received one?"

"Blair Bainbridge."

Harry held up the card to the light. "Nice print job. Did you call Sheriff Shaw?"

"Yes. And I called Charlottesville Press, Papercraft, Kaminer and Thompson, King Lindsay, every printer in Charlottesville. No one has any record of such an order."

"Could a computer with a graphics package do something like this?"

"You're asking me? That's what children are for, to play with computers." Mrs. Hogendobber put her hands on her hips.

"Well, here come Rick and Cynthia. Maybe they'll know."

The officers thought the postcards could have been printed with an expensive laser printer but they'd check with computer experts in town.

As they drove slowly away Cynthia watched new storm clouds approaching from the west. "Boss?"

"What?"

"Why would a killer do something like this? It's stupid."

"On the one hand, yes; on the other hand . . . well, I don't know." Rick gripped the wheel tighter and slowed to a crawl. "We have next to nothing. He or she knows that, but there's something inside this person, something that wants to show off. He doesn't want to get caught but he wants us and everyone else to know he's smarter than the rest of us put together. Kind of a classic conflict."

"He needs to reaffirm his power, yet stay hidden." She waved to Fair, stuck in the snow. "We'd better stop. I think we can get him out."

Rick rolled his eyes and stared at the ceiling. "Look, I know this is illegal so I won't ask you directly but wouldn't it be odd if these postcards were misplaced for a day—just a day?" He paused. "We got someone smart, incredibly smart, and someone who likes to play cat and mouse. Dammit. Christmas!"

"Huh?"

"I'm afraid for every Christmas present under every tree right now."

48

A stupendous Douglas fir scraped the high ceiling in Mim Sanburne's lovely mansion. The heart-pine floors glowed with the reflection of tree lights. Presents were piled under the tree, on the sideboard in the hall, everywhere—gaily colored packages in green, gold, red, and silver foil wrapping paper topped off with huge multicolored bows.

Approximately 150 guests filled the seven downstairs rooms of the old house. Zion Hill, as the house was named, originated as a chinked log cabin, one room, in 1769. Indians swooped down to kill whites, and Zion Hill had no neighbors until after the Revolutionary War. There were rifle slits in the wall where the pioneers retreated to shoot attacking Indians. The Urquharts, Mim's mother's family, prospered and added to the house in the Federal style. Boom times covered the United States in a glow in the 1820's. After all, the country had won another war against Great Britain, the West was opening up, and all things seemed possible. Captain Urquhart, the third generation to live at Zion Hill, invested in the pippin apple, which people said was brought into the county from New York State by Dr. Thomas Walker, physician to Thomas Jefferson. The Captain bought up mountain land dirt-cheap and created miles of orchards. Fortunately for the Captain, Americans loved apple pie, apple cider, applesauce, apple tarts, apple popovers, apples. Horses liked them too.

Before the War Between the States, the next generation of Urquharts bought into the railroad heading west and more good fortune was heaped upon their heads. Then the War Between the States ravaged them; three out of four sons were sacrificed. Two generations later, only one daughter and one son survived. The daughter had the good sense to marry a Yankee who, although locally despised, arrived with money and frugal New England values. The brother, never free of his war wounds, worked for his sister's husband, not a comfortable arrangement but better than starvation. The stigma of Yankee blood had slightly faded by World War II, faded enough so that Mim didn't mind using her paternal family name, Conrad, although she always used her mother's name first.

Architecture buffs liked an invitation to Zion Hill because the rooms had been measured by the distance from the foreman's elbow to the end of his middle finger. The measurements weren't exact, yet visually the rooms appeared perfect. Gardeners enjoyed the boxwoods and the perennial and annual gardens lovingly tended for over two centuries. Then, too, the food pleased everyone. The fact that the hostess lorded it over them pleased no one, but there were so many people to talk to at the Christmas party, you only had to say

"Hello" to Mim and "Thank you for the wonderful time" as you left.

The lushes of Albemarle County, glued to the punch bowl as well as the bar, had noses as red as Santa's outfit. Santa appeared precisely at 8:00 P.M. for the children. He dispensed his gifts and then mommies and daddies could take home their cherubs for a good night's rest. Once the small fry were evacuated, folks kicked into high gear. Someone could be depended on to fall down dead drunk every year, someone else would start a fight, someone would cry, and someone would seduce a hapless or perhaps fortunate partygoer.

This year Mim hired the choir from the Lutheran Church. They would go on at 9:30 P.M. so the early risers could carol and go home.

The acid-green of Mim's emeralds glittered on her neck. Her dress, white, was designed to show off the jewels. Dangling emerald earrings matched the necklace, the aggregate value of which, retail at Tiffany's, would have topped $200,000. Hot competition in the jewelry department came from Boom Boom Craycroft, who favored sapphires, and Miranda Hogendobber, who was partial to rubies. Miranda, not a wealthy woman, had inherited her sumptuous ruby and diamond necklace and earrings from her mother's sister. Susan Tucker wore modest diamond earrings and Harry wore no major stones at all. For a woman, Mim's Christmas party was like entering the lists. Who wore what counted for more than it should have and Harry couldn't compete. She wished she were above caring but she would have liked to have one stunning pair of earrings, necklace, and ring. As it was she was wearing the misshapen gold earring.

The men wore green, red, or plaid cummerbunds with their tuxedos. Jim Sanburne wore mistletoe as a boutonniere. It produced the desired effect. Fitz-Gilbert sported a kilt, which also produced the desired effect. Women noticed his legs.

Fair escorted Boom Boom. Harry couldn't figure out if this had been a longstanding date, if he was weakening, or if he was just a glutton for punishment. Blair accompanied Harry, which pleased her even if he did ask at the last minute.

Fitz-Gilbert passed out Macanudos. He kept his Cuban Montecristos for very special occasions or his personal whim, but a good Macanudo was as a Jaguar to the Montecristo Rolls-Royce. Blair gladly puffed on the gift cigar.

Susan and Ned joined them, as did Rick Shaw, in a tuxedo, and Cynthia Cooper wearing a velvet skirt and a festive red top. The little group chatted about the University of Virginia's women's basketball team, of which everyone was justly proud. Under the astute guidance of coach Debbie Ryan, the women had evolved into a national power.

Ned advised, "If only they'd lower the basket, though. I miss the dunking. Other than that it's great basketball and those ladies can shoot."

"Especially the three-pointers." Harry smiled. She loved that basketball team.

"I'm partial to the guards myself," Susan added. "Brookie's hero is Debbie Ryan. Most girls want to grow up to be movie stars or players. Brookie wants to be a coach."

"Shows sense." Blair noticed Susan's daughter in the

middle of a group of eighth-graders. What an awkward age for everyone, the young person and the adults.

Market Shiflett joined them. "Some party. I wait for this each year. It's the only time Mim invites me here unless she wants a delivery." His face shone. He'd been downing Johnnie Walker Black, his special brand.

"She forgets," Harry diplomatically told him.

"The hell she does," Market rejoined. "How'd you like your last name to be Shiflett?"

"Market, if you're living proof I'd be honored to have Shiflett as my last name." Blair's baritone soothed.

"Hear, hear." Ned held up his glass.

The tinkle of shattered glass diverted their attention. Boom Boom had enraged Mrs. Drysdale by swinging her breasts under Patrick Drysdale's aquiline nose. Patrick, not immune to such bounty, forgot he was a married man, a condition epidemic at such a large party. Missy threw a glass at Boom Boom's head. Instead, it narrowly missed Dr. Chuck Beegle's head and smashed against the wall.

Mim observed this. She cocked her head in Little Marilyn's direction.

Little Marilyn glided over, "Now, Missy, honey, how about some coffee?"

"Did you see what that vixen did? Obviously, she has nothing to recommend her other than her . . . her tits!"

Boom Boom, half in the bag, laughed, "Oh, Missy, get over it. You've been jealous of me since sixth grade, when we were studying pirates and those boys called you a sunken chest."

Her remark inflamed Missy, who reached into a bowl

of cheese dip. The gooey yellow handful immediately decorated Boom Boom's bosom.

"Damn you for getting that stuff on my sapphires!" Boom Boom pushed Missy.

"Is that what you call them . . . sapphires?" Missy shrieked.

Harry nudged Susan. "Let's go."

"May I assist?" Blair volunteered.

"No, this is women's work," Susan said lightly.

Under her breath Harry whispered to her friend, "If she swings she'll take a roundhouse. Boom Boom can't throw a straight punch."

"Yeah, I know."

Susan swiftly wrapped an arm around Boom Boom's small waist, propelling her into the kitchen. The sputtering died away.

Harry, meanwhile, ducked a punch and came up behind Missy, putting both hands on Missy's shoulders, and steered her toward the powder room. Little Marilyn followed.

"God, I hate her. I really hate her," Missy seethed, her frosted hair bobbing with each step. "If I were really awful I'd wish her upon Patrick. She ruins every man she touches!" Missy realized who was shepherding her. "I'm sorry, Harry. I'm so mad I don't know what I'm saying."

"It's all right, Missy. You do know what you're saying and I agree."

This opened a new line of conversation and Missy calmed down considerably. Once in the immense bathroom, Little Marilyn ran a washcloth under cold water and applied it to Missy's forehead.

"I'm not drunk."

"I know," Little Marilyn replied. "But when I get rattled this works for me. Mother, of course, supports Upjohn Industries."

"What?" Missy didn't get the joke.

"Mummy has pills to calm her down, pills to pep her up, and pills to put her to sleep, forgive the expression."

"Marilyn"—Missy put her hand over Little Marilyn's—"That's serious."

"I know. She won't listen to her family and if Hayden McIntire won't prescribe them she simply goes to another doctor and pays him off. So Hayden goes on writing out the prescriptions. That way he has an idea of how much she's taking."

"Are you okay now?" Harry inquired of Missy.

"Yes. I lost my temper and I'll go apologize to your mother, Marilyn. Really, Patrick's not worth fussing over. He can look at anything he wants on the menu but he can't order, that's all."

This was an expression both Harry and Little Marilyn heard frequently from married couples. Little Marilyn smiled and Harry shrugged. Little Marilyn stared at Harry, bringing her face almost nose to nose.

"Harry!"

"What?" Harry stepped backward.

"I had earrings like that, except that one looks—"

"Squashed?"

"Squashed," Little Marilyn echoed. "And you only have one. Now that's peculiar because I lost one. I wore them all the time, my Tiffany disks. Anyway, I thought I lost it on the tennis court. I never did find it."

"I found this one."

"Where?"

"In a possum's nest." Harry studied Little Marilyn intently. "I traded the possum for it."

"Come on." Missy reapplied her lipstick.

"Scout's honor." Harry raised her right hand. "Did you keep the mate?" she asked Little Marilyn.

"I'll show you tomorrow. I'll bring it to the post office."

"I'd love to see what it looks like in pristine condition."

Little Marilyn took a deep breath. "Harry, why can't we be friends?"

Missy stopped applying her lipstick in mid-twirl. A Sanburne was being emotionally honest, sort of.

In the spirit of the season Harry smiled and replied, "We can try."

Three quarters of an hour later Harry, having spoken to everyone on her way back from the bathroom, managed to reach Susan. She whispered the news in Susan's ear.

"Impossible." Susan shook her head.

"Impossible or not, she seems to think it's hers."

"We'll see tomorrow."

Boom Boom swooped upon them. "Harry and Susan, thank you ever so much for relieving me of Missy Drysdale's tedious presence."

Before they could reply, and it would have been a tart reply, Boom Boom threw her arms around Blair, who was relieved to find his date finally sprung from the powder room. "Blair, darling, I need a favor—not a humongous favor but a teeny-weeny one."

"Uh . . ."

"Orlando Heguay says he'll come down for New

Year's Eve and I can't put him up at my place—I hardly know the man. Would you?"

"Of course." Blair held out his hands as if in benediction. "It's what I meant to do all along."

Susan whispered to Harry, "Has Fair spent a lot on his Christmas present for Our Lady of the Sorrows?"

"He says he can't return it. He had a coat specially made from Out of the Blue."

"Ouch." Susan winced. Out of the Blue, an expensive but entertaining ladies' apparel store, couldn't take back a personalized item. Anyway, few women fit Boom Boom's specifications.

"Tim-ber!" Harry cupped her hands to her mouth at the exact moment Fitz-Gilbert Hamilton hit the floor, drunk as a skunk.

Everyone laughed except for the two Marilyns.

"I'd better make up for that." Harry wiggled through the crowd to Little Marilyn. "Hey, we're all under pressure," she whispered. "Too much party tonight. Don't get too mad at him."

"Before this night is out we'll have them stacked like cordwood."

"Where are you going to put them?"

"In the barn."

"Sensible." Harry nodded.

The Sanburnes thought of everything. The loaded guests could sleep it off in the barn and puke in the barn —no harm done to the Persian rugs. And no guilt over someone being in an accident after the party.

Before the night was over Danny Tucker's girlfriend cried because he didn't ask her to dance enough.

The juiciest gossip of all was that Missy Drysdale left Patrick, drunk and soon a stable candidate. She traipsed out of the party with Fair Haristeen, who dumped Boom Boom when he overheard her talking about Orlando Heguay's visit.

Boom Boom consoled herself by confiding to Jim Sanburne how misunderstood she was. She would have made real progress if Mim hadn't yanked him away.

Another Christmas party: Peace on Earth, Goodwill toward Men.

49

Harry sat in the middle of an avalanche of paper. Mrs. Murphy jumped from envelope pile to envelope pile while Tucker, head on paws, tail wagging, waited for the cat to dash through the room.

"You're it." Mrs. Murphy jumped over Tucker, who leapt up and chased her.

"Stay on the ground. It's not fair if you go to the second story." Tucker made up the rules as she ran.

"Says who?" Mrs. Murphy arced upward, landing on the counter.

Mrs. Hogendobber barely noticed the two animals, a sign that she had become accustomed to their antics.

"One more day of this, Harry. There's a bit of aftermath, as you well know, but the worst will be over tomorrow and then we can take off Christmas Eve and Christmas Day."

Harry, sorting out mail as fast as she could, replied, "Miranda, I barely recover from one Christmas before the next one is on the way."

Reverend Jones, Little Marilyn, and Fitz-Gilbert pushed through the door in a group, Market on their heels. Everyone plucked the offending postcards out of their boxes.

Mrs. Hogendobber headed off their protests. "We got them too. The sheriff knows all about it, and face it, we had to deliver them. We'd violate a federal law if we withheld your mail."

"Maybe we wouldn't mind so much if he were literate," Fitz joked.

"Christmas is almost upon us. Let's concentrate on the meaning of that," Herb counseled.

Pewter scratched at the front door. While the humans talked, Mrs. Murphy and Tucker told Pewter about Simon and the earring.

As if on cue, Little Marilyn reached into her pocket and pulled out the undamaged Tiffany earring. "See."

Harry placed the damaged earring next to the shiny gold one. "A pair. Well, so much for a Tiffany earring. It was the only way I was going to get one."

"Put not thy faith in worldly goods." The Reverend smiled. "Those are pretty worldly goods, though."

Fitz poked at the bent-up earring. "Honey, where did you lose this? They were your Valentine's present last year."

"Now, Fitz, I didn't want to upset you. I was hoping I'd find it and then you'd—"

"Never know." He shook his head. "Marilyn, you'd lose your head if it weren't fastened to your shoulders." After he said this he wished he could have retracted it, considering the Halloween horror. His wife didn't seem to notice.

"I don't know where I lost it."

"When's the last time you remember wearing them?" Miranda asked the logical question.

"The day before the hard rains—oh, October, I guess. I wore my magenta cashmere sweater, played tennis over at the club, changed there, and when I got back into the car I couldn't find one earring when I got home."

"Maybe it popped off when you pulled your sweater over your head. Mine do that sometimes," Harry mentioned.

"Well, I did take my sweater off in the car and I had a load of dry cleaning on the front seat. If the earring flew off, it might have landed in the clothing and I wouldn't have heard that tinkle, like when metal hits the ground."

"Which car were you in, honey?" Fitz asked.

"The Range Rover. Well, it doesn't matter. I thank you for finding this, Harry. I wonder if Tiffany's can repair it. Did you really find it in a possum's nest?"

"I did." Harry nodded.

"What are you doing ransacking possums' nests?" Fitz pinched Harry's elbow.

"I have this little guy who lives with me."

"You found my earring on your property?" Little Marilyn was astonished. "I was nowhere near your property."

"I found it but who knows where the possum found it? Maybe he's a member of Farmington Country Club."

This made everyone laugh, and after more chatter they left and the next wave of people came in, also upset when they pulled the "Don't stick your nose where it don't belong" postcards out of their boxes.

The animals observed the human reactions. Pewter washed behind her ears and asked Mrs. Murphy again, *"You believe that earring is connected to the first murder?"*

"I don't know. I only know it's very peculiar. I keep hoping someone will find the teeth. That would be a big help. If the earring was dropped, what about the teeth?"

"Since those would identify the first victim, you can bet the killer got rid of the teeth," Tucker said.

"Once the snow melts, let's go back to the graveyard. Can't hurt to look."

"I want to come." Pewter pouted.

"You'd be a big help," Mrs. Murphy flattered her, *"but I don't see how we can get Mother to bring you out. You can do one thing, though."*

"What?" Pewter's eyes enlarged, as did her chest. She was puffing up like a broody hen.

"Pay atttention to each human who comes to the store. Let me know if anyone seems stressed."

"Half of Crozet," Pewter grumbled but then she brightened. *"I'll do my best."*

Tucker cocked her head and stared at her friend. *"What's wrong, Murphy?"*

"What's wrong is the postcard. It's kind of smartass. I mean, if it is from the killer, which we don't know, but if it is, it's also a warning. It means, to me, that maybe this person thinks someone just might get too close."

50

Using the Sheaffer pen that had once been his father's, Cabell wrote his wife a note. The black ink scrawled boldly across the pale-blue paper.

My Dearest Florence,
    Please forgive me. I've got to get away to sort out my thoughts. I've closed my personal checking account. Yours remains intact, as does our joint account and the investments. There's plenty of money, so don't worry.
    I'll leave the car at the bank parking lot behind the downtown mall. Please don't call Rick Shaw. And don't worry about me.

                                                            Love,
                                                            Cabell

Taxi did just that. The letter was propped up against the coffee machine. She read it and reread it. In all the years she had known her husband, he had never done anything as drastic as this.

She dialed Miranda Hogendobber. She'd been friends

with Miranda since kindergarten. It was seven-thirty in the morning.

"Miranda."

Mrs. H. heard the strain in her friend's voice immediately. "Florence, what's the matter?"

"Cabell has left me."

"What!"

"I said that wrong. Here. Let me read you the letter." As she finished, Florence sobbed, "He must be suffering some kind of breakdown."

"Well, you've got to call the sheriff."

"He forbids me to do that." Florence cried harder.

"He's wrong. If you don't call him I will."

By the time Rick and Cynthia arrived at the beautiful Hall residence, Miranda had been there for a half hour. Sitting next to her friend, she supplied support during the questioning.

Rick, who liked Taxi Hall, smoked half a pack of cigarettes while he gently asked questions. Cynthia prudently refrained from smoking, or the room would have been filled with blue fog.

"You said he's been preoccupied, withdrawn."

Taxi nodded, and Rick continued. "Was there any one subject that would set him off?"

"He was terribly upset about Ben Seifert. He calmed down once the books were audited but I know it still bothered him. Ben was his protégé."

"Was there resentment at the bank over Ben's being groomed to succeed your husband?"

She folded her arms across her chest and thought about this. "There's always grumbling but not enough for murder."

"Did your husband ever specifically name anyone?"

"He mentioned that Marion Molnar couldn't stand Ben but she managed to work with him. Really, the politics of the bank are pretty benign."

Rick took a deep breath. "Have you any reason to suspect that your husband is seeing another woman?"

"Is that necessary?" Miranda bellowed.

"Under the circumstances, yes, it is." Rick softened his voice.

"I protest. I protest most vigorously. Can't you see she's worried sick?"

Taxi patted Miranda's hand. "It's all right, Miranda. Everything must be considered. To the best of my knowledge Cabell is not involved with another woman. If you knew Cabby like I do, you'd know he'd much rather play golf than make love."

Rick smiled weakly. "Thank you, Mrs. Hall. We will put out an all-points alert. We'll fax photos of Cabby to other police and sheriff's departments. And the first time he uses a credit card we'll know. Try to relax and know that we are doing everything we can."

Outside the door Rick dropped a cigarette, which sizzled in the snow.

Cooper observed the snow melting around the hot tip. "Well, looks like we know who killed Ben Seifert. Why else would he run?"

"Goddammit, we're going to find out." He stepped on the extinguished cigarette. "Coop, nothing makes sense. Nothing!"

51

Harry wondered where Mrs. Hogendobber was, for she was scrupulously punctual. Being a half hour late was quite out of line. The mail bags clogged the post office and Harry was falling behind. If it had been any time other than Christmas, Harry would have left her post and gone to Miranda's house. As it was, she called around. No one had seen Mrs. Hogendobber.

When the back door opened relief flooded through Harry. Those emotional waters instantly dried up when Mrs. Hogendobber told her the news.

Within fifteen minutes of Miranda's arrival—half an hour before the doors opened to the public—Rick Shaw knocked on the back door.

He walked through the mail bags and up to the counter, glanced at the composite picture of the reconstructed head. "Lot of good that's done. Not a peep! Not a clue! *Nada!*" He slammed his hand on the counter, causing Mrs. Murphy to jump and Tucker to bark.

"Hush, Tucker," Harry advised the dog.

Rick opened his notebook. "Mrs. Hogendobber, I wanted to ask you a few questions. No need to cause Mrs. Hall further upset."

"I'm glad to help."

Rick looked at Harry. "You might as well stay. She'll tell you everything anyway, the minute I leave." He poised his pencil. "Have you noticed anything unusual in Cabell Hall's behavior?"

"No. I think he's exhausted, but he hasn't been irritable or anything."

"Have you noticed a strain in the marriage?"

"See here, Rick, you know perfectly well that Florence and Cabby have a wonderful marriage. Now this line of questioning has got to stop."

Rick flipped shut his notebook, irritation, frustration, and exhaustion dragging down his features. He looked old this morning. "Dammit, Miranda, I'm doing all I can!" He caught himself. "I'm sorry. I'm tired. I haven't even bought one Christmas present for my wife or my kids."

"Come on, sit down." Harry directed the worn-out man to a little table in the back. "We've got Miranda's coffee and some Hotcakes muffins."

He hesitated, then pulled up a chair. Mrs. Hogendobber poured him coffee with cream and two sugars. A few sips restored him somewhat. "I don't want to be rude but I have to examine all the angles. You know that."

"Yeah, we do."

Rick said, "Well, you tell me how one partner in a marriage knows what the other's doing if she's asleep."

Miranda downed a cup of coffee herself. "You don't.

My George could have driven to Richmond and back, I'm such a sound sleeper, but well, you know things about your mate and about other people. Cabell was faithful to Taxi. His disappearance has nothing to do with an affair. And how do we know he wrote that letter voluntarily?"

"We don't," Rick agreed. A long silence followed.

"I have a confession to make." Harry swallowed and told Rick about the misshapen earring.

"Harry, I could wring your neck! I'm out of here."

"Where are you going?" Harry innocently asked.

"Where do you think I'm going, nitwit? To Little Marilyn's. I hope I get there before she mails off that earring to New York. If you ever pull a stunt like this again I'll have your hide—your hide! Do you understand?"

"Yes," came the meek voice.

Rick charged out of the post office.

"Oh, boy, I'm in the shit can," Harry half-whispered.

Rick opened the door and yelled at both of them, "Almost forgot. Don't open any strange Christmas presents." He slammed the door again.

"Just what does that mean?" Mrs. Hogendobber kicked a bag of mail. She regretted that the instant she did it, because there was so much mail in the bag.

"Guess he's afraid presents will be booby-trapped or something."

"Don't worry. We can sniff them first," Tucker advised.

Harry interpreted the soft bark to mean that Tucker wanted to go outside. She opened the back door but the dog sat down and wouldn't budge.

"What gets into her?" Harry wondered.

"She's trained you," Mrs. Hogendobber replied.

"You guys are dumb," Tucker grumbled.

"There goes our expedition," Mrs. Murphy said to her friend. *"Look."*

Tucker saw the storm clouds rolling in from the mountains.

Harry pulled a mail bag over to the back of the boxes. She started to sort and then paused. "It's hard to concentrate."

"I know but let's do our best." Miranda glanced at the old wooden wall clock. "Folks will be here in about fifteen minutes. Maybe someone will have an idea about all this . . . crazy stuff."

As the day wore on, people trooped in and out of the post office but no one had any new ideas, any suspects. It took until noon for the news of Cabell's vanishing act to make the rounds. A few people thought he was the killer but others guessed he was having a nervous breakdown. Even the falling snow and the prospect of a white Christmas, a rarity in Central Virginia, couldn't lift spirits. The worm of fear gnawed at people's nerve endings.

52

Christmas Eve morning dawned silver gray. The snow danced down, covering bushes, buildings, and cars, which were already blurred into soft, fantastic shapes. The radio stations interrupted their broadcasts for weather bulletins and then returned to "God Rest Ye Merry Gentlemen." A fantastic sense of quiet enshrouded everything.

When Harry turned out Tomahawk and Gin Fizz, the horses stood for a long time, staring at the snowfall. Then old Gin kicked up her heels and romped through the snow like a filly.

Chores followed. Harry picked up Tucker while Mrs. Murphy reclined around her neck. She waded through the snow. A snow shovel leaned against the back porch door. Harry put the animals, protesting, into the house and then turned to the odious task of shoveling. If she waited until the snow stopped she'd heave twice as much snow. Better to shovel at intervals than to tackle it later, because the weather report promised another two feet. The path to the barn seemed a mile long. In actuality it was about one hundred yards.

"Let me out. Let me out," Tucker yapped.

Mrs. Murphy sat in the kitchen window. *"Come on, Mom, we can take the cold."*

Harry relented and they scampered out onto the path she had cleared. When they tried to go beyond that, the results were comical. Mrs. Murphy would sink in way over her depth and then leap up and forward with a little cap of snow on her striped head. Tucker charged ahead like a snowplow. She soon tired of that and decided to stay behind Harry. The snow, shoveled and packed, crunched under her pads.

Mrs. Murphy, shooting upward, called out, *"Wiener, wiener! Tucker is a wiener!"*

"You think you're so hot," Tucker grumbled.

Now the tiger cat turned somersaults, throwing up clots of snow. She'd bat at the little balls, then chase them. Leaping upward, she tossed them up between her paws. Her energy fatigued Tucker while making Harry laugh.

"Yahoo!" Mrs. Murphy called out, the sheer joy of the moment intoxicating.

"Miss Puss, you ought to be in the circus." Harry threw a little snowball up in the air for her to catch.

"Yeah, the freak show," Tucker growled. She hated to be outdone.

Simon appeared, peeping under the barn door. *"You all are noisy today."*

Harry, bent over her shovel, did not yet notice the bright eyes and the pink nose sticking out from under the door. As it was, she was only halfway to her goal, and the snow was getting heavier and heavier.

"No work today." Mrs. Murphy landed head-deep in the snow after another gravity-defying leap.

"Think Harry will make Christmas cookies or pour syrup in the snow?" Simon wondered. *"Mrs. MacGregor was the best about the syrup, you know."*

"Don't count on it," Tucker yelled from behind Harry, *"but she got you a Christmas present. Bet she brings it out tomorrow morning, along with the presents for the horses."*

"Those horses are so stupid. Think they'll even notice?" Simon criticized the grazing animals. He nourished similar prejudices against cattle and sheep. *"What'd she get me?"*

"Can't tell. That's cheating." Mrs. Murphy decided to sit in the snow for a moment to catch her breath.

"Where are you, Murph?" Tucker always became anxious if she couldn't see her best friend and constant tormentor.

"Hiding."

"She's off to your left, Tucker, and I bet she's going to bust through the snow and scare you," Simon warned.

Too late, because Mrs. Murphy did just that and both Tucker and Harry jumped.

"Gotcha!" The cat swirled and shot out of the path again.

"That girl's getting mental," Tucker told Harry, who wasn't listening.

Harry finally noticed Simon. "Merry Christmas Eve, little fellow."

Simon ducked away, then stuck his head out again. *"Uh, Merry Christmas, Harry."* He then said to Mrs. Murphy, who made it to the barn door, *"It unnerves me talking to humans. But it makes her so happy."*

A deep rumble alerted Simon. *"See you, Murphy."* He

hurried back down the aisle, up the ladder, and across the loft to his nest. Murphy, curious, stuck her head out of the barn door. A shiny new Ford Explorer, metallic hunter-green with an accent stripe and, better yet, a snow blade on the front, pulled into the driveway. A neat path had been cleared.

Blair Bainbridge opened his window. "Hey, Harry, out of the way. I'll do that."

Before she could reply, he quickly plowed a walkway to the barn.

He cut the motor and stepped out. "Nifty, huh?"

"It's beautiful." Harry rubbed her hand over the hood, which was ornamented with a galloping horse. Very expensive.

"It's beautiful and it's your chariot for the day with me as your driver. I know you don't have four-wheel drive and I bet you've got presents to deliver, so go get them and let's do it."

Harry, Mrs. Murphy, and Tucker spent the rest of the morning dropping off presents for Susan Tucker and her family, Mrs. Hogendobber, Reverend Jones and Carol, Market and Pewter, and finally Cynthia Cooper. Harry was gratified to discover they all had gifts for her too. Every year the friends exchanged gifts and every year Harry was surprised that they remembered her.

Christmas agreed with Blair. He enjoyed the music, the decorations, the anticipation on children's faces. By tacit agreement Cabell would not be discussed until after Christmas. So as Blair accompanied Harry, the cat, and the dog into various houses, people marveled at the white Christmas, and at the holiday bow tied on Tucker's collar, compliments of Susan. Eggnog would be offered, whiskey sours, tea, and coffee. Cookies would be passed around in the shapes of trees and bells and angels, covered with red or green sparkles. This Christmas there were as many fruitcakes as Claxton, Georgia, could produce, plus the homemade variety drowning in rum. Cold turkey for sandwiches, cornbread, cranberry sauce, sweet potato pie, and mince pie would be safely stowed in Tupperware containers and given to Harry, since her culinary deficiencies were well known to her friends.

After dropping off Cynthia's present, they would drive through the snow to the SPCA, for Harry always left gifts there. The sheriff's office was gorged with presents but not for Rick or Cynthia. These were "suspicious" gifts. Cynthia was grateful for her nonsuspicious one.

Blair remarked, "You're a lucky woman, Harry."

"Why?"

"Because you have true friends. And not just because the back of the car is crammed with gifts." He slowed. "Is this the turn?"

"Yes. The hill's not much of a grade but in this weather nothing is easy."

They motored up the hill and took a right down the little lane leading to the SPCA. Fair's truck was parked there.

"Still want to go in?"

"Sure." She ignored the implication. "The doors are probably locked anyway."

Together they unloaded cases of cat and dog food. As they carted their burden to the door, Fair opened it and they stepped inside.

"Merry Christmas." He gave Harry a kiss on the cheek.

"Merry Christmas." She returned it.

"Where is everybody?" Blair inquired.

"Oh, they go home early on Christmas Eve. I stopped by to check a dog hit by a car. He didn't make it." Harry knew that Fair never could get used to losing an animal. Although he was an equine vet, he, like other veterinarians, donated his services to the SPCA. Every Christmas during their marriage, Harry brought food, so Fair naturally took those days to work at the shelter.

"Sorry." Harry meant it.

"Come here and look." He led them over to a carton. Inside were two little kittens. One was gray with a white bib and white paws and the other was a dark calico. The poor creatures were crying piteously. "Some jerk left them here. They were pretty cold and hungry by the time I arrived. I think they'll make it, though. I checked them over and gave them their shots, first series. No mites, which is a miracle, and no fleas. Too cold for that. Scared to death, of course."

"Will you fill out the paperwork?" Harry asked Fair.

"Sure."

She reached into the carton and picked up a kitten in each hand. Then she put them into Blair's arms. "Blair, this is the only love that money can buy. I can't think of anything I'd rather give you for Christmas."

The gray kitten had already closed her eyes and was purring. The calico, not yet won over, examined Blair's face.

"Say yes." Fair had his pen poised over the SPCA adoption forms. If he was surprised by Harry's gesture, he wasn't saying so.

"Yes." He smiled. "Now what am I going to call these companions?"

"Christmas names?" Fair suggested.

"Well, I guess I could call the gray one Noel, and the calico Jingle Bells. I'm not very good at naming things."

"That's perfect." Harry beamed.

On the way home Harry held the carton on her lap. The kittens fell asleep. Mrs. Murphy poked her head over the side and made an ungenerous comment. She soon went to sleep herself. The cat had eaten turkey at every stop. She must have gobbled up half a bird all totaled.

Tucker took advantage of Mrs. Murphy's food-induced slumber to give Blair the full benefit of her many opinions. *"A dog is more useful, Blair. You really ought to get a dog that can protect you and keep rats out of the barn too. After all, we're loyal and good-natured and easy to keep. You can housebreak a corgi puppy in a week or two,"* she lied.

Blair patted her head. Tucker chattered some more until she, too, fell asleep.

Harry could recall less stressful Christmases than this one. Christmases filled with youth and promise, parties and laughter, but she could not remember giving a gift that made her so blissfully happy.

53

Highly potent catnip sent Mrs. Murphy into orbit. Special dog chewies pleased Tucker. She also received a new collar with corgis embroidered on it. Simon liked his little quilt, which Harry had placed outside his nest. It was a small dog blanket she had bought at the pet store. The horses enjoyed their carrots, apples, and molasses treats. Gin Fizz received a new turn-out blanket and Tomahawk got a new back-saver saddle pad.

After chores Harry opened her presents. Susan gave her a gift certificate to Dominion Saddlery. If Harry added some money to it she might be able to afford a new pair of much needed boots. When she opened Mrs. Hogendobber's present she knew she would be able to afford them, because Mrs. H. had also given her a certificate. Susan and Miranda had obviously put their heads together on this one and Harry felt a surge of affection wash over her. Herbie and Carol Jones gave her a gorgeous pair of formal deerskin gloves, also for hunting. Harry kept rubbing them between her fingers; the buttery texture felt cool and soft. Market had wrapped up a knuckle bone for Tucker, more turkey for Mrs. Murphy, and a tin of shortbread cookies for Harry. Cynthia Cooper's present was a surprise, a facial at an upscale salon in Barracks Road Shopping Center.

No sooner had she opened her packages than the phone rang. Miranda, another early riser, loved her earrings. She also promised Harry she'd bring all the food gifts she'd received to work so that whoever came to the post office could help themselves, thereby removing the temptation from Mrs. Hogendobber's lips. Hanging up the phone, Harry realized that she and Miranda would wipe out the food before anyone walked through the door.

As the day progressed the sun appeared. The icicles sparkled and the surface of the snow at times shone like a rainbow, the little crystals reflecting red, yellow, blue, and purple highlights. The Blue Ridge Mountains loomed baby-blue. Wind devils picked up snow in the meadows and swirled it around.

More friends called, including Blair Bainbridge, who said he'd never had so much fun in his life as he did watching the kittens. He said he'd take her to work tomorrow and promised to give her a Christmas present before tomorrow night. He enjoyed being mysterious about it.

Then Susan called. She also loved her earrings. Harry spent too much money on her, but that's what friends were for. The noise in the background tried Susan's patience. She gave up and said she'd see Harry tomorrow. She, Ned, and the kids were going outside to make syrup candy in the snow.

Harry thought that was a great idea, and armed with

a tin of Vermont maple syrup, she plunged into the snow, now mid-thigh in depth. Mrs. Murphy shot down the path to the barn, covered from yesterday's snow but at least not over her head.

"Simon," the cat called out, *"syrup in the snow."*

The possum slid down the ladder. He hurried outside the barn and then stopped.

"Come on, Simon. It's okay," Tucker encouraged him.

Emboldened by the smell and halfway trusting Harry, the gray creature followed in Mrs. Murphy's footsteps. He sat near Harry and when she poured out the syrup he gleefully leapt toward it with such intensity that Harry took a step backward.

Watching him greedily eat the frozen syrup reminded Harry that life ought to be a feast of the senses. Living with the mountains and the meadows, the forest and the streams, Harry knew she could never leave this place, because the country nourished her senses. City people drew their energy from one another. Country people drew their energy, like Antaeus, from the earth herself. Small wonder that the two types of humans could not understand each other. This deep need for solitude, hard physical labor, and the cycle of the seasons removed Harry from the opportunity for material success. She'd never grace the cover of *Vogue* or *People.* She'd never be famous. Apart from her friends no one would even know she existed. Life would be a struggle to make ends meet and the older she got the harsher the struggle. She knew that. She accepted it. Standing in the snow, surrounded by the angelic tranquillity, guarded by the old mountains of the New World, watching Simon eat his syrup, cat and dog next to her, she was grateful that she knew where she belonged. Let others make a shout in the world and draw attention to themselves. She regarded them as conscripts of civilization. Her life was a silent rebuke to the grabbing and the getting, the buying and the selling, the greediness and lust for power that she felt infected her nation. Americans died in sordid martyrdom to money. Indeed, they were dying for it in Crozet.

She poured out more syrup into the snow, watching it form lacy shapes, and wished she had heated chocolate squares and mixed the two together. She reached down and scooped up a graceful tendril of hard syrup. It tasted delicious. She poured more for Simon and thought that Jesus was wise in being born in a stable.

54

"We need a pitchfork." Harry, using her broom, jabbed at the mail on the floor. "I don't remember there being this much late mail last year."

"That's how the mind protects itself—it forgets what's unpleasant." Mrs. Hogendobber was wearing her new earrings, which were very becoming. The radio crackled; Miranda walked over, tuned it, and turned up the volume. "Did you hear that?"

"No." Harry pushed the mail-order catalogues across the floor with her broom. Tucker chased the broom.

"Another storm to hit tomorrow. My lands, three snowstorms within—what's it been—ten days? I don't ever recall that. Well now, maybe I do. During the war we had a horrendous winter—'44, I think, or was it '45?" She sighed. "Too many memories. My brain needs to find more room."

Mim, swathed in chinchilla, swept through the front door. A gust of wind blew in snow around her feet. "How was it?" She referred to Christmas.

"Wonderful. The service at the church, well, those children in the choir outshone themselves." Miranda glowed.

"And you, out there all alone?" Mim stamped the snow from her feet as she addressed Harry.

"Good. It was a good Christmas. My best friends gave me certificates to Dominion Saddlery."

"Oh." Mim's eyebrows shot upward. "Nice friends."

Mrs. Hogendobber tilted her head, earrings catching the light. "How about these goodies? Harry gave them to me."

"Very nice." Mim appraised them. "Well, Jim gave me a week at the Greenbrier. Guess I'll take it in February, the longest month of the year," she joked. "My daughter framed an old photo of my mother, and she gave me season's tickets to the Virginia Theater. Fitz gave me an auto emergency kit and a Fuzzbuster." She smiled. "A Fuzzbuster, can you imagine? He said I need it." Her face changed. "And someone gave me a dead rat."

"No." Mrs. Hogendobber stopped sorting mail.

"Yes. I am just plain sick of all this. I sat up last night by myself in Mother's old sewing room, the room I made my reading room. I've gone over everything so many times I'm dizzy. A man is killed. We don't know him or anything about him other than that he was a vagrant or a vagabond. Correct?"

"Correct."

Mim continued: "Then Benjamin Seifert is strangled and dumped in Crozet's first tunnel. I even thought about the supposed treasure in the tunnels, but that's too far-fetched." She was referring to the legend that Claudius Crozet had buried in the tunnels the wealth he received from his Russian captor. The young engineer, an officer in Napoleon's army, was seized during the horrendous retreat from Moscow and taken to the estate of a fabulously wealthy aristocrat. So useful was the personable engineer, building many devices for the Russian, that when prisoners were finally freed, he bestowed upon Crozet jewels, gold, and rubies. Or so they said.

Harry spoke. "And now Cabell has . . ." She clicked her fingers in the air to indicate disappearance.

Mim waved a dismissive hand. "Two members of the same bank. Suspicious. Maybe even obvious. What isn't so obvious is why am I a target? First the"—she grimaced—"torso in the boathouse. Followed by the head in the pumpkin when my husband was judging. And then the rat. Why me? I can't think of any reason why, other than petty spite and envy, but people aren't killed for that."

Harry weighed her words. "Did Ben or Cabell have access to your accounts?"

"Certainly not, even though Cabell is a dear friend. No check goes out without my signature. And of course I studied my accounts. As a precaution I'm having my accountant audit my own books. And then"—she threw up her hands—"that earring. Well, Sheriff Shaw acted as though my daughter was a criminal. Forgive me, Harry, but a possum with an earring doesn't add up to evidence."

"No, it doesn't," Harry concurred.

"So . . . why me?"

"Maybe you should review your will." Miranda was blunt.

This knocked Mim back. But she didn't lash out. She thought about it. "You don't mince words, do you?"

"Mim, if you think this is somehow directed at you, then you may be in danger," Mrs. Hogendobber counseled. "What would someone want of you? Money. Do you own land impeding a developer? Are you in the way of anything that converts to profit? Do you have business ventures we don't know about? Is your daughter your sole beneficiary?"

"When Marilyn married I settled a small sum upon her as a dowry and to help them with their house. She will, of course, inherit our house and the land when Jim and I die and I've created a trust that jumps a generation, so most of the money will go to her children should she have them. If not, then it will go to her and she'll have to pay oodles of taxes. My daughter isn't going to kill me for money, and she wouldn't bother with a banker." Mim was forthright.

"What about Fitz?" Harry blurted out.

"Fitz-Gilbert has more money than God. You don't think we let Marilyn marry him without a thorough investigation of his resources."

"No." Harry's reply was tinged with regret. She'd have hated for her parents to do that to the man she loved.

"A shirttail cousin?" Miranda posited.

"You know my relatives as well as I do. I have one surviving aunt in Seattle."

"Have you talked to the sheriff and Coop about this?" Harry asked.

"Yes, and my husband too. He's hiring a bodyguard to protect me. If one can ever get through the snow. And another storm is coming." Mim, not a woman easily frightened, was worried. She headed for the door.

"Mim, your mail." Miranda reached into her box and held it out to her.

"Oh." Mim took the mail in one Bottéga Veneta–gloved hand and left.

A bit later Fitz arrived. He and Little Marilyn had indulged in an orgy of spending. He listed the vast number of gifts with glee and no sense of shame. "But the best is, we're going to the Homestead for a few days starting tonight."

"I thought Mim was going to the Greenbrier." Miranda was getting confused.

"Yes, Mother is going, she says, in February, but we're going tonight. A second honeymoon maybe, or just getting away from all this. You heard that Mim received an ugly present." They nodded and he continued: "I think she ought to go to Tahiti. Oh, well, there's no talking to Mim. She'll do as she pleases."

Blair came in. "Hey, I've got good news for you. Orlando Heguay is coming down on the twenty-eighth and he can't wait to see you."

"Orlando Heguay." Fitz pondered the name. "Miami?"

"No. Andover."

Fitz clapped his hand to his face. "My God, I haven't seen him since school. What's he doing?" Fitz caught his breath. "And how do you know him?"

"We'll catch up on all that when he gets here. He's looking forward to seeing you."

"How about dinner at the club Saturday night?" Fitz smiled.

"I'm not a member."

"I'll take care of it." Fitz clapped him on the back. "Be fun. Six?"

"Six," Blair answered.

As Fitz left with an armful of mail, Blair looked after him. "Does that guy ever work?"

"He handled a real estate closing last year," Harry laughed.

"Are you going to be home after work?" Blair asked her.

"Yes."

"Good. I'll stop by." Blair waved goodbye and left. Alone again, Miranda smiled. "He likes you."

"He's my neighbor. He has to like me."

$$\boxed{55}$$

Four bags of sweet feed, four bags of dog crunchies, and four bags of cat crunchies, plus two cases of canned cat food astounded Harry. Blair unloaded his Explorer to her protests that she couldn't accept such gifts. He told her she could stand there and complain or she could help unload and then make them cocoa. She chose the latter.

Inside, as they sipped their chocolate drinks, he reached into his pocket and pulled out a small light-blue box.

"Here, Harry, you deserve this."

She untied the white satin ribbon. TIFFANY & CO. in black letters jumped out at her from the middle of the blue box. "I'm afraid to open this."

"Go on."

She lifted the lid and found a dark-blue leather box with TIFFANY written in gold. She opened that to behold an exquisitely beautiful pair of gold and blue-enameled earrings nestled in the white lining. "Oh," was all she could say.

"Your colors are blue and gold, aren't they?"

She nodded yes and carefully removed the earrings. She put them in her ears and looked at herself in the mirror. "These are beautiful. I don't deserve this. Why do you say I deserve this? It's . . . well, it's . . ."

"Take them, Mom. You look great," Murphy advised.

"Yeah, it was bad enough you tried to give back our crunchies. You need something pretty," Tucker chimed in.

Blair admired the effect. "Terrific."

"Are you sure you want to give me these?"

"Of course I'm sure. Harry, I'd be lost out here without you. I thought I was hardworking and reasonably intelligent but I would have made a lot more mistakes without you and I would have spent a lot more money. You've been helpful to someone you hardly know, and given the circumstances, I'm grateful."

"What circumstances?"

"The body in the graveyard."

"Oh, that." Harry laughed. She'd thought he was talking about Boom Boom. "I don't mean that quite the way it sounds, Blair, but I'm not worried about you. You're not killer material."

"Under the right—or perhaps I should say wrong— circumstances I think anyone could be killer material, but I appreciate your kindness to a stranger. Wasn't it Blanche DuBois who said, 'I have always depended on the kindness of strangers'?"

"And it was my mother who said, 'Many hands make light work.' Neighbors help one another to make light work. I was glad to do it. It was good for me. I learned that I knew something."

"What do you mean?"

"I take bush-hogging, knowing when to plant, knowing how to worm a horse, those kinds of things, as a given. Helping you made me realize I'm not so dumb after all."

"Girls who go to Seven Sisters colleges are rarely dumb."

"Ha." Harry exploded with mirth and so did Blair.

"Okay, so there are some dumb Smithies and Holy Jokers but then, there are some abysmal Old Blues and Princeton men too."

"Have you ever tracked, after a snow?" Harry changed the subject, since she didn't like to talk about herself or emotions.

"No."

"I've got my father's old snowshoes. Want to go out?"

"Sure."

Within minutes the two suited up and left the house. Not much sunlight remained.

"These snowshoes take some getting used to." Blair picked up a foot.

They trekked into the woods where Harry showed him bobcat and deer tracks. The deer followed air currents. Seeing these things and smelling the air, feeling the difference in temperature along the creek and above it, Blair began to appreciate how intelligent animal life is. Each species evolved a way to survive. If humans humbled themselves to learn, they might be able to better their own lives.

They moved up into the foothills behind Blair's property. Harry was making a circle, keeping uppermost in her mind that light was limited. She put her hand on his forearm and pointed up. An enormous snowy owl sat in a walnut tree branch.

She whispered, "They rarely come this far south."

"My God, it's huge," he whispered back.

"Owls and blacksnakes are the best friends a farmer can have. Cats too. They kill the vermin."

Long pink shadows swept down from the hills, like the skirts of the day swirling in one last dance. Even with snowshoes, walking could be difficult. They both breathed harder as they moved out of the woods. At the edge of the woods Harry stopped. Her blood turned as cold as the temperature. She pointed them out to Blair. Snowshoe footprints. Not theirs.

"Hunters?" Blair said.

"No one hunts here without permission. The Mac-Gregors and Mom and Dad were fierce about that. We used to run Angus, and the MacGregors bred polled Herefords. You can't take the chance of some damn fool shooting your stock—and they do too."

"Well, maybe someone wanted to track, like we're doing."

"He wanted to track all right." The sharp cold air filled her lungs. "He wanted to track into the back of your property."

"Harry, what's wrong?"

"I think we're looking at the killer's tracks. Why he wants to come back here I don't know, but he dumped hands and legs in your cemetery. Maybe he forgot something."

"He wouldn't find it in the snow."

"I know. That's why I'm really worried." She knelt down and examined the tracks. "A man, I think, or a heavy woman." She stepped next to the track and then

picked up her snowshoe. "See how much deeper his track is than mine?"

Blair knelt down also. "I do. If we follow these, maybe we'll find out where he came from."

"We're losing the light." She pointed to the massing clouds tethered to the peaks of the mountains. "And here comes the next snowstorm."

"Is there an old road back up in here?"

"Yes, there's an old logging road from 1937, which was the last time this was select-cut. It's grown over but he might know it. He could take a four-wheel drive off Yellow Mountain Road and hide it on the logging road. He couldn't take it far but he could get it out of sight, I reckon."

A dark shadow, like a blue finger, crept down toward them. The sun was setting. The mixture of clear sky and clouds was giving way to potbellied clouds.

"What would anyone want back up here?" Blair rubbed his nose, which was getting cold.

"I don't know. Come on, let's get back."

In the good weather the walk back to Harry's would have taken twenty minutes but pushing along through the snow they arrived at Harry's back door in the dark one hour later. Their eyes were running, their noses were running, but their bodies stayed warm because of the exercise. Harry made more cocoa and grilled cheese sandwiches. Blair gratefully accepted the supper and then left to take care of his kittens.

As soon as he left, Harry called Cynthia Cooper.

Cynthia and Harry knew each other well enough not to waste time. The officer came to the point. "You think someone is after Blair?"

"Why else would someone be up there scoping the place?"

"I don't know, Harry, but then nothing about these murders makes any sense except for the fact that Ben was up to no good. But just what kind of no good we still don't know. I think Cabell knows, though. We'll find him. Ben died a far richer man than he lived. Bet that took discipline."

"What?"

"Not spending the money."

"Oh, I never thought of that," Harry replied. "Look, Coop, is there any way you can put someone out in Blair's barn? Hide someone? Whoever this is doesn't intend to barge down his driveway. He'll sweep down from the mountainside."

"Harry, can you think of any reason, any reason at all, why someone would want to kill Blair Bainbridge?"

"No."

A long sigh came through the phone. "Me neither. And I like the guy, but liking someone doesn't mean they can't be mixed up in monkey business. We called his mother and father—routine, plus I wondered why he didn't go home for Christmas or why they didn't come here. His mother was very pleasant. His father wasn't rude but I could tell there's tension there. He disapproves of his son. Calls him a dilettante. No wonder Blair didn't go home. Anyway, there wasn't much from them. No red flags went up."

"Will you put a man out there?"

"I'll go out myself. Feel better?"

"Yes. I owe you one."

"No, you don't. Now sleep tight tonight. Oh, you heard about the dead rat present to Mim?"

"Yeah. That's odd."

"I can think of about one hundred people who would like to do that."

"But would they?"

"No."

"Are you nervous about this? It's not over yet. I can feel it in my bones."

A silence from Coop told Harry what she needed to know. Cynthia finally said, "One way or the other, we'll figure this out. You take care."

56

The wind lashed across the meadows in the early morning darkness. Even silk long johns, a cotton T-shirt, a long-sleeved Patagonia shirt, and a subzero down jacket couldn't stave off the bitter cold. Harry's fingers and toes ached by the time she reached the barn.

Simon was grateful for the food she brought him. He had stayed in last night. Harry even tossed out some raw hamburger for the owl. Given the mice that crept into the barn when the weather became cruel, Harry needn't have fed the owl. She dined heartily on what the barn itself could supply, a fact that greatly irritated Mrs. Murphy, who believed that every mouse had her name on it.

When the chores were finished and Harry ventured back out, the wind was blowing harder. She couldn't see halfway across the meadow, much less over to Blair's. She was glad she had kept the horses in this morning, even if it would mean more mucking chores.

Tucker and Mrs. Murphy followed on her heels, their heads low, their ears swept back.

"If this ever stops I'm asking the owl to look where those prints were," Tucker said.

"They're covered now." Mrs. Murphy blinked to keep out the snow.

"Who knows what she'll find? She can see two miles. Maybe more."

"Oh, Tucker, don't believe everything she says. She's such a blowhard, and she probably won't cooperate."

Both animals scooted through the door when Harry opened it. The phone was ringing inside. It was seven o'clock.

Cynthia's voice greeted her "hello" with "Harry, all's well over here."

"Good. How was Blair?"

"At first he thought it was silly for me to sleep out in the barn but then he came around."

"Is he awake yet?"

"Don't see any lights on in the house. That boy's got to get himself some furniture."

"We're waiting for a good auction."

"Got enough to eat? I think the electricity might go out and the phone lines might come down if this keeps up."

"Yeah. Can you get out okay?" Harry asked.

"If not, I'll spend an interesting day with Blair Bainbridge, I guess." A distant rumble alerted the young policewoman. "Harry, I'll call you right back."

She ran outside and strained her ears. A motor, a deep rumble, cut through even the roar of the wind. The snow was blowing so hard and fast now that Cynthia could barely see. She'd parked her cruiser in front of the house. She heard nothing for a moment and then she heard that deep rumble again. She ran as fast as she could through the deep snow but it was no use. Whoever was rolling down the driveway finally saw the police car and backed out. She ran back into the barn and called Harry.

"Harry, if anyone comes down your driveway other than Susan or Mrs. Hogendobber, call me."

"What's the matter?"

"I don't know. Listen, I've got to get out on the driveway before all the tracks are covered. Do as I say. If I'm not back at the barn, call Blair. If he doesn't pick up, you call Rick. Hear?"

"I hear." Harry hung up the phone. She patted Tucker and Mrs. Murphy and was very glad for their sharp ears.

Meanwhile, Cynthia struggled through the blinding snow. She thought she knew where she was going until she bumped into an ancient oak. She'd veered to the right off the driveway. She got back on the driveway again and reached the backup tracks. The tread marks were being covered quickly. If only she had a plaster kit, but she didn't. By the time she got one this would be gone. She knelt on her hands and knees and puffed away a little snow. Wide tires. Deep snow treads. Tires like that could be on any regular-sized pickup truck or large, heavy, family four-wheel drive like a Wagoneer, a Land Cruiser, or a Range Rover. She hunkered down in the snow and smashed her fist into the powder. It flew up harmlessly. Half of the people in Crozet drove those types of vehicles and the other half drove big trucks.

"Damn, damn, damn!" she shouted out loud, the wind carrying away her curses.

On her way back to the barn she slammed into the corner of the house. There'd be no getting out of Foxden today. She hugged the side of the building and slowly made her way to the back porch. She opened the back door, stepped inside the porch, closed the door behind her, and leaned against it. It wasn't eight yet and she was exhausted. She could no longer see the barn.

She used the dachshund foot scraper and cleaned off her boots. She unzipped her heavy parka and shook off the snow. She hung it on the hook outside the door to the kitchen.

She stepped into the kitchen and dialed Harry. "You okay?"

"Yeah, no one's coming down my driveway."

"Okay, here's the plan. You can't get to work today. Mrs. Hogendobber will go in if she can even get down the alleyway. Call her."

"I've never missed a day because of weather."

"You're missing today," Cynthia ordered her. "Blair has that Explorer. We'll pack up his kittens and him and we're coming over there. I don't want you alone, or him alone, for a while anyway."

"Nobody wants *me*."

"You don't know that. I can't take any chances. So, I'll get him up and we'll be over there within the hour."

57

"What pests." Mrs. Murphy flicked her tail away from Jingle Bells, the calico, who was madly chasing it.

"Human babies are worse." Tucker ignored the gray kitty, Noel, who climbed up one side of her body only to slide down the other screaming *"Wheee!"*

Harry, Blair, and Cynthia busied themselves making drawings of each room of Blair's house. Then they drew furniture for each room, cut it out, and fiddled with different placements.

"Have you told us everything?" Cynthia asked again.

"Yes." Blair pushed a sofa with his forefinger. "Doesn't go there."

"What about this, and put a table behind it? Then put the lamps on that." Harry arranged the pieces.

"What about a soured business deal?" Cynthia asked.

"I told you, the only deal I made was to buy Foxden . . . and the tractor at the auction. If something is on my property that is valuable or germane to the case, don't you think whoever this is would have taken it?"

"I don't know," Cynthia said.

"Whoops," Harry yelled as the lights went out. She ran to the phone and put the receiver to her ear. "Still working."

The sky darkened and the wind screamed. The storm continued. Fortunately, Harry kept a large supply of candles. They wouldn't run out.

After supper they sat around the fireplace and told ghost stories. Although the storm slackened, a stiff wind still rattled the shutters on the house. It was perfect ghost story time.

"Well, I've heard that Peter Stuyvesant still walks the church down on Second Avenue in New York. You can hear his peg leg tap on the wood. That's it for me and ghost stories. I was always the kid who fell asleep around the campfire." Blair smiled.

"There's a ghost at Castle Hill." Cynthia mentioned a beautiful old house on Route 22 in Keswick. "A woman appears carrying a candle in one of the original bedrooms. She's dressed in eighteenth-century clothing and she tells a guest that they ought not to spend the night. Apparently she has appeared to many guests over the last two hundred years."

"What? Don't they meet her social approval?" Harry cracked.

"We know their manners won't be as good," Blair said. "Socializing has been in one long downward spiral since the French Revolution."

"Okay." Cynthia jabbed at Harry. "Your turn."

"When Thomas Jefferson was building Monticello, he brought over a Scotsman by the name of Dunkum. This highly skilled man bought land below Carter's Ridge and he built what is now Brookhill, owned by Dr.

Charles Beegle and his family, wife Jean, son Brooks, and daughters Lynne and Christina. The Revolutionary War finally went our way and after that Mr. Dunkum built more homes along the foot of the ridge. You can see them along Route Twenty—simple, clean brick work and pleasing proportions. Anyway, as he prospered, less fortunate relatives came to stay with him, one being a widowed sister, Mary Carmichael. Mary loved to garden and she laid out the garden tended today by Jean Beegle. One hot summer day Jean thought she'd run the tractor down the brick path to the mess of vines at the end which had resisted her efforts with the clippers. Jean was determined to wipe them out with the tractor. To her consternation, no sooner did she plunge into the vines than she dropped into a cavity. The tractor didn't roll over—it just sat in the middle of a hole in the earth. When Jean looked down she beheld a coffin. Needless to say, Jean Beegle burnt the wind getting off that tractor.

"Well, Chuck borrowed a tractor from Johnny Haffner, the tractor man, and together the two men pulled out the Beegles' tractor. Curiosity got the better of them and they jumped back into the grave and opened the casket. The skeleton of a woman was inside and even a few tatters of what must have been a beautiful dress. A wave of guilt washed over both Chuck and Johnny as they closed up the coffin and returned the lady to her eternal slumbers. Then they filled in the cavity.

"That night a loud noise awakened Jean. She heard someone shout three times. Someone—a voice she didn't recognize—was calling her. 'Jean Ritenour Beegle, Jean, come to the garden.'

"Well, Jean's bedroom didn't have a window on that side, so she went downstairs. She wasn't afraid, because it was a woman's voice. I would have been afraid, I think. Anyway, she walked out into her garden and there stood a tall well-figured woman.

"She said, 'My name is Mary Carmichael and I died here in 1791. As I loved the garden, my brother buried me out here and planted a rosebush over my grave. When he died the new owners forgot that I was buried here and didn't tend to my rosebush. I died in the kitchen, which used to be in the basement of the house. The fireplace was large and it was so cold. They kept me down there.'

"Jean asked if there was anything she could do to make Mary happy.

"The ghost replied, 'Plant a rosebush over my grave. I love pink roses. And you know, I built a trellis, which I put up between the two windows.' She pointed to the windows facing the garden, which would be the parlor. 'If it would please you and it does look pretty, put up a white trellis and train some yellow tearoses to climb it.'

"So Jean did that, and she says that in the summers on a moonlit night she sometimes sees Mary walking in the garden."

As the humans continued their ghost stories, Mrs. Murphy gathered the two kittens around her. *"Now, Noel and Jingle, let me tell you about a dashing cat named Dragoon. Back in the days of our ancestors . . ."*

"When's that?" the gray kitten mewed.

"Before we were a country, back when the British ruled. Way back then there was a big handsome cat who used to hang around with a British officer, so they called him Dragoon. Oh, his whiskers were silver and his paws were white,

his eyes the brightest green, and his coat a lustrous red. The humans had a big ball one night and Dragoon came. He saw a young white Angora there, wearing a blue silk ribbon as a collar. He walked over to her as other cats surrounded her, so great was her beauty. And he talked to her and wooed her. She said her name was Silverkins. He volunteered to walk Silverkins home. They walked through the streets of the town and out into the countryside. The crickets chirped and the stars twinkled. As they neared a little stone cottage with a graveyard on the hill, the pretty cat stopped.

" 'I'll be leaving you here, Dragoon, for my old mother lives inside and I don't want to wake her.' Saying that, she scampered away.

"Dragoon called after her, 'I'll come for you tomorrow.'

"All the next day Dragoon couldn't keep his mind on his duties. He thought only of Silverkins. When night approached he walked through the town, ignoring the catcalls of his carousing friends. He walked out on the little country path and soon arrived at the stone cottage. He knocked at the door and an old cat answered.

" 'I've come to call on Silverkins,' he said to the old white cat.

" 'Don't jest with me, young tom,' the old lady cat snarled.

" 'I'm not jesting,' said he. 'I walked her home from the ball last evening.'

" 'You'll find my daughter up on the hill.' The old cat pointed toward the graveyard and then shut the door.

"Dragoon bounded up the hill but no Silverkins was in sight. He called her name. No answer. He leapt from tombstone to tombstone. Not a sign of her. He reached the end of a row of human markers and he jumped onto a small

square tombstone. It read, 'Here lies my pretty pet, Silverkins. Born 1699. Died 1704.' And there on her grave was her blue silk ribbon."

The kittens screamed at the end of the story.

Harry glanced over at the scared babies. Mrs. Murphy was lying on her side in front of them, eyes half-closed.

"Mrs. Murphy, are you picking on those kittens?"

"Hee hee" was all Mrs. Murphy would say.

58

No goblins bumped in the night; no human horrors either. Harry, Cynthia, and Blair awoke to a crystal-clear day. Harry couldn't remember when a winter's day had sparkled like this one.

Perhaps Harry had overreacted. Maybe those tracks belonged to someone looking, illegally, for animals to trap. Maybe the truck or car Cynthia heard coming down Blair's driveway was simply someone who had lost his way in the snow.

By the time Harry arrived at work she felt a little sheepish about her concerns. Outside the windows she saw road crews maneuvering the big snowplows. One little compact car by the side of the road was being completely covered by snow.

Mrs. Hogendobber bustled around and the two gossiped as they worked. Boom Boom was the first person at the post office. She'd borrowed a big four-wheel-drive Wagoneer from the car dealer just before the storm. She hadn't bought it yet. "How fortunate to have such a long-term loan," was Mrs. Hogendobber's comment.

"Orlando arrives today. The ten-thirty. Blair said he'd pick him up and we'd get together for dinner. Wait until you meet him. He really is special."

"So's Fair," Harry defended her ex. If she'd thought about it she probably would have kept her mouth shut, but that was the trouble: She didn't think. She said what came into her head at that exact moment.

Boom Boom's long eyelashes fluttered. "Of course he is. He's a dear sweet man and he's been such a comfort to me since Kelly died. I'm very fond of him but well, he is provincial. All he really knows is his profession. Face it, Harry, he bored you too."

Harry threw the mail she was holding onto the floor. Mrs. Hogendobber wisely came alongside Harry . . . just in case.

"We all bore one another occasionally. No one is universally exciting." Harry's face reddened.

Mrs. Murphy and Tucker pricked their ears.

"Oh, come off it. He wasn't right for you." Boom Boom derived a sordid pleasure from upsetting others. Emotions were the only coin Boom Boom exchanged. Without real employment to absorb her, her thoughts revolved around herself and the emotions of others. Sometimes even her pleasures became fatiguing.

"He was for a good long time. Now why don't you pick up your mail and spare me your expertly made-up face." Harry gritted her teeth.

"This is a public building and I can do what I want."

Miranda's alto voice resonated with authority. "Boom Boom, for a woman who proclaims exaggerated sensitivity, you're remarkably insensitive to other people. You've created an uncomfortable situation. I suggest you think on it at your leisure, which is to say the rest of the day."

Boom Boom flounced off in a huff. Before the day reached noon she would call everyone she knew to inform them of her precarious emotional state due to the personally abusive behavior of Harry and Mrs. Hogendobber, who crudely ganged up on her. She would also find it necessary to call her psychiatrist and then to find something to soothe her nerves.

Mrs. Hogendobber bent over with some stiffness, scooping up the mail Harry had tossed on the floor.

"Oh, Miranda, I'll do that. I was pretty silly."

"You still love him."

"No, I don't," Harry quietly replied, "but I love what we were to each other, and he's worth loving as a friend. He'll make some woman out there a good companion. Isn't that what marriage is about? Companionship? Shared goals?"

"Ideally. I don't know, Harry, young people today want so much more than we did. They want excitement, romance, good looks, lots of money, vacations all the time. When I married George we didn't expect that. We expected to work hard together and improve our lot. We scrimped and saved. The fires of romance burned brighter sometimes than others but we were a team."

Harry thought about what Mrs. Hogendobber said. She also listened as Miranda turned the conversation to church gossip. The best soprano in the choir and the best tenor had started a row over who got the most solos. Mrs. Hogendobber interspersed her pearls of wisdom throughout.

At one o'clock Blair brought in Orlando Heguay.

The airplane was late, the terminal crowded, but all was well. Orlando charmed Mrs. Hogendobber. Harry thought he was exactly right for Boom Boom: urbane, wealthy, and incredibly attractive. Whether or not he was a man who needed to give a woman the kind of constant attention Boom Boom demanded would be known in time.

As Blair opened his post box a hairy paw reached out at him. He yanked back his hand.

"Scared you," Mrs. Murphy laughed.

"You little devil." Blair reached back into his box and grabbed her paw for a minute.

Orlando walked around and then paused before the photograph of the unidentified victim. Studying it intently, he let out a low whistle. "Good God."

"I beg your pardon," Mrs. Hogendobber said.

Harry walked over to explain why it was on the wall but before she could open her mouth Orlando said, "That's Tommy Norton."

Everyone turned to him, ashen-faced. Harry spoke first. "You know this man?"

"It's Tommy Norton. I mean, the hair is wrong and he looks thinner than when I knew him but yes, if it isn't Tommy Norton it's his aging double."

Miranda dialed Rick Shaw before Orlando finished his sentence.

$$59$$

After profuse apologies for disrupting Orlando's holiday, Rick and Cynthia closed the door to Rick's office.
Blair waited outside and read the newspaper.

"Continue, Mr. Heguay."

"I met Fitz-Gilbert in 1971. We were not close at
school. He had a good friend in New York, Tommy
Norton. I met Tommy Norton in the summer of 1974.
He worked as a gofer in the brokerage house of Kincaid,
Foster and Kincaid. I was seventeen that summer and I
guess he was fifteen or sixteen. I worked next door at
Young and Fulton Brothers. That convinced me I never
wanted to be a stockbroker." Orlando took a breath and
continued. "Anyway, we'd have lunch once or twice a
week. The rest of the time they'd work us through
lunch."

"We?" Cynthia asked.

"Tommy, Fitz-Gilbert Hamilton, and myself."

"Go on." Rick's voice had a hypnotic quality.

"Well, there's not much to tell. He was a poor kid

from Brooklyn but very bright and he wanted to be like Fitz and me. He imitated us. It was sad, really, that he couldn't go to prep school, because it would have made him so happy. They weren't giving out as many scholarships in those days."

"Did he ever come up to Andover to visit?"

"Well, Fitz's parents were killed in that awful plane crash that summer, and the next year, at school, Fitz was really out of control. Tommy and Fitz were close, though, and Tommy did come up at least once that fall. He fit right in. Since I was a year older than Tommy, I lost touch after graduating and going to Yale. Fitz went to Princeton, once he straightened out, and I don't know what happened to Tommy. Well, I do remember that he worked again at Kincaid, Foster and Kincaid the following summer and so did Fitz."

"Can you think of anyone else who might know Tommy Norton?" Rick asked.

"The head of personnel in those days was an officious toad named Leonard, uh, Leonard Imbry. Funny name. If he's still there he might remember Tommy."

"What makes you think the photograph reconstruction is Norton?" Cynthia thought Orlando, with his dark hair and eyes, was extremely handsome and she wished she were in anything but a police uniform.

"I wouldn't want to bet my life on it but the reconstruction had Tommy's chin, which was prominent. The nose was a little smaller maybe, and the haircut was wrong." He shrugged. "It looked like an older version of that boy I knew. What happened to him? Before I could get the story from the ladies in the post office you whisked me away."

Cynthia answered. "The man in the photograph was

murdered, his face severely disfigured, and his body dismembered. The fingerprints were literally cut off the fingerpads and every tooth was knocked out of his head. Over a period of days people here kept finding body parts. The head turned up in a pumpkin at our Harvest Festival. It was really unforgivable and there are children and adults who will have nightmares for a long time because of that."

"Why would anyone want to kill Tommy Norton?" Orlando was shocked at the news.

"That's what we want to know." Rick made more notes.

"When was the last time you saw Fitz-Gilbert Hamilton?" Cynthia wished she could think of enough questions to keep him there for hours.

"At my graduation from Andover Academy. His voice had deepened but he was still a little slow in developing. I don't know if I would recognize him today. I'd like to think that I would."

"You said he attended Princeton—after he straightened out."

"Fitz was a mess there for a while after his parents died. He was very withdrawn. None of us boys was particularly adept at handling a crisis like that. Maybe we wouldn't be adept today either. I don't know, but he stayed in his room playing Mozart's *Requiem*. Over and over."

"But he stayed in school?" Rick glanced up from his notes.

"Where else could they put him? There were no other relatives, and the executor of his parents' estate was a New York banker with a law degree who barely knew the boy. He got through the year and then I heard that summer of '75 that he started to come out of his shell, working back at Kincaid, Foster and Kincaid with Tommy. They were inseparable, those two. Then there was the accident, of course. I never heard of any trouble at Princeton but Fitz and I weren't that close, and anything I did hear would have been through the grapevine, since we'd all gone off to different colleges. He was a good kid, though, and we all felt so terrible for what happened to him. I look forward to seeing him."

They thanked Orlando, and Blair, too, for waiting. Then Cynthia got on the horn and called Kincaid, Foster and Kincaid. Leonard Imbry still ran personnel and he sounded two years older than God.

Yes, he remembered both boys. Hard to forget after what happened to Fitz. They were hard workers. Fitz was unstable but a good boy. He lost track of both of them when they went off to college. He thought Fitz went to Princeton and Tommy to City College.

Cynthia hung up the phone. "Chief."

"What?"

"When are Little Marilyn and Fitz returning from the Homestead?"

"What am I, social director of Crozet? Call Herself." *Herself* was Rick's term for Big Marilyn Sanburne.

This Cynthia did. The Hamiltons would be back tonight. She hung up the phone. "Don't you find it odd that Orlando recognized the photograph, if it is Tommy Norton, and Fitz-Gilbert didn't?"

"I'm one step ahead of you. We'll meet them at their door. In the meantime, Coop, get New York to see if anyone in the police department, registrar, anyone, has records on Tommy Norton or Fitz-Gilbert Hamilton. Don't forget City College."

"Where are you going?" she asked as he took his coat off the rack.

"Hunting."

60

In just a few days at the Homestead, Little Marilyn knew she'd gained five pounds. The waffles at breakfast, those large burnished golden squares, could put a pound on even the most dedicated dieter. Then there were the eggs, the rolls, the sweet rolls, the crisp Virginia bacon. And that was only breakfast.

When the telephone rang, Little Marilyn, languid and stuffed, lifted the receiver and said in a relaxed voice, "Hello."

"Baby."

"Mother." Little Marilyn's shoulder blades tensed.

"Are you having a good time?"

"Eating like piggies."

"You'll never guess what's happened here."

Little Marilyn tensed again. "Not another murder?"

"No, no, but Orlando Heguay—he knows Fitz from prep school—recognized the unidentified murdered man. He said it was someone called Tommy Norton. I hope this is the breakthrough we've been waiting for, but Sheriff Shaw, as usual, appears neither hopeful nor unhopeful."

The daughter smiled, and although her mother couldn't see it, it was a false smile, a knee-jerk social response. "Thank you for telling me. I know Fitz will be relieved when I tell him." She paused. "Why did Rick Shaw tell you who the victim was?"

"He didn't. You know him. He keeps his cards close to his chest."

"How did you find out?"

"I have my sources."

"Oh, come on, Mother. That's not fair. Tell me."

"This Orlando fellow walked into the post office and identified the photograph. Right there in front of Harry and Miranda. Not that anyone is one hundred percent sure that's the victim's true identity, but well, he seems to think it is."

"The whole town must know by now," Little Marilyn half-snorted. "Mrs. Hogendobber is not one to keep things to herself."

"She can when she has to, but no one instructed her not to tell and I expect that anyone would do the same in her place. Anyway, I think Rick Shaw went over there, slipping and sliding in the snow, and had a sit-down with both of them. I gave him the key to Fitz's office. Rick said he needed to get back in there too. He thought the fingerprint people might have missed something."

"Here comes Fitz back from his swim. I'll let you tell him everything." She handed the phone to her husband and mouthed the word "Mother."

He grimaced and took the phone. As Mim spun her

story his face whitened. By the time he hung up, his hand was shaking.

"Darling, what's wrong?"

"They think that body was Tommy Norton. I *knew* Tommy Norton. I didn't think that photo looked like Tommy. Your mother wants me to come home and talk to Rick Shaw immediately. She says it doesn't look good for the family that I knew Tommy Norton."

Little Marilyn hugged him. "How awful for you."

He recovered himself. "Well, I hope there's been a mistake. Really. I'd hate to think that was . . . him."

"When was the last time you saw him?"

"I think it was 1976."

"People's appearances change a lot in those years."

"I ought to recognize him though. I didn't think that composite resembled him. Never crossed my mind.

"He had a prominent chin. I remember that. He was very good to me and then we lost track when we went to separate colleges. Anyway, I don't think boys are good at keeping up with one another the way girls are. You write letters to your sorority sisters. You're on the phone. Women are better at relationships. Anyway, I always wondered what happened to Tom. Listen, you stay here and enjoy yourself. I'll drive back to Crozet, if for no other reason than to calm Mother and look at the drawing with new eyes. I'll fetch you tomorrow. The major roads are plowed. I'll have no trouble getting through."

"I don't want to be here without you, and you shouldn't have to endure a blast from Mother alone. God forbid she should think our social position is compromised the tiniest bit—the eensiest."

He kissed her on the cheek. "You stay put, sweetie. I'll be back in no time. Eat a big dinner for me."

Little Marilyn knew she wouldn't change his mind. "I think I've already eaten enough."

"You look gorgeous."

He changed his clothes and kissed her goodbye. Before he could reach the door the phone rang. Little Marilyn picked up the receiver. Her eyes bugged out of her head.

"Yes, yes, he's right here." Little Marilyn, in a state of disbelief, handed the phone to Fitz.

"Hello." Fitz froze upon hearing Cabell Hall's voice. "Are you all right? Where are you?"

Little Marilyn started for the suite's other phone. Fitz grabbed her by the wrist and whispered, "If he hears the click he might hang up." He returned to Cabell. "Yes, the weather has been bad." He paused. "In a cabin in the George Washington National Forest? You must be frozen." Another pause. "Well, if you go through Rockfish Gap I could pick you up on the road there." Fitz waited. "Yes, it would be frigid to wait, I agree. You say it's warm in the cabin, plenty of firewood? What if I hiked up to the cabin?" He paused again. "You don't want to tell me where it is. Cabell, this is ridiculous. Your wife is worried to death. I'll come and get you and take you home." He held the receiver away from his ear. "He hung up. Damn!"

"What's he doing in the George Washington National Forest?" Marilyn asked.

"Says he'd been taking groceries up there for a week before he left. He's got plenty of food. Went up there because he wanted to think. About what I don't know. Sounds like his elevator doesn't go to the top anymore."

"I'll call Rick Shaw," she volunteered.

"No need. I'll see him after I visit Taxi. She needs to know Cabby's physically well, if not mentally."

"Do you know exactly where he is?"

"No. In a cabin not far from Crabtree Falls. The state police can find him though. You stay here. I'll take care of everything."

He kissed her again and left.

61

Sheriff Shaw had investigated the theft at Fitz-Gilbert's office when it was first reported. Now, alone in the office, he sat at the desk. He hoped for a false-bottomed drawer but there wasn't one. The drawers were filled with beautiful stationery, investment brochures, and company year-end reports. He also found a stack of *Playboy* magazines. He fought the urge to thumb through them.

Then he got down on his hands and knees. The rug, scrupulously clean, yielded nothing.

The kitchen, however, yielded a bottle of expensive port, wine and scotch, crackers, cheese, and sodas. The coffee maker appeared brand-new.

He again got down on his hands and knees, once he opened the closet door. Again it was clean, except for a tuft of blond hair stuck in the corner on the floor.

Rick placed the hair in a small envelope and slipped it into his jacket pocket.

As he closed the door to the office he knew more

than when he walked in, but he still didn't know enough.

He needed to be methodical and cautious before some high-ticket lawyer smashed his case. Those guys could get Sherman's March reduced to trespassing.

62

Cynthia Cooper discovered that Tommy Norton had never matriculated at City College of New York. By two in the afternoon her ear hurt, she'd been on the phone so long. Finally she hit pay dirt. In the summer of 1976, a Thomas Norton was committed to Central Islip, one of the state's mental institutions. He was diagnosed as a hebephrenic schizophrenic. Unfortunately, the file was incomplete and the woman on the other end of the phone couldn't find the name of his next of kin. She didn't know who admitted him.

Cynthia was then transferred to one of the doctors, who remembered the patient. He was schizophrenic but with the help of drugs had made progress toward limited self-sufficiency in the last five years. Recently he was remitted to a halfway house and given employment as a clerical worker. He was quite bright but often disoriented. The doctor gave a full physical description of the man and also faxed one for Cynthia.

When the photo rolled out of the office fax she knew they'd found Tommy Norton.

She then called the halfway house and discovered that Tommy Norton had been missing since October. The staff had reported this to the police but in a city of nine million people Tommy Norton had simply disappeared.

She roused Rick on his radio. He was very interested in everything she knew. He told her to meet him at Fitz-Gilbert Hamilton's house with a search warrant.

63

The pale-orange sun set, plunging the temperature into the low twenties. As Venus rose over the horizon she seemed larger than ever in the biting night air. A violent orange outline ran across the top of the Blue Ridge Mountains, transforming the deep snows into golden waves. So deep was the snow that even the broomstraw was engulfed. A thin crust of ice covered the snow.

Giving Orlando the full tour of Crozet wasn't possible because many of the side roads remained snowed under. Blair asked his friend's indulgence as he turned down Harry's driveway at 5:10 P.M. He'd picked up a round black de-icer for her to try in the water trough and he thought tonight would be a good test. If it didn't work, Paul Summers at Southern States said he could bring it back and get his money refunded.

"I don't remember you being the country type." Orlando reached for a hand strap as the vehicle slowly rocked down the driveway. "In fact, I don't remember you getting up before eleven."

"Times change and people change with them." Blair smiled.

Orlando laughed. "Couldn't have anything to do with the postmistress."

"Hmmn" was Blair's comment.

Orlando, serious for a moment, said, "It's none of my business but she seems like a good person and she's easy on the eyes. Fresh-looking. Anyway, after what you've been through you deserve all the happiness you can find."

"I loved Robin but I could keep a distance from her. You know, if we'd gotten married I don't think it would have lasted. We lived a pretty superficial life."

Orlando sighed. "I guess I do too. But look at the business I'm in. If you want the clients with deep pockets, you shmooze with them. I envy you."

"Why?"

"Because you had the guts to get out."

"I'll still go on shoots from time to time until I get too wrinkled or they don't want me anymore. See, you were smarter than I was. You picked a career where age is irrelevant."

Orlando smiled when the clapboard house and barn came into view. "Clean lines."

"She has little sense of decoration, so tread lightly, okay? I mean, she's not a blistering idiot but she hasn't a penny, really, so she can't do much."

"I read you loud and clear."

They pulled up in front of the barn and the two men got out. Harry was mucking the stalls. Her winter boots bore testament to the task. The doors to the stalls hung open as the used shavings were tossed into the wheelbarrow. At the end of the aisle another wheelbarrow, filled with sweet-smelling shavings, stood. The door to the tack room was open also. Tucker greeted everyone and Mrs. Murphy stuck her head out of the loft opening. An errant sliver of hay dangled on her whisker. When Harry saw the two men she waved and called out, "Hola!" This amused Orlando.

"Who is it?" Simon asked.

"Blair and his friend Orlando."

"She won't bring them up here, will she?" The possum nervously paced. *"She brought Susan up once and I didn't think that was right."*

"Because of the earring. That was a special case. They won't climb up the ladder. The one guy's too well-dressed, anyway."

"Shut up down there." The owl ruffled her feathers, turned around, and settled down while expanding on everyone's deficiencies.

Down below Orlando admired the barn and the beautiful construction work. The barn had been built in the late 1880's, the massive square beams prepared to bear weight for centuries to come.

Tucker barked, *"Someone's coming."*

A white Range Rover pulled up next to Blair's Explorer. Fitz-Gilbert Hamilton opened the door and hurried into the barn.

"Orlando, I've been looking at Blair's for you, and then thought you might be here."

"Fitz . . . is it really you?" Orlando squinted. "You look different."

"Fatter, older. A little bald." Fitz laughed. "You look the same, only better. It's amazing what the years do to people—inside and outside."

As the two men shook hands, Harry noticed a bulge,

chest-high, in Fitz's bomber jacket. This wasn't an ordinary bomber jacket—it was lined with goose down so Fitz could be both warm and dashing.

Tucker lifted her nose and sniffed. *"Murphy, Murphy."*

The cat again stuck her head out the opening. *"What?"*

"Fitz has the stench of fear on him."

Mrs. Murphy wiggled her nose. A frightened human being threw off a powerful, acrid scent. It was unmistakable, so strong that a human with a good nose—for a human—could even smell it once they had learned to identify it. *"You're right, Tucker."*

"Something's wrong," Tucker barked.

Harry leaned down to pat the corgi's head. "Pipe down, short stuff."

Mrs. Murphy called down, *"Maybe he found another body."* She stopped herself. If he'd found another body he would have said that immediately. *"Tucker, get behind him."*

The little dog slunk behind Fitz, who continued to chat merrily with Orlando, Blair, and Harry. Then he changed gears. "What made you think that picture was Tommy Norton?"

Orlando tipped his head. "Looked like him to me. How is it you didn't notice?"

Fitz unzipped his jacket and pulled out a lethal, shiny .45. "I did, as a matter of fact. You three get against the wall there. I don't have time for an extended farewell. I need to get to the bank and the airport before Rick Shaw finds out I'm here and I'll be damned if you're going to wreck things for me—so."

As Orlando stood there, puzzled, Tucker sank her

teeth up to the gums into Fitz's leg. He screamed and whirled around, the tough dog hanging on. The humans scattered. Harry ran into one of the stalls, Orlando dove into the tack room, shutting the door, and Blair lunged for the wall phone in the aisle, but Fitz recovered enough to fire.

Blair grunted and rolled away into Gin's stall.

"You all right?" Harry called. She didn't see Blair get hit.

"Yeah," Blair, stunned, said through gritted teeth. The force of being struck by a bullet is as painful as the lead intruding into the flesh. Blair's shoulder throbbed and stung.

Tucker let go of Fitz's leg and scrambled to the barn doors, bullets flying after her. Once she wriggled out of the barn she slunk alongside the building. Tucker didn't know what to do.

Mrs. Murphy, who had been peering down from the loft, ran to the side and peeked through an opening in the boards. *"Tucker, Tucker, are you all right?"*

"Yes." Tucker's voice was throaty and raw. *"We've got to save Mother."*

"See if you can get Tomahawk and Gin Fizz up to the barn."

"I'll try." The corgi set out into the pastures. Fortunately, the cold had hardened the crust of the snow and she could travel on the surface. A few times she sank into the powder but she struggled out.

Simon, scared, shivered next to Mrs. Murphy.

Down below, Fitz slowly stalked toward the stalls. The cat again peered down. She realized that he would be under the ladder in a few moments.

Harry called out, "Fitz, why did you kill those people?" She played for time.

Mrs. Murphy hoped her mother could stall him, because she had a desperate idea.

"Ben got greedy, Harry. He wanted more and more."

As Fitz spoke, Orlando, flattened against the wall, moved nearer to the door of the tack room.

"Why did you pay him off in the first place?"

"Ah, well, that's a long story." He moved a step closer to the loft opening.

Tucker, panting, reached Tomahawk first. *"Come to the barn, Tommy. There's trouble inside. Fitz-Gilbert wants to kill Mom."*

Tomahawk snorted, called Gin, and they thundered toward the barn, leaving Tucker to follow as best she could.

Inside, the tiger cat heard the hoofbeats. Their pasture was on the west side of the barn. She vaulted over hay bales and called through a space in the siding. *"Can you jump the fence?"*

Gin answered, *"Not with our turn-out rugs in this much snow."*

Simon wrung his pink paws. *"Oh, this is awful."*

"Crash the fence then. Make as much noise as you can but count to ten." Tucker caught up to the horses. *"Tucker,"* Mrs. Murphy called, *"help them count to ten. Got it? Slow."* She spun around and called to Simon over her shoulder. *"Help me, Simon."*

The gray possum shuttled over the timothy and alfalfa as quickly as he could. He joined Mrs. Murphy at the south side of the barn. Hay flew everywhere as the cat clawed at a bale.

"What are you doing?"

"*Getting the blacksnake. She's hibernating, so she won't curl around us and spit and bite.*"

"*Well, she's going to wake up!*" Simon's voice rose.

"*Worry about that later. Come on, help me get her out of here.*"

"*I'm not touching her!*" Simon backed up.

At that moment Mrs. Murphy longed for her corgi friend. Much as Tucker griped and groaned at Mrs. Murphy, she had the heart of a warrior. Tucker would have picked up the snake in a heartbeat.

"*Harry has taken good care of you,*" the cat pleaded.

Simon grimaced. "*Ugh.*" He hated the snake.

"*Simon, there's not a moment to lose!*" Mrs. Murphy's pupils were so large Simon could barely see the gorgeous color of her iris.

A shadowy, muffled sound overhead startled them. The owl alighted on the hay bale. Outside, the horses could be heard making a wide circle. Within seconds they'd be smashing to bits the board fencing by the barn. In her deep, operatic voice the owl commanded, "*Go to the ladder, both of you. Hurry.*"

Bits of alfalfa wafted into the air as Mrs. Murphy sped toward the opening. Simon, less fleet of foot, followed. The owl hopped down and closed her mighty talons over the sleeping four-foot-long blacksnake. Then she spread her wings and rose upward. The snake, heavy, slowed her down more than she anticipated. Her powerful chest muscles lifted her up and she quietly glided to where the cat and the possum waited. She held her wings open for a landing, flapped once to guide her, and then softly touched down next to Mrs. Murphy. She left the snake, now groggy, at the cat's paws. She opened her wide wingspan and soared upward to her roost. Mrs. Murphy had no time to thank her. Outside, the sound of splintering wood, neighing, and muffled hoofbeats in the snow told her she had to act. Tucker barked at the top of her lungs.

"Pick up your end," Mrs. Murphy firmly ordered Simon, who did as he was told. He was now more frightened of Mrs. Murphy than of the snake.

Fitz, distracted for a moment by the commotion outside, turned his head toward the noise. He was close to the loft opening. The cat, heavy snake in her jaws, Simon holding its tail, flung the snake onto Fitz's shoulders. By now the blacksnake was awake enough to curl around his neck for a moment. She was desperately trying to get her bearings and Fitz screamed to high heaven.

As he did so Mrs. Murphy launched herself from the loft opening and landed on Fitz's back.

"Don't do it!" Simon yelled.

The cat, no time to answer, scrambled with the snake underfoot as Fitz bellowed and attempted to rid himself of his tormentors. Mrs. Murphy mercilessly shredded his face with her claws. As she tore away at Fitz she saw, out of the corner of her eye, Blair come hurtling out of the stall.

"Orlando!" Blair called.

No sooner had he hollered for his friend than Harry, having shed her winter parka, moved from Tomahawk's stall like a streak.

Mrs. Murphy grabbed for Fitz's right eye.

He fired the gun in the air as the cat blinded him. Instinctively he covered the damaged eye with his right hand, the gun hand, and that fast, Harry hit him at the knees. He went down with an "oomph." The snake hit the ground with him. Mrs. Murphy gracefully jumped off. Tucker wiggled back into the barn.

"Get his gun hand!" Mrs. Murphy screeched.

Tucker raced for the flailing man. Fitz kicked Harry away and she lurched against the wall with a thud. Blair struggled to keep Fitz down but his one arm dangled uselessly. Orlando crept out of the tack room and, seeing the situation, swallowed hard, then joined the fight.

"Jesus!" Fitz bellowed as the dog bit clean through his wrist, pulverizing some of the tiny bones. His fingers opened and the gun was released.

"Get the gun!" Blair hit Fitz hard with his good fist, striking him squarely in the solar plexus. If he hadn't been wearing the down bomber jacket, Fitz would have been gasping.

Harry dove for the gun, skidding across the aisle on her stomach. She snatched it as Fitz kicked Blair in the groin. Orlando hung on his back like a tick. Fitz possessed the strength of a madman, or a cornered rat. He raced backward and squashed Orlando on the wall. Tucker kept nipping at his heels.

Fitz whirled around and beheld Harry pointing the gun at him. Blood and clear fluid coursed down from his sightless right eye. He moved toward Harry.

"You haven't got the guts, Mary Minor Haristeen."

Blair, panting from the effort and the pain, got between Fitz and Harry while Orlando, flat on his back, the wind knocked out of him, sucked wind like a fish out of water.

Her fur puffed out so she was double her size, Mrs. Murphy balanced herself on a stall door. If she had to, she'd launch another attack. Meanwhile, the blacksnake, half in a daze, managed to slither into Tomahawk's stall to bury herself in shavings. Simon stuck his head out of the loft opening. His lower jaw hung slack.

"You haven't got a prayer, Fitz. Give up." Blair held out his hand to stop the advancing man.

"Fuck off, faggot."

Blair had been called a faggot so many times it didn't faze him—that and the fact that the gay men he knew were good people. "Hold it right there."

Fitz swung at Blair, who ducked.

"Get out of the way, Blair." Harry held the gun steady and true.

"You'll never shoot. Not you, Harry." Fitz laughed, a weird, high-pitched sound.

"Get out of the way, Blair. I mean it." Harry sounded calm but determined.

Orlando struggled to his feet and ran to the phone. He dialed 911 and haltingly tried to explain.

"Just tell them Harry Haristeen, Yellow Mountain Road. Everybody knows everybody," she called to Orlando.

"But everybody doesn't know everybody, Harry. You don't know me. You didn't want to know me." Fitz kept stalking her.

"I liked you, Fitz. I think you've gone mad. Now stop." She didn't back up as he advanced.

"Fitz-Gilbert Hamilton is dead. He went to pieces." Fitz laughed shrilly.

Orlando hung up the phone. Blair's face froze. They couldn't believe their ears.

"What do you mean?" Orlando asked.

Fitz half-turned to see him with his good eye. "*I'm* Tommy Norton."

"But you can't be!" Orlando's lungs still ached.

"Oh, but I am. Fitz lost his mind, you know. Off and on, and then finally . . . off." Fitz, the man they knew as Fitz, waved his hand in the air at "off." "Half the time he didn't know his own name but he knew me. I was his only friend. He trusted me. After that car accident we both had to have plastic surgery. A little nose work for him, plus my chin was reduced while his was built up. He emerged looking more like Tommy Norton and I looked more like Fitz-Gilbert Hamilton. Once the swelling went down, anybody would have taken us for brothers. And as we were still young men, not fully matured, people would readily accept those little changes when I next met them: the deeper voice, the filled-out body. It was so easy. When he finally lost it completely, the executor and I put the new Tommy in Central Islip. As for my family—my father had left my mother when I was six. She was generally so damned drunk she was glad to be rid of me, assuming she even noticed."

"The executor! Wasn't Cabell the executor?" Harry asked.

"Yes. He was handsomely paid and was a good executor. We stayed close after he moved from New York to Virginia. Cabell even introduced me to my wife. He took his cut and all went well. Until 'Tommy' showed up."

A siren wailed in the distance.

"All you rich people. You don't know what it's like. Money is worth killing for. Believe me. I'd do it again. Fitz would still be alive if he hadn't wandered down here looking for me. I guess he was like England's George the Third—he would suffer years of insanity and then snap out of it. He'd be lucid again. I was easy to find. Little Marilyn and I regularly appear in society columns. Plus, all he would have to do was call his old bank and track down his executor. He was smart enough to do that. As pieces of his past came back to him he knew he was Fitz-Gilbert Hamilton. Well, I couldn't have that, could I? I was better at being Fitz-Gilbert than he was. He didn't need his money. He would have just faded out again and all that money would have been useless, untouchable."

The siren howled louder now and Tommy Norton, thinking Harry had grown less vigilant, leapt toward her. A spit of flame flashed from the muzzle of the gun. Tommy Norton let out a howl, deep and guttural, and clutching his knee, fell to the ground. Harry had blown apart his kneecap. Undaunted, he crawled toward her.

"Kill me. I'd rather be dead. Kill me, because if I get to you, I'll kill you."

Blair got behind him, putting his knee in Tommy's back while wrapping his good arm around the struggling man's neck. "Give it up, man."

The metal doors of the barn squeaked as they were rolled back. Rick Shaw and Cynthia Cooper, guns drawn, burst into the barn. Behind them stood Tomahawk and Gin Fizz, splinters of the fence scattered in the snow, the fronts of their blankets a mess.

"Did we do a good job?" they nickered.

"The best," Mrs. Murphy answered, her fur now returning to normal.

Cynthia attended to Blair. "I'll call an ambulance."

"I think I'd get there faster if I drove myself in the Explorer."

"I'll take you."

Tommy sat on the floor, blood spurting from his

knee and his eye, yet he seemed beyond pain. Perhaps his mind couldn't accept what had just happened to him emotionally and physically.

"No, you won't. Both these men need care." Rick pointed for Orlando to call the hospital and he gave the number. "Tell them Sheriff Shaw is here. On the double."

As Harry and Blair filled in the officers, Tommy would laugh and correct little details.

"What was Ben Seifert's connection?" Rick wanted to know.

"Accidental. Stumbled on Cabell Hall's second set of books, the ones where he accounted for my payments. Cabell is somewhere up in the mountains, by the way. He ran away because he thought I'd kill him, I guess. He'll come down in good time. Anyway, Ben proved useful. He fed me information on who was near bankruptcy, and I'd buy their land or lend them money at a high interest rate. So I started to pay him off, too, but . . ." Tommy gasped as a jolt of pain finally reached his senses.

Harry walked over to Mrs. Murphy and picked her off the stall door. She buried her face in the cat's fur. Then she hunkered down to kiss Tucker. Tears rolled down Harry's cheeks.

Blair put his good arm around her. She could smell the blood soaking through his shirt and his jacket.

"Let's take this off." She helped him remove the jacket. He winced. Cynthia came over, while Rick kept his revolver trained on Tommy.

"Still in there." Cynthia referred to the bullet. "I hope it didn't shatter any bone."

"Me too." Blair was starting to feel woozy. "I think I better sit for a minute."

Harry helped him to a chair in the tack room.

Orlando stood next to Rick. He stared at this man whom he once knew. "Tom, you passed, you know."

Tiny bits of patella were scattered on the barn aisle. A faint smile crossed Tom's features as he fought back his agony. "Yeah, I fooled everybody. Even that insufferable snob, that bitch of a mother-in-law." A dark pain twisted his face. His features contorted and he fought for control. "I would never have been able to marry Little Marilyn. Fitz-Gilbert could marry her. Tommy Norton couldn't."

"Maybe you're selling her short." Orlando's voice was soothing.

"She's controlled by her mother" was the matter-of-fact reply. "But you know what's funny? I learned to love my wife. I never thought I could love anybody." He looked as if he would weep.

"How much was the Hamilton fortune worth?" Sheriff Shaw asked.

"When I inherited it, so to speak, it was worth twenty-one million. With Cabell's management and my own attention to it, once I came of age it had grown to sixty-four million. There are no heirs. No Hamiltons are left. Before I killed Fitz, I asked if he had children and he said no." Tommy deliberately did not look at his knee, as if not seeing it would control the pain.

"Who will get the money?" Orlando wanted to know. After all, money is fascinating.

"Little Marilyn. I made sure of that twice over. She's the recipient of my will and Fitz-Gilbert's, the one he signed in my office that October day. Trusting as a lamb. It might take a while but one way or the other my wife gets that money."

"Exactly how did you kill Fitz-Gilbert Hamilton?" Cynthia inquired.

"Ben panicked. Typical. Weak and greedy. I always told Cabell that Ben could never run Allied after Cabell retired. He didn't believe me. Anyway, Ben was smart enough to get Fitz in his car and out of the bank before he caused an even greater scene or blurted out who he was. He drove him to my office. Ben was prepared to hang around and become a nuisance. I told him to go back to the bank, that Fitz and I would reach some accord. I said this in front of Fitz. Ben left. Fitz was all right for a bit. Then he became angry when I told him about his money. I made so much more with it than he ever could have! I offered to split it with him. That seemed fair enough. He became enraged. One thing led to another and he swung at me. That's how my office was wrecked."

"And you stole the office money from yourself?" Cynthia added.

"Of course. What's two hundred dollars and a CD player, which is what I listed as missing?" Sweat drenched Tommy's face.

"So, how did you kill him?" She pressed on.

"With a paperweight. He wasn't very strong and the paperweight was heavy. I caught him just right, I suppose."

"Or just wrong," Harry said.

Tommy shrugged and continued. "No matter. He's dead now. The hard part was cutting up the body. Joints are hell to cut through."

Rick picked up the questioning. "Where'd you do that?"

"Back on the old logging trail off Yellow Mountain Road. I waited until night. I stored the body in the closet in my office, picked him up, and then took him out on the logging road. Burying the hands and legs was easy until the storm came up. I never expected it to be that bad, but then everything was unexpected."

"What about the clothes?" Rick scribbled in his notebook.

"Threw them in the dumpster behind Safeway—the teeth too. If it hadn't rained so hard and that damned dog hadn't found the hand, nobody would know anything. Everything would be just as it was . . . before."

"You think Ben and Cabell wouldn't have given you trouble?" Harry cynically interjected.

"Ben would have, most likely. Cabell stayed cool until Ben turned up dead." Tom leaned his head against the wall and shook with pain and fatigue. "Then he got squirrely. Take the money and run became his theme song. Crazy talk. It takes weeks to liquidate investments. Months. Although as a precaution I always kept a lot of cash in my checking account."

"Well, you might have gotten away with murder, and then again you might not have." Rick calmly kept writing. "But the torso and the head in the pumpkin—you were pushing it, Tommy. You were pushing it."

He laughed harshly. "The satisfaction of seeing Mim's face." He laughed again. "That was worth it. I knew I was safe. Sure, the torso in the boathouse pointed to obvious hostility against Marilyn Sanburne but so what? The pieces of body in the old cemetery— considering what happened to Robin Mangione—was sure to throw you off the track at some point. I copied her murder to make Blair the prime suspect, just in case something should go wrong. I had backup plans to contend with people—not dogs." He sighed, then smiled. "But the head in the pumpkin—that was a stroke of genius."

"You ruined the Harvest Fair for the whole town," Harry accused him.

"Oh, bullshit, Harry. People will be telling that story for decades, centuries. Ruined it? I made it into a legend!"

"How'd you do it? In the morning?" Cynthia was curious.

"Sure. Jim Sanburne and I catalogued the crafts and the produce. Since he was judging the produce, we decided it wouldn't be fair for him to prejudge it in any way. I planned to put the head in a pumpkin anyway— another gift for Mim—but this was too good to pass up. Jim was in the auditorium and I was in the gym. We were alone after the people dropped off their entries. It was so easy."

"You were lucky," Harry said.

Tom shook his head as if trying to clear it. "No, I wasn't that lucky. People see what they want to see. Think of how much we miss every day because we discount evidence, because odd things don't add up to our vision of the world as it ought to be, not as it is. You were all easy to fool. It never occurred to Jim to tell Rick that I was alone with the pumpkins. Not once. People were looking for a homicidal maniac . . . not me."

The ambulance siren drew closer. "My wife saw what she wanted to see. That night I came home from Sloan's she thought I was drunk. I wasn't. We had our sherry nightcap and I took the precaution of putting a sleeping pill in hers. After she went to sleep I went out, got rid of that spineless wonder, Ben Seifert, and when I got back I crawled into bed for an hour and she was none the wiser. I pretended to wake up hung over, as opposed to absolutely exhausted, and she accepted it."

"Then what was the point of the postcards?" Harry felt anger rising in her face now that the adrenaline from the struggle was ebbing.

"Allied National has one of those fancy desk-top computers. So do most of the bigger businesses in Albemarle County, as I'm sure you found out, Sheriff, when you tried to hunt one down."

"I did," came the terse reply.

"They're not like typewriters, which are more individual. By now Cabell was getting nervous, so we cooked up the postcard idea. He thought it would cast more suspicion on Blair, since he didn't receive one. Although by that time few people really believed Blair had done it. Cabell wanted to play up the guilty newcomer angle and get you off the scent. Not that I worried about the scent. Everyone was so far away from the truth, but Cabell was worried. I did it for fun. It was enjoyable, jerking a string and watching you guys jump. And the gossip mill." He laughed again. "Unreal—you people are absolutely unreal. Someone thinks it's revenge. Someone else thinks it's demonology. I learned more about people through this than if I had been a psychiatrist."

"What did you learn?" Harry's right eyebrow arched upward.

"Maybe I reconfirmed what I always knew." The ambulance pulled into the driveway. "People are so damn self-centered they rarely see anybody or anything as it truly is because they're constantly relating everything back to themselves. That's why they're so easy to fool. Think about it." And with that his energy drained away. He could no longer hold his head up. Pain conquered even his remarkable willpower.

As the ambulance carried Tommy Norton away, Harry knew she'd be thinking about it for years to come.

64

The fire crackled, arching up the chimney. Outside the fourth storm of this remarkable winter crept to the top of the mountains' peaks.

Blair, his arm in a sling, Harry, Orlando, Mrs. Hogendobber, Susan and Ned, Cynthia Cooper, Market and Pewter, and the Reverend Jones and Carol gathered before the fire.

While Blair was in the hospital enduring the cold probe to find the bullet, Cynthia had called Susan and Miranda to tell them what happened and to suggest that they bring food to Harry's. Then she dispatched an officer to Florence Hall's to break the news to her of her husband's complicity as gently as possible. The state police might not find Cabell tonight but after the storm they'd flush him out of his cabin.

Orlando had stayed at the farm while Harry had followed the ambulance in the Explorer. He cooked pasta while the friends arrived. Tomorrow night would be time enough for him to see Boom Boom.

Rick organized guards for Norton while the doctors patched him up. He and Cynthia then enjoyed telling the reporters and TV crews how they apprehended this dangerous criminal. Then Rick let Cynthia join her friends.

While the women organized the food, Reverend Jones, after declaring himself a male chauvinist, went out and repaired the fence lines. His version of being a male chauvinist meant doing the chores he thought were hard and dirty. The result was that, behind his back, the women dubbed him the "male chauvinist pussycat." Market lent him a hand and within forty-five minutes they had replaced the panels and cleaned up the mess. Then they attended to the horses. Fortunately, the blankets had absorbed the damage. Both Tomahawk and Gin Fizz were none the worse for wear and they patiently waited in their stalls with the doors open—in the hurry to get Blair and Tommy to the hospital, no one had thought to put the horses in their stalls and close the doors.

Sitting on the floor, plates in their laps, the friends tried to fathom how something like this could happen. Mrs. Murphy, Pewter, and Tucker circled the seated people like sharks, should a morsel fall from a plate.

"What about the tracks behind my house?" Blair stabbed at his hot chicken salad.

Cynthia said, "We found snowshoes in Fitz's—I mean Tommy Norton's—Range Rover. He dropped the earring back there. There wasn't anything he could do about that mistake but it was the earring that rattled him. I mean, after the real Fitz initially shocked him. Anyway, he wanted to know how quickly he could get back here in the snow if he had to, if you or Orlando, most likely, proved difficult. He was performing a dry run, I think, or he was hoping to head you off before Orlando got here. He must have been getting pretty shaky knowing about Orlando's visit. Anything to prevent it would have been worth the risk."

"What would I have done?" Orlando asked.

"He wasn't sure. Remember, his whole life, the plan of many years, was jeopardized when the real Fitz showed up. Ben Seifert used the event to extort more money out of him. He was getting nervous. What if you noticed something, which, unlikely as it may have seemed to you, was not unlikely to him? You knew him before he was Fitz-Gilbert. The impossible was becoming possible," Cynthia pointed out. "And it turned out you did cause trouble. You recognized the face in the photograph. The face that must have cost a fortune in plastic surgery."

"What about the earring?" Carol was curious.

"We'll never really know," Harry answered. "But I remember Little Marilyn saying that she thought it must have popped off when she took her sweater off in the car, the Range Rover. Tommy had the body in a plastic bag on the front floor, and the sharp part of the earring, the part that pierces one's ear, probably got stuck on the bag or in a fold of the bag. Given his hurry he didn't notice. All we do know is that Little Marilyn's earring showed up in a possum's nest miles away from where she last remembered wearing it, and there's no way the animal would have traveled the four miles to her place."

"Does Little Marilyn know?" Mrs. Hogendobber felt sympathy for the woman.

"She does," Cynthia told her. "She still doesn't believe it. Mim does, of course, but then she'll believe bad about anybody."

This made everyone laugh.

"Did anyone in this room have a clue that it might be Fitz?" Mrs. Hogendobber asked. "Tommy. I can't get used to calling him Tommy. I certainly didn't."

Neither had anyone else.

"He was brilliant in his way." Orlando opened a delicate biscuit to butter it. "He knew very early that people respond to surfaces, just as he said. Once he realized that Fitz was losing it, he concocted a diabolically clever yet simple plan to become Fitz. When he showed up at Princeton as a freshman, he *was* Fitz-Gilbert Hamilton. He was more Fitz-Gilbert Hamilton than Fitz-Gilbert Hamilton. I remember when I left for Yale my brother said that now I could become a new person if I wanted to. It was a new beginning. In Tommy's case that was literal."

Blair took that in, then said, "I don't believe he ever thought he would have to kill anyone. I just don't."

"Not then," Cynthia said.

"Money changes people." Carol stated the obvious, except that to many the obvious is overlooked. "He'd become habituated to power, to material pleasures, and he loved Little Marilyn."

"Love or money," Harry half-whispered.

"What?" Mrs. Hogendobber wanted to know everything.

"Love or money. That's what people kill for. . . ." Harry's voice trailed off.

"Yes, we did have that discussion once." Mrs. Hogendobber reached for another helping of macaroni and cheese. It was sinfully tasty. "Maybe the road to Hell is paved with dollar bills."

"If that's the center of your life," Blair added. "You know, I read a lot of history. I like knowing other people have been here before me. It's a comfort. Well, anyway, Marie Antoinette and Louis the Sixteenth became better people once they fell from power, once the money was taken away. Perhaps somebody else would actually become a better person if he or she *did* have money. I don't know."

The Reverend considered this. "I suppose some wealthy people become philanthropists, but it's usually at the end of their lives when Heaven has not been secured as the next address."

As the group debated and wondered about this detail or that glimpse of the man they knew as Fitz, Harry got up and put on her parka. "You all, I'll be back in a minute. I forgot to feed the possum."

"In another life you were Noah," Herbie chuckled.

Mrs. Hogendobber cast the Lutheran minister a reproving glare. "Now, Reverend, you don't believe in past lives, do you?"

Before that subject could flare up, Harry was out the back door, Mrs. Murphy and Tucker tagging along. Pewter elected to stay in the kitchen.

She slid back the barn doors just enough for her to squeeze through to switch on the lights. It was hard to believe that a few hours ago she nearly met her death in this barn, the place that always made her happy.

She shook her head as if to clear the cobwebs. Mostly she wanted to reassure herself she was alive. Mrs. Murphy led the way, and Harry crawled up the ladder,

Tucker under her arm, and handed the food to Simon, who was subdued.

Mrs. Murphy rubbed against the little fellow. *"You done good, Simon."*

"Mrs. Murphy, that was the worst thing I've ever seen. There's something wrong with people."

"Some of them," the cat replied.

Harry watched the two animals and wondered at their capacity to communicate and she wondered, too, at how little we really know of the animal world. We're so busy trying to break them, train them, get them to do our bidding, how can we truly know them? Did the masters on the plantation ever know the slaves, and does a man ever know his wife if he thinks of himself as superior—or vice versa? She sat in the hay, breathing in the scent, and a wave of such gratitude flushed through her body. She didn't know much but she was glad to be alive.

Mrs. Murphy crawled in her lap and purred. Tucker, solemnly, leaned against Harry's side.

The cat craned her head upward and called, *"Thanks."*

The owl hooted back, *"Forget it."*

Tucker observed, *"I thought you didn't like humans."*

"Don't. I happen to like the blacksnake less than I like humans." She spread her wings in triumph and laughed.

The cat laughed with her. *"You like Harry—admit it."*

"I'll never tell." The owl lifted off her perch in the cupola and swept down right in front of Harry, startling her. Then she gained loft and flew out the large fan opening at the end of the barn. A night's hunting awaited her, at least until the storm broke.

Harry backed down the ladder, Tucker under her

arm. Harry stood in the center of the aisle for a moment. "I'll never know what got into you two," she addressed the horses, "but I'm awfully glad. Thank you."

They looked back with their gentle brown eyes. Tomahawk stayed in one corner of his stall while Gin, sociable, hung her head over the Dutch door.

"And Mrs. Murphy, I still don't know how the blacksnake came flying out of the loft, followed by you. I guess I'll never know. I guess I won't know a lot of things."

"Put her back up in her place," Mrs. Murphy suggested, *"or she'll freeze to death."*

"She doesn't know what you're talking about." Tucker scratched at Tomahawk's stall door and whined. *"Is this the one she hid in?"* the dog asked the cat.

"Under the shavings in there somewhere." The tiger's whiskers swept forward as she joined Tucker in clawing at the door.

She knew the snake would be there but nonetheless it always made her jump when she saw one. Harry, curious, opened the door. Now she knew why Tomahawk was in one corner of his stall. He did not like snakes and he said so.

"Here she is." Tucker stood over the snake.

Harry saw the snake, partially covered by shavings. "Is she alive?" She knelt down and placed her hand behind the animal's neck. Gently she lifted the snake and only then did she realize how big the reptile was. Harry suffered no special fear of snakes but it couldn't be said that she wanted to hold one, either. Nonetheless, she felt some responsibility for this blacksnake. The animal moved a bit. Tomahawk complained, so they backed out of the stall.

Mrs. Murphy climbed up the ladder. *"I'll show you."*

Harry racked her brain to think of a warm spot. Other than the pipes under her kitchen sink, only the loft came to mind, so she climbed back up.

The cat ran to her and ran away. Harry watched with amusement. Mrs. Murphy had to perform this act four times before Harry had enough sense to follow her.

Simon grumbled as they passed him, *"Don't you put that old bitch near me."*

"Don't be a fuss," the cat chided. She led Harry to the snake's nest.

"Look at that," Harry exclaimed. She carefully placed the snake in her hibernating quarters and covered her with loose hay. "The Lord moves in mysterious ways his wonders to perform," she said out loud. Her mother used to say that to her. The Lord performed his or her wonders today with a snake, a cat, a dog, and two horses. Harry had no idea that she'd had more animal help than that, but she did know she was here by the grace of God. Tommy Norton would have shot her as full of holes as Swiss cheese.

As she closed up the barn and walked back to the house, a few snowflakes falling, she recognized that she had no remorse for shooting that man in the kneecap. She would have killed him if it had been necessary. In that respect she realized she belonged to the animal world. Human morality often seems at a variance with Nature.

Fair Haristeen's truck churned, sliding down the driveway. He hurriedly got out and grabbed Harry in his arms. "I just heard. Are you all right?"

"Yes." She nodded, suddenly quite exhausted.

"Thank God, Harry, I didn't know what you meant to me until I, until I . . ." He couldn't finish his sentence. He hugged her.

She hugged him hard, then released him. "Come on. Our friends are inside. They'll be glad to see you. Blair was shot, you know." She talked on and felt such love for Fair, although it was no longer romantic. She wasn't taking him back, but then he wasn't asking her to come back. They'd sort it out in good time.

When they walked into the kitchen, a guilty, fat gray cat looked at them from the butcher block, her mouth full. She had demolished an entire ham biscuit, the incriminating crumbs still on her long whiskers.

"Pewter," Harry said.

"I eat when I'm nervous or unhappy." And indeed she was wretched for having missed all the action. *"Of course, I eat when I'm relaxed and happy too."*

Harry petted her, put her down, and then thought her friends deserved better than canned food tonight. She put ham biscuits on the floor. Pewter stood on her hind legs and scratched Harry's pants.

"More?"

"More," the gray cat pleaded.

Harry grabbed another biscuit, plus some turkey Miranda had brought and placed it on the floor.

"I don't see why you should get treats. You didn't do anything," Mrs. Murphy growled as she chewed her food.

The gray cat giggled. *"Who said life was fair?"*

ABOUT THE AUTHORS

Rita Mae Brown is the bestselling author of *Rubyfruit Jungle, In Her Day, Six of One, Southern Discomfort, Sudden Death, High Hearts, Bingo, Venus Envy, Dolley: A Novel of Dolley Madison in Love and War,* and *Starting from Scratch: A Different Kind of Writers' Manual.* She is co-author with Sneaky Pie Brown of *Wish You Were Here, Rest in Pieces,* and *Murder at Monticello.* Rita Mae Brown is also an Emmy-nominated screenwriter and a poet. She lives in Charlottesville, Virginia.

Sneaky Pie Brown, a tiger cat born on August 27, 1982, somewhere in Albemarle County, Virginia, was discovered by Rita Mae Brown at her local SPCA. Sneaky Pie refuses to divulge her contributions to the novels of her adopted mother, Rita Mae. She admits, however, that her life has inspired her art . . . particularly in her uncanny resemblance to Mrs. Murphy.

RITA MAE BROWN
& SNEAKY PIE BROWN

"Charming . . . Ms. Brown writes with wise, disarming wit."
—*The New York Times Book Review*

Sneaky Pie Brown has a sharp feline eye for human foibles. She and her human co-author, Rita Mae Brown, offer wise and witty mysteries featuring small-town postmistress Mary Minor Haristeen (known to all as Harry) and her crime-solving tiger cat, Mrs. Murphy.

WISH YOU WERE HERE ___28753-2 $5.99/$7.99 Canada
The recipients of mysterious postcards start turning up murdered and Harry may be the only one able to link the victims. Mrs. Murphy and Harry's Welsh corgi, Tee Tucker, begin to scent out clues to the murderer before Harry finds herself on the killer's mailing list.

REST IN PIECES ___56239-8 $5.99/$7.50
When pieces of a dismembered corpse begin turning up around town, the primary suspect is the new drop-dead-gorgeous romantic interest in Harry's life. Mrs. Murphy decides to investigate and has hair-raising encounter with the dark side of human nature.

MURDER AT MONTICELLO ___57235-0 $5.99/$7.99
Mrs. Murphy and Tee Tucker are helped out by Pewter, the corpulent cat from a nearby grocery, in solving a two-hundred-year-old murder that someone in Crozet wants left undiscovered.

Ask for these books at your local bookstore or use this page to order.

Please send me the books I have checked above. I am enclosing $____ (add $2.50 to cover postage and handling). Send check or money order, no cash or C.O.D.'s, please.

Name _____

Address _____

City/State/Zip _____

Send order to: Bantam Books, Dept. MC 43, 2451 S. Wolf Rd., Des Plaines, IL 60018
Allow four to six weeks for delivery.
Prices and availability subject to change without notice.   MC 43 8/95

RITA MAE BROWN

___56497-8	**VENUS ENVY**	$5.99/$6.99 in Canada
___28220-4	**BINGO**	$5.99/$6.99
___27888-6	**HIGH HEARTS**	$5.99/$6.99
___27573-9	**IN HER DAY**	$4.99/$5.99
___27886-X	**RUBYFRUIT JUNGLE**	$5.99/$6.99
___27446-5	**SOUTHERN DISCOMFORT**	$5.99/$6.99
___26930-5	**SUDDEN DEATH**	$5.99/$6.99
___27887-8	**SIX OF ONE**	$5.99/$6.99
___34630-X	**STARTING FROM SCRATCH:**	$10.95/$13.95

A DIFFERENT KIND OF WRITER'S MANUAL

- -

Ask for these books at your local bookstore or use this page to order.

Please send me the books I have checked above. I am enclosing $_____ (add $2.50 to cover postage and handling). Send check or money order, no cash or C.O.D.'s, please.

Name _____

Address _____

City/State/Zip _____

Send order to: Bantam Books, Dept. RMB, 2451 S. Wolf Rd., Des Plaines, IL 60018
Allow four to six weeks for delivery.
Prices and availability subject to change without notice.   RMB 5/95